Praise for
Natasha Gordon-Chipembere's
FINDING LA NEGRITA

"This well-told story is a clarion call for true feminism, an inspiration for women all over the world regardless of age, race, class, ethnicity and gender identities. Evoking the sights, scents and sounds of Costa Rica, Gordon-Chipembere immerses the reader in the untold lives of the freed and enslaved Black people of Costa Rica as well as the mixed-race. Long after the last page of *Finding La Negrita* is closed, these vividly painted characters will resonate in the hearts and minds of readers."

—**Elizabeth Nunez**, author of *Prospero's Daughter, Bruised Hibiscus*, and *Now Lila Knows*

"A powerfully evocative emotional narrative . . . a journey into a community created by free and enslaved Africans and filled with joy, pain, and wisdom."

—**Dorothy E. Mosby**, author of Place, Language and Identity in *Afro-Costa Rican Literature*

FINDING LA NEGRITA

Natasha Gordon-Chipembere

JADED IBIS PRESS

Finding La Negrita
Copyright © 2022 by Natasha Gordon-Chipembere

Published by Jaded Ibis Press
A nonprofit, feminist press publishing socially engaged literature jadedibispress.com

Cover design by Crystal J. Hairston
Special thanks to Costa Rican muralist Guadalupe Alvarez Rojas, who painted the cover art that appears at the Municipal Museum of Cartago in Costa Rica. Thanks also goes out to the mayor of Cartago, Silvia Alvarado Maritnez, as well as the Municipal Museum of Cartago for allowing the press to reprint the artwork.

Trade Paperback ISBN: 978-1-938841-89-7
eBook ISBN: 978-1-938841-90-3
First Edition: 2022 Printed and bound in the United States of America.

For Tia Maj

Because you cleared the way

The most universal definition of the slave is a stranger. Torn from kin and community, exiled from one's country, dishonored, and violated, the slave defines the position of the outsider. She is the perpetual outcast, the coerced migrant, the foreigner, the shamefaced child in the lineage. Contrary to popular belief, Africans did not sell their brothers and sisters into slavery. They sold strangers: those outside the web of kin and clan relationships.[1]

---

[1] Hartman, S. (2007). *Lose Your Mother: A Journey Along the Atlanic Slave Route*. New York: Farrar, Straus and Giroux, 5.

Preface

This is a story I was meant to write. As a child of an Afro-Costa Rican mother born in Brooklyn, I have always been fascinated with the ways that Costa Rica (mis)understood race as a *mestizo* society with Anglo-values, juxtaposed against the national worship of their Black Madonna, *La Negrita*. I was a tenured professor in New York in 2013, when I received a small grant to visit the National Archives in Costa Rica to research the Black Madonna. What I found was breathtaking. This black, twenty centimeter stone carving of the Virgin Mary and Child found in 1635 in the colonial capital of Costa Rica was discovered (according to folklore and narrated by the Catholic Church) by a free Black girl named Juana Maria. The Catholic Church built a sanctuary in the Madonna's honor and put the free *pardos* (Blacks) who lived in *La Puebla de Los Pardos* in charge of her veneration for over 200 years.

During the call for independence and the emergence of nationhood in Costa Rica, the Catholic Church removed *La Negrita* (the little Black one) from the community of free Blacks who venerated her and used her as a national symbol of unity when forming the Costa Rican nation in 1821. Today, the icon is housed in the National Basilica in Cartago and is the patron saint of Costa Rica. August 2nd is her annual veneration day and thousands of people pilgrimage to the Basilica for her blessings, especially on their health.

I made my own pilgrimage to the Basilica in January 2013. My goal was to bear witness to the Black Madonna while honoring the Afro-descended people who worshipped her hundreds of years before. As I made my way to the altar, two nuns knelt to my right in prayer. When I bowed my head, I felt an incredible pressure in my mind's eye, and I could see the altar filled with the spiritual presence of Black people surrounding the icon. When I was jarred out of my meditation, I realized that I had been weeping, overcome with the message I received. These ancestors had asked me to tell their stories: of their lives, loves, fears, and triumphs. I had been asked to write about the free and enslaved Black people who lived in colonial Costa Rica yet are not found in the national archives or the folkloric celebrations that define Costa Rica's history.

I agreed. I asked for every door to be opened to write this story, for the characters to present themselves. Dakarai was the first to grace my page. He held my hand and walked me into their world. For this, I am forever grateful.

I have taken creative liberties with imagining this seventeenth century world as I built the interior lives of the community of Afro-descendants who lived in *La Gotera* and Cartago. However, the foods, fauna, sounds, slave-owning, and community dynamics, especially amongst the Spaniards of that time, are based in historical truths. Costa Rica was considered a backwater, forgotten colony in the Spanish world, as it did not have a cash crop to compete with Brazil's sugar markets or the silver mines in Mexico and Peru. Slavery existed in Costa Rica from about 1600–1823, over 200 years. However, the numbers of enslaved people were smaller than in traditional plantation system societies. Cattle ranching in the north, cacao production on the Caribbean coast and domestic labor in Cartago were the three main areas that enslaved people worked. Contrary to other slave-owning societies, the Spaniards were not wealthy, and many could not afford to keep enslaved peoples. A township on the outskirts of Cartago, called *La Gotera* ("the leak"), was designated living space for free Black and mixed-race peoples. It is their lives that this book opens into and to which you are invited.

Prologue

Fragrant, luxurious indigo blue. This is the color of night that engulfs Towela as she enters Lupita's family compound near the center of town. The houses are lumpy shadows as the dark descends. The evening's twilight wraps around her like music. At twenty-five, Towela is poised in the beauty of her youth. Her mahogany skin accentuates her cheekbones and firmly set brown eyes. Though she leans more on the side of slender, her full lips have invited many to dream about their taste. It has been almost a year since she has seen her best friend and she is grateful for this trip with her father so she can visit with Lupita. Since she married seven years ago, and moved with Dakarai near the Zambezi, it is not often that her father plucks her from her sculpting work to accompany him on one of his lecturing trips.

But, two weeks ago, her father appeared at their front door without ceremony and requested her presence with him at the palace in Benguela on the Angolan coast. He was being asked to interpret a new document that had come from northern Timbuktu. She was very familiar with the journey, as she and Dakarai used the same roads on their annual market trip to sell their sculptures. Dakarai had seemed withdrawn when she told him that she would be away for two weeks. With a gentle embrace, she left him, ready to change the routine of her world and see Lupita. There was so much on her heart to share; things she could not tell her father. She had noticed his slower gait and even suggested they rest more often, but he remained determined to get there within the usual six days.

And so now, with the evening air humid with ocean breeze from the coast and the expanse of sky a midnight blue with the orange rays of a sun no longer visible, Towela enters the party. There is a fire to the left of the main house in the compound and that is the source of all activity. Colorful cushions and blankets are strewn around the fire as the crowd of mostly young people sways to the melodic singing of a young man, standing with his back towards her. Even from the compound walls' dung-colored entrance, Towela can see, because of the fire, that his dark skin is smooth like the *rapoko* stone she uses to carve her Shona statues. Such a beauty. He is reed thin but passionate as his hands wave, enunciating the words he sings without accompaniment. Everyone is mesmerized. His words are in Kikongo, a language she cannot understand, but as she listens while she walks closer to the group, she gets the meaning of his words. They are a lament, perhaps of things to come. His voice pierces the night and even the dogs settle into stillness. Towela holds her breath.

Closing her eyes, she gulps down the sounds, the pitch of his voice stinging the inside of her chest, and tears appear suddenly. She is startled when she feels arms around her, and it takes a second to realize that Lupita is embracing her. The joy she feels at being held by her friend brings the tears faster and as she rests her head on Lupita's soft, round shoulder, her body shakes with sobs. Lupita simply holds her, perhaps assuming that she is moved by the music as much as the rest of the crowd. They release each other when the song comes to an end, joining the group of about twenty-five people, mostly in their twenties, in a rousing applause.

"Come, let's go sit away from everyone so you can fill me in on life. I have missed you so much, Towela," Lupita says as she grabs Towela's hand and leads her towards the main house. The nearly full moon allows for some light in the darkness as they move away from the fire. In the distance, Towela can hear that the singer has been convinced to sing a favorite local tune, and other voices eagerly join in once he begins to sing again.

Towela and Lupita enter a small house, round in shape with a thatched cone roof that has an opening in the center for smoke. There is a fire in the middle of the room that brings warmth to the three sleeping children on wooden beds. This is where Lupita lives with her mother and three smaller siblings. Her father resides in the main house and both he and her mother are gone to visit the palace for the presentation by Towela's father. Towela knew the feast afterwards would extend for hours and this was why she had asked permission to visit with Lupita, who remained in the compound to care for her younger brothers and sister.

Lupita is a small wonder. At twenty-four, Lupita is chocolate-brown, short and round, with full hips, plump breasts, a perpetual blush from the beach's constant sun tinging her cheeks, and a ready twinkle in her eye. Her hair is always plaited in the newest styles and bejeweled with shells. She is the object of desire for most young men in the village but her father's wealthy status in the community leaves most of them pining from afar. Allowed great freedom to invite local friends to share their art at the family compound, Lupita has become known as a great hostess and the center of the cultural scene in Benguela.

Once settled in the darkened space, Towela quietly fills her friend in on her life with Dakarai. She tells about the seven years of waiting to become a mother and the despair and sadness she feels. Then she is silent. Unburdening her heart has been helpful. Lupita holds her hand and just listens. As she is going to speak, Lupita is suddenly called from outside. Getting up, she indicates to Towela that she should remain seated while she sorts out what is happening outside.

Towela barely has time to close her eyes when Lupita comes back in, grabbing her hand to pull her upright in excitement.

"Towela! It's the poet, the famous Agostinho! Someone invited him here and, oh! I cannot believe that he actually came. This is a real honor," Lupita almost shouts, forgetting her sleeping siblings.

Towela cannot say much before she is dragged outside towards the fire. She can already sense the anticipation in the air as Agostinho clears his throat. What she does not expect is to have the breath knocked out of her when she faces him across the fire. He looks nothing like a poet, who in her mind's eye should be languid, short, and intense. Cinnamon-brown with short, thick hair and broad shoulders, he stands a little under six feet tall; Agostinho looks more like a prince than a wandering wordsmith. They lock eyes and he smiles with just the left side of his lips curving up to acknowledge her blush.

Looking down at her feet, Towela does not pay much attention as he begins to recite a poem in Portuguese, which causes an instant uproar amongst the crowd as they protest the use of the white man's tongue. Hushing the crowd to listen carefully, Agostinho starts again, skillfully intertwining Kikongo with Portuguese in a political poem, condemning the increased slave trade that is happening on their shores and in the marketplace just outside of Lupita's family compound. Soon, his words are heralded as several young men spring to their feet with rapturous applause.

When the night grows late and the crowd begins to fade, Towela holds back. On the arrival of Lupita's parents, all those lingering say their quick goodbyes. Towela gets special greetings as they love her deeply: they embrace her with the warmth and exhaustion of enjoying a long evening out. They immediately retire after giving instructions to the servants to put out the fire. After a few more poems by Agostinho, Lupita finally introduced him to Towela. She finds that he is Mbunda and also twenty-five. He now lingers at the compound entrance as Towela gives Lupita a final hug. Without words, she walks alongside Agostinho as they take the central road into town.

In their quiet conversation about nothing and everything, Agostinho switches into Tumbuka, which she speaks, and explains that he is a teacher in his village. As they walk side by side, they occasionally touch hands. At the intersection of the road that leads towards his lodgings, Agostinho looks at Towela. With his right hand, he reaches out to touch her lips. Their eyes had long adjusted to the darkness, and she gently gives a soft nod of consent and follows him to his place, which is not far away and easy to get to in the flickering moonlight. Towela's heart races as she wants this moment outside of time. She thinks only fleetingly of Dakarai when they enter Agostinho's room, and he turns to kiss her. They make love quickly, no sounds, only breathing and then respite, as if starved. She holds onto him when he climaxes inside of her, as she has little fear of pregnancy since it has not happened in seven years of marriage. When he softens, he gently removes himself from her, kisses her shoulder and settles into sleep.

She watches him as he snores, noticing the hairs of his short beard move. For some reason, this makes her giggle. She thinks of Dakarai's clean face, and this is when she remembers who she is. She quietly dresses in the encroaching dawn light and makes it back to her own lodgings without another to serve as witness. She washes up quickly in cold water, traces of the sun already peeking in the rose-pink sky. Grateful that she has a room separate from her father's, she crawls into bed. The sleep that overtakes her is the most peaceful she's had in months.

1635, Costa Rica

According to the Catholic Church of Costa Rica, in the area that is today known as the Puebla de los Pardos [*formally known as* La Gotera], *in Costa Rica, there lived a young woman of African descent named Juana Maria. In 1635, upon a rock, near a spring, this* parda *found an extraordinary icon of the Virgin Mary and Child. She took it home and put it in a box. The next day, it was gone. When she returned to the rock in the forest a second time, the same sculpture was there.*

This happened a second time and when the woman came near the rock again, she encountered the same icon a third time. Afraid and unsure, she ran to the priest and explained her case. After hearing the story, the priest placed the icon in the Tabernacle of the Santiago Apostol Church in Cartago. However, the next day, she was not there. Resolved, both the parish priest and congregation went to the rock, where she was originally found, and the icon was there once more ... Therefore, a thatched roof was built over the rock where her Sanctuary was eventually constructed.

Imagine a story, passed from mouth to mouth, tumbling like sacred stone, carved from African lives lived. Imagine this story, heard across seas, and stretched over time, about how a Black girl found an icon of a mother and child. Perhaps the story passed from mouth to mouth, ear to ear is remembered, at its source, differently than the Church told ...

FINDING
LA NEGRITA

Natasha Gordon-Chipembere

Jendayi

La Gotera (the outskirts) of Colonial Cartago, Costa Rica, October 1634

Josefina wakes Jendayi this morning. She is Jendayi's neighbor, Mama Petronila's daughter and like her sister. They were raised together for seven years before Jendayi's father came to get her and set up their house next door. Josefina was born in an Angolan slave caste and her father was a Portuguese governor, who kept her mother for two years before they made the passage across the sea because her mother was replaced with a newer, younger enslaved African woman. Jendayi had been told this story only once, when she asked why Josefina looked so different from her with her thick, curly, blonde hair and green eyes, and it was never spoken of again. Though Josefina is just two years older than her, Jendayi feels like Josefina knows the secrets of the world. There is a sadness that she has felt between Josefina and her mother whenever she was with them in recent days, but maybe it had been there all along and she is just realizing it now.

"Juana Maria, Juana Maria," Jendayi hears the singsong fragments of Josefina's words in the corners of her mind. Instantly, she is annoyed. With her eyes still closed she says, "Stop calling me that. You know my name is Jendayi. Only the *panas* call me that, and as far as I know you are not one of them."

"Fine, but get up already Jendayi, I am not getting the water today," Josefina impatiently states as she stands over Jendayi in bed, her tall, wiry body vibrating with the sound of her voice. Jendayi can feel it even though she stays wrapped in the warm cocoon of her bed.

"Ahhh, has Baba already gone into town?" Jendayi asks groggily, chasing the fragments of a dream as she struggles to sit up.

"Yes, he has already gone. You must get water and take it to the church before school. You know your job. Plus, I have something to tell you, so hurry up!" Josefina says as she pokes Jendayi's shoulder.

Jendayi trusts Josefina as her sister since she is the only girl in *La Gotera* who allows her to hang around and ask as many questions about life as she wants. Josefina has never delivered the water to the Church of Santiago Apostol, though at one point years ago, there was some talk about the girls taking turns. The first few times it was Josefina's responsibility to take the water to Padre for the altar, she pretended that she was sick, so Jendayi eventually took on the work herself and it became her singular job before attending school—a job she doesn't mind doing in exchange for Josefina's companionship.

Josefina even refuses to attend the school that Padre runs because she will not go inside the building. Jendayi has always found this strange, not because she is a fan of Padre's religion, but because she loves going to school. But Josefina is firm about never setting a foot inside the church. It is a rebuilt church, still in the reconstruction phase since the earthquake four years ago. Every time there is a bit of a tremble, Josefina gets that terrified look in her eyes as if the ancestors were calling her home. But Jendayi is not afraid of earthquakes or the Volcano Irazú that peeks at them daily. She was born on the sea; moving earth does not frighten her in the way it does many others from *La Gotera*.

Jendayi gets up and stretches. She is so tired because her night was framed from beginning to end with dreams of her mother. Josefina's voice tore her away from hearing something her mother was trying to say to her. Jendayi feels this deeply, though she has never met her mother and has no real idea what she looked like beyond her father's brief recollections. Towela was her name, and Jendayi knows she was a sculptor and scribe for her grandfather. She died in childbirth while crossing the sea in the slave ship. Jendayi is all that remains of her.

Jendayi shakes her head and sees Josefina looking at her frayed pink nightgown, which is getting much too small. The curves of Jendayi's full breasts and slender but shapely hips make it clear that she needs grown-women clothes now. But there is nothing she can do because even free Africans, like Jendayi's father, do not earn much money making furniture or working on the cacao plantations or with the cattle in the north. Maybe it is time that I find some paying work in Cartago, Jendayi thinks as she changes into her light-blue day dress, puts her well-worn brown leather sandals on her feet and rushes to the earthen basin to wash her face and clean her teeth. She stares quickly into the mirror over the clay basin, looking into her brown, almond shaped eyes that sit squarely in her round, chocolate-brown face. She ties her thick black braids back with a headscarf as she does not have time to properly untwist, oil and retwist her hair. She knows without feeling vain that she is very pretty, even at fifteen, because it is evident in the stares that she gets from Black and white men during Thursday's market; it was why her father often had a bewildered frown on his face when they were in public together. She is not interested in those looks and doesn't care about any of those men but in her belly, she is unsure of what they want, and it makes her afraid. She is most happy at school, at home or on the *finca*, in the safety of *La Gotera*.

Josefina remains standing in the doorframe as if she is afraid that Jendayi will vanish into thin air and not take the water to the church as she promised and somehow, she will be forced to do it. Josefina clears her throat, indicating that Jendayi needs to stop preening in the mirror and get moving.

Once ready, Jendayi pushes past Josefina who is straight as a sapling, with not a curve in sight for seventeen years. Yet, she is beautiful. Josefina is like a dancer to Jendayi, walking so that the air caresses the bottom of her feet, head high with a smile slow and sometimes wicked. Jendayi knows that Josefina has a *novio* in Cartago, Nicolas, who is a *zambo*, half Bribri and African, and very poor. He is also a *pardo* and so perhaps that is what binds them. Jendayi has seen him bring horses into town from Guanacaste with his employer, Don Jimenez, who is Cartago's Mayor. She thinks Nicolas is very handsome, with his broad, muscular shoulders, *café-con-leche* skin and rugged smile, even when he is muddy and sweaty from his backbreaking work. She doubts that Mama Petronila knows about their romance, but Josefina is obsessed with him. She has told Jendayi that he is only eighteen but had been laboring for Don Jimenez out in Guanacaste for three years and there was talk that he would be brought to Cartago soon for a big project Don Jimenez was about to undertake. Jendayi thinks these are just rumors and nothing worth listening to. She has told Josefina that her pipe dreams are just wishes to have Nicolas closer to her. Josefina has taken Jendayi as her "cover" a few times so she could meet Nicolas near the plaza whenever he sent word that he would be in town. So, Jendayi has spent boring hours sitting on the church steps, looking at the sky and watching people pass by while they went off to who knows where. While Jendayi was carrying pots and pots of water to Padre and learning her lessons, Josefina was making excuses to go into town to see him. Perhaps Josefina has the better end of the stick, but Jendayi is happy to help her. Either way, Nicolas will not take away the heavy pots of water that Jendayi must carry, and she is already late; the plaza and the church are on the outskirts of Cartago, and she has about ten minutes of walking.

The water pump near the center of *La Gotera* is closer to the church than the one in Cartago, so this is where Jendayi always stops for the water that once delivered to the church, would be cleaned by an enslaved woman who lives in the small shack behind the church's schoolroom. Dakarai, Jendayi's father, does not encourage her to talk to Esmeralda, the African lady who cleans the church, though of course Jendayi wants to know everything about her. Esmeralda is said to be blind in her left eye and to have burn marks on her left arm, but she never comes out while there are people milling around the church or the small schoolroom. Jendayi has only seen her once at a far distance. She tries her best to listen in on stories, told by the whispering adults in *La Gotera*, about Esmeralda's burnt body, but to no avail. Esmeralda is a shadow to Jendayi, but she can sense Esmeralda is well-respected by their people there, though she does not fully understand why.

The water pump is the daily center of activity that is managed by the Black and Brown women of *La Gotera*. Jendayi has to take water to the church every day except Saturday, and she is normally the first one there. The iron water pump is planted on firm wooden slats and the area around it is muddy and messy. Normally there is a long line of mothers and daughters who come to collect their water to begin the day of washing, cooking, and cleaning before they must go into work in Cartago as domestics, cooks, and nannies for those Spanish families who do not have their own enslaved people. The water pump, with its constant creaking and water splashing, is where all gossip happens in *La Gotera*. Young girls are assessed by the older women who are the gatekeepers of respectability. The air is humid and moist, full of the smell of just-awakened unwashed bodies and the muddy earth. The sounds of chatter are plentiful against the fresh splash of ice-cold water. On misty mornings, which are many in Cartago, collecting the water is a burden as the cold water and the cold air would become a painful mix. But today is not misty. The sun is bright overhead, beating down on all the Brown heads in line. Jendayi has two rust-colored clay gourds for the water, and she stands in the line that is now long because she overslept. Josefina gives her an "I told you so" look, but Jendayi ignores her and stares high up to the Volcano Irazú. Though the sun sits in the sky, the volcano's peak is shrouded in mist. As far as the eye can stretch, the land is green and lush, flowers and birds fighting for space on the horizon. Normally this view causes Jendayi to pause, but today she is too tired to appreciate the abundance of Costa Rica. Summer will be here soon after so many months of heavy rain and *neblina.*

As Jendayi waits her turn, she absentmindedly watches the brown, muddy water course down the firmly packed dirt road. She mumbles good morning, *buenas dias* or *hola* to the various women in line, who she knows are already taking stock of her old leather sandals and untidy hair, tied back quickly in a yellow headscarf. Jendayi also knows that the younger girls are whispering behind her back about the boys in *La Gotera* who seem to find her interesting. Normally, she does not have to undergo these gossipy stares because she is the first to get her water and leave. Jendayi keeps her back straight and tries to be polite without saying a word. Yet, Josefina is greeting everyone as her normal, bubbly self. Jendayi can tell it is all fake, but she is impressed by Josefina's ability to manage a crowd of nosey women. A random thought flits through her mind: there are no boys in this line collecting water. Before she can get too upset about this, the line begins to move. As she gets closer to the water pump, the air, filled with spraying water, grows chillier. After Jendayi is finally able to fill her containers, she quickly balances her long stick across her shoulders, cloth wrapped around the pole where it rests on her neck. Josefina lifts both gourds, placing their leather cords on either end of the stick. Jendayi moves with impatience and splashes Josefina with water as she leaves the line.

"Hold still already, Jendayi," Josefina says as she looks down at her wet dress. Jendayi doesn't even bother to apologize because she knows that within five minutes the sun will quickly dry the thin material. Her mouth is still tired from all the talking she did in her dreams last night. Jendayi is afraid to ask her father if she called out in her sleep. Her mind wanders to their house as she adjusts the water on her shoulders. Jendayi and her father live closest to the road into Cartago. From their front door, they can see the Cruz de Caravaca and the Volcano Irazú. Her father is meticulous with their house and whitewashes it annually, once the rains subside. Like Mama Petronila's house next door, they have a profusion of red, orange, and pink flowers planted in clay pots by the front door as they do not have much of a front yard. It is Jendayi's job to maintain the clay pots of herbs, especially lemongrass for tea, along the back of the house. She loves *zacate de limon* and savors its full muskiness in her mouth after allowing it to steep for a few minutes. In the back of their house, there is a small path that leads to the outhouse and her father's work shed.

Their house, like many of the others in *La Gotera,* has three rooms: the kitchen with a sizable hearth and a big wooden table for cooking, cleaning, and eating and two small bedrooms. In the kitchen, there are two wooden benches Jendayi's father carved under the table, which they would push in and out when working or eating. The walls inside the house are also whitewashed and there are several shelves her father has constructed that hold a cast-iron pot, a kettle, plates and utensils, clean cloths and four red-clay pots with flour and grains. Displayed on two walls are small handwoven fabrics that Jendayi has created over the years during her school breaks. She has always been creative with her hands, so weaving comes naturally to her. The colors of thread she chose match the vibrant colors of Costa Rica's tropical flowers, many of which Jendayi can see outside the window. Her favorites are the honeysuckle, lemongrass, and oregano that grow wildly in the back of their house that she uses to make oils to keep the bugs out. If she pinches the leaves, their sharp, lemony tang will be on her fingers like perfume throughout the day.

The kitchen is the center of Jendayi and her father's life, as this is where they are most together. Last year, Mama Petronila gifted her a large mortar and pestle for her fourteenth birthday, with a clear message about Jendayi's cooking duties. It holds a rarely used place of honor at the center of the wooden table along with a clay pot filled with flowers and a candelabra of melted candles. What Jendayi loves most about their simple house is that her father has several of his Shona sculptures on small tables and some shelves throughout the room. When she is working alone or her father is carving by the hearth, that is when she feels most at peace, admiring the beauty of what his hands have produced. She, too, wishes to do the same one day. The kitchen opens to a small hallway that has two wooden doors side-by-side to each other.

Their bedrooms are small and utilitarian, holding a bed, a chair, two circular tables and some shelves. Jendayi has tried to add color to her room by putting up blue curtains in her one window and placing smaller sculptures from her father on the shelves he has erected. Most of these are gifts marking a birthday or the new year. Mama Petronila taught her how to weave palm-frond mats, so she makes them every year for their rooms to stave off the Cartago cold first thing in the morning when she gets out of bed. Her favorite piece of furniture in the room is a magnificently hand-carved table her father made of one entire tree trunk. It is a masterpiece really, with all its intricate twists and turns and burnished mahogany wood. Sadly, the wax from too many candlesticks covers its surface these days, taking away some of its beauty. Jendayi has a small mirror, a washbasin, and another serviceable table near the window for washing up. Her father's room is stark: he has no sculptures, colors, or decorations, though she tries to add fresh flowers for him whenever she remembers. He is usually so exhausted after a day of work that his sole focus is the bed when he comes home. The single chair in his room has a stack of his clean pants and shirts that Jendayi has learned to mend (and what a disaster that first was!). Two pairs of sandals sit underneath the bed along with his chamber pot, just in case of midnight emergencies.

Jendayi can reconcile the blandness of her father's bedroom because of all the life he has infused into his work shed. Though it is a small space, it fits a sleeping pallet, a worktable and two chairs. She really loves that space, though she is not allowed in often. The floor and shelves hold her father's beautiful sculptures in various heights, made of the famed teak wood of Costa Rica. He keeps slabs of wood against a wall, many candles on the table and a lantern by the door, which Jendayi continually adds new candles to, as her father often works late into the night when he cannot sleep. The smell is always comforting—woodsy with lemon balm and candle wax.

"Jendayi, come. I will walk with you to the main road into Cartago, until the plaza. I told you there is something I want to share with you," Josefina shakes Jendayi out of her daydreaming by giving her a side look, indicating that she has forgiven Jendayi's water spill. Josefina puts her own gourd of water on her head and begins to walk alongside Jendayi.

Jendayi is too focused on carrying the gourds without spilling them that she does not say anything but soon, they are walking in time with each other. Jendayi stops briefly as they pass the road that goes off to their homes and she watches

Josefina deliver the water to her mother. Mama Petronila is in the yard, waiting as some chickens peck over the grains she has just spread. She stops and waves to Jendayi, shouting a traditional blessing from her home beyond the sea. Jendayi cannot wave back as she is balancing the water and it is very heavy, so she just smiles. As the sun gets higher in the sky, she begins to sweat.

When Josefina rejoins Jendayi, she reaches to take a gourd of water. Jendayi sighs with relief as she can now carry one on her head and remove the stick from her neck and shoulders, which she hoists under her arm.

"Well?" Jendayi says, expecting a story about Nicolas.

Josefina looks around and slowly says, "I overheard Mama and a few others speaking last night about the story about the church. I knew there was a reason why I cannot cross my foot in there."

"Wait. What story?" Jendayi asks, looking at the road straight ahead.

"Well, from what I heard, the *panas*[2] in Cartago and especially Padre at Santiago Apostol do not want people in *La Gotera* to know about it because they want to continue collecting the taxes and tributes to the Grand Church in Guatemala. I have no idea how they can keep convincing our people to put money towards a church that is always in a

---

[2] Derogatory name given to indicate a Spanish colonist by Black people in Costa Rica.

state of repair. It's a never-ending hole for money to fall into. I know they are certainly cursed."

Jendayi murmurs a quick yes, pretending to know what she is speaking about.

"Well, the story goes that there were two Spanish brothers living nearby in Cartago. One was said to be very handsome but lazy and the other brother became a priest. By some chance they fell in love with the same woman, but she only wanted to be with the handsome brother. One Sunday, as the brother who was a priest was giving Mass, he noticed that his brother and this woman were in the church. Supposedly, the priest flew into a rage and killed his brother with a knife right there in front of everyone in the church! It is said that he buried his brother's body under the grounds of the church, the same one you are so dedicated to with your classes. What madness! Can you imagine what the people were thinking in the middle of Mass?"

Jendayi stops walking and turns in her tracks to face Josefina. She imagines the details of the killing near the altar, people screaming as brother fights brother over a woman. Josefina does not stop with Jendayi, and she has to run a bit to catch up with Josefina, splashing the water over the sides of the gourd.

"What else," Jendayi says, knowing there is more to come. The hair stands on her arms and it is not from the sloshing water.

"So, people believe that the priest, who died shortly after killing his brother, has been trying to do penance for his behavior since 1575, but only bad things have been happening with the church. It never seems to be finished and there are always problems with it. Look, remember the earthquake four years ago? Nothing else in all of Cartago was damaged except the church. Even after four years, they are still not finished with the repairs from that time. I know there is so much rubble in the back. My mama says that the priest's soul wanders around the church at night, crying for forgiveness from a brother who refuses to grant it. I always knew there was something bad in that church; no *m' hija*, I am not putting one foot into that place," Josefina says defiantly, as if this is not just gossip she is sharing, but real live news with facts.

They cross the marker of La Cruz de Caravaca, which the Spaniards put up to show the boundary line of where free Blacks could work but not live. It is a daily reminder of how Blacks are never considered good enough: they are integrated into the Spaniards' lives and their economy, but they are not good enough to live within Cartago, unless they are the Spaniards' slaves. Only Africans, mulattoes and mestizos who are free can live in *La Gotera* and work for the Spaniards or like Jendayi's father, have a small business with both African and Spanish customers. Jendayi always stops by La Cruz and silently curses it. This is just an instinct because it is a painful reminder that at one time, when her father was enslaved, they lived on separate sides of that marker. Jendayi was raised by Mama Petronila until he was able to buy his freedom. Happily, Jendayi has very little memory of those seven years apart. She cannot think of anything to say to Josefina about the story she has shared, but the hairs on her arms are raised as they near the church.

With the main doors open, Jendayi can see Padre inside by the altar and she knows to go around the back, near the small kitchen, to deliver the water before she goes inside the school. The kitchen is the area of the church that remains most unfinished since the last earthquake. Jendayi is late, but her head is still turning with all that Josefina has told her. Josefina silently hands her the gourd she has carried and helps Jendayi put the stick on her back in order to balance the two water jugs. Turning towards the main road in town beyond the plaza, Josefina waves goodbye. Jendayi doesn't have time to ask her if she is going to see Nicolas because Padre sees her and points to the back of the church.

The road is muddy from last night's rain and Jendayi is completely drenched in sweat. She did not notice it while Josefina was speaking but now, maneuvering over bits of rubble in the path, she is suddenly aware of how tired she feels. No one is in the small cooking area near the back, so she slowly kneels and places the gourds of water on the ground. She knows that Esmeralda has been waiting for this to get on with her day's work, and she momentarily feels guilty for staying in her dreams too long.

Jendayi deposits the water and wipes her hands on her dress, standing. Her body locks into its shadow and she is unable to move. This is not like her, but her mind is far away. Her breathing comes fast as she goes over the details of Josefina's story.

How unfair it is that she is already so sure of herself that she can say she will never enter this church. I certainly do not understand my own feelings to make such pronouncements, Jendayi thinks, with a pit in her stomach. The story leaves her feeling jumpy, like the *hermanos muertos* have their death eyes on her, peering inside her head in some kind of warning. Jendayi feels the ghost of a warm breath pass her check, startling her out of her reverie. She quickly leaves for the schoolroom, not turning back to see if anyone is indeed behind her.

Jendayi watches her father's dark brown hands carefully. They are long and strong with nails that are cut almost to the quick. He does not have elegant hands, rather there are scars that cover all parts of his skin, each telling their own story. He wields his tiny chisel effortlessly, cutting into the stone that he has told her is like their *rapoko* stone from home beyond the sea. Jendayi is supposed to be sifting the maize for their meal, but she cannot stop studying her father's movements. Her stomach clenches as a familiar emptiness fills her: a longing for a dead mother whose hands only caressed her once and then were gone. She imagines a sculptor's fingers, long and firm, like her father's. Jendayi holds her mother's imagined eyes in her memory, her voice a shadow on the inside of her ear. Yet, Jendayi knows her mother is with her in the darkest nights when she cannot sleep and sadness covers her skin like cloth. On those nights, they talk in whispers as Jendayi recounts her day's work and how her father sometimes labors in the cacao fields of Don Lindo on Saturdays, though he now has his own carpentry shop near the *campo santo*[3] of the Santiago Apostol Church in Cartago. How even at home, he makes time to carve, sometimes long into the night rather than sleep. How she can smell the sadness and longing on him, but she is too much of this place to hold his feelings.

Her father has said they came by *barco* from the place across the sea. The ship was so big that it fought even their god of the water. These are the stories that her father has told her over the years, and she trusts him with her life. He saved her when they finally came to this place, though he could not save her mother. Jendayi does not know what it means to have been born on the sea, between homes, taking her first steps in a place where many of their people were enslaved. Inside, she always feels ready to fly back to Africa, where she could watch her mother and father carve the beautiful figures that made them famous. It was their hands and eyes and the mastery of their carving that brought them to the Dondo traders near the Benguela palace on the Angolan coast. Once a year, Jendayi's parents made the six-day trek across forests and savannas, careful to stay with other groups of traders and not wander alone, lest they disturb animals hungry for their next meal. She always wondered about their lives and the time that brought the final sadness. Maybe, it was because they were so well-known, her mother so beautiful and her father so full of love for his wife, a woman who struggled to

---

[3] The cemetery space next to the Church; "sacred land."

produce a child for him even after seven years of marriage. Or maybe it was because they became too comfortable in their business on the coast. However, it was during this time when Jendayi's mother was finally pregnant with her that they took their time in trading at the coast. Her father boasted that finally he was to have a child and not just a carving of a child to hold in his arms. Her father told her, with shaking hands and skin weeping with sweat, that it was then when they got caught by the Portuguese slavers, first him and then her. No matter how much Jendayi begged for him to tell her more, her father always stopped there, as if he was on the edge of a cliff, a scream locked in his throat. He could not, would not, move any further in his mind's eye.

Jendayi knows that her mother gave birth to her on that ship and died while she lived. Jendayi has never asked what happened to her mother's body or how she managed to stay alive as they were at sea for several months but here she is, watching her father's hands and knowing that he once held her mother's in a place of love, knowing her mother once held her small body in her arms before she died.

Mama Petronila and Josefina were also on that ship with them. Mama always greets her father with an air of deference as she understands that he is a master carver who is considered royalty at home across the sea. She remembers that his name is Dakarai in their language. It means "joy." Jendayi wants to believe that there were times of great joy in his life when he was carving with her mother, when he understood the meaning of his name. He is now called Juan Carlos by the *panas.* Even in freedom, he answers to the name Juan Carlos. Her mother's name, Towela, means "beauty." She was from the Tumbuka people, but after she came to marry Jendayi's father, they lived near the Zambezi, where it was easy to get stone to carve and sell. Her mother died without ever being forced to have a name placed on her by an owner with a lazy tongue.

The *panas* call Jendayi Juana Maria, not her real name, given by her mother, or so her father claims. Jendayi means "to give thanks" in Shona. She guesses even in the bottom of that ship with her mother dying, they both felt that she was a blessing rather than a curse. Only the people in *La Gotera* call Jendayi by her proper name. The Spaniards here do not like them to speak in any language other than Spanish, which she speaks perfectly. Jendayi's father tried to teach her their language from home and it is easy for her, but she has no one other than her father to practice with, even though she knows that Mama Petronila can speak it. She once heard Mama Petronila and her father speaking in their language, remembering that time on the ship.

When Jendayi was a child, Mama Petronila just watched her from the corner of her eyes as she cared for the babies in *La Gotera.* Mama Petronila was eventually given her freedom when she landed in Portobello, Panama as no one would buy her because she was no longer of child-bearing age and could not work in the fields or clean house—she had a severe limp because her right leg was shorter than the other, making it is impossible for her to stand for long periods of time. Neither

Jendayi nor Josefina know what happened to her leg. And so, at fifty-five, she is now the babysitting *abuelita* to African and mestizo children who are free. There is so much that Jendayi wants to ask Mama Petronila about her mother, but she can feel Mama Petronila holding the words tightly, like round stones in her mouth. Maybe she is afraid that if she starts spilling their history, she will never stop speaking of that time. So, she remains quiet and sings the songs of her people softly for the babies that she cares for. Once they are grown, they will be forced to attend the Catholic school that the Padre had made mandatory for all *pardos* in *La Gotera*. Jendayi hates that word, *pardo*. It means a free African, but she thinks no one can give or take freedom. Her father said that at one time he was not a *pardo* but an enslaved man and so he took his freedom seriously. Jendayi has never been enslaved; she is simply an African born far away from home.

Jendayi shakes her head as her father gives her a look that instantly puts her back on task. It is humid that day and she is late preparing their meal. *Domingo* is the only day that they are together for much of the afternoon. During the week, after school, she comes home and teaches Spanish to the small children in Mama Petronila's care, so their parents can go to work on the cacao plantations and in Cartago. There is so much that she wants to know but it seems as if there is a silent bond with all the adults who managed to survive slavery and are now living freely in *La Gotera*. Since Jendayi can read, write and speak Spanish and a bit of her mother tongue, she is considered a girl apart. She tries not to make herself too noticeable, but languages are easy for her and when she gets a lot of practice, as she does teaching the little ones, she becomes better at it. She wants to learn English. Once when they went to the east coast to check Don Jimenez's cacao plantations in Matina, her father met a few Miskito *zambos* and they tried to speak to him in English, or rather a Creole that her father said came from their trade with the British along the shores of that area. They seemed to have understandings that Jendayi did not get. Maybe it had to do with their mixed identity: they were both African and Indigenous and all that wrapped up made them fierce and free. Her father was calm and managed to communicate with them, somehow. When leaving, she saw him give them a small bird he had carved during their journey.

More than languages, Jendayi wants to learn how to carve like her mother and father. But her father refuses to teach her. She feels asking causes him such pain that she stopped all together. But inside her heart, she wants to create. She feels it. Carving is the language that her parents spoke. It connected them to a home with their ancestors.

Esmeralda

My name is Esmeralda. It is only at this time in the morning, when the first birds are remembering the sounds of their voices—calling to the sun to warm their wings after a night of nestled perching—that I can stand outside. I am fifty-one years old as far as I have been able to count, which I learned only after being given to the church. I have always been owned by one form of oppression or another.

As an enslaved person, my life is one of interiors. I clean the church for Padre, and I live tucked away in a shack behind the looming gravity of stained glass and burnt candle stubs. Today, I stand in my doorway, edged slightly against the frame, so if anyone were to pass, they would have to look twice to see me. Instead of staring up into the fleeing night sky and seeing the shadow of Volcano Irazú, I look down at my shriveled left arm, hanging aimlessly against my thin green dress, its color lost years ago with constant washing. It is hard to see the width of this place around me as my left eye remains glassy and visionless. I do not think back to the fire but shrug off those memories that want to take over. I have been in this place, Costa Rica, for my entire life but came here to Cartago at the age of sixteen when my mother and brother died and I was gifted to the church. Thirty-five years have passed, and I serve as witness, now with one eye, to the comings and goings of this very different place. I do not remember the land beyond the sea that many speak about in *La Gotera* and I force myself not to take on their longing. Guatemala is the center of the universe in this place of mountains and volcanoes, and trees thick with arms that stretch into the nocturnal homes of hundreds of birds.

The air is chilled this morning. Padre has yet to stir, though at times I have been called to light candles in the small chapel alongside the altar this early in the morning when he has woken from a restless sleep and prayer is possibly his medicine. I don't know and I do not care about the things that move his world. I only care when his world collides with mine. Today, I think about this town that feels forgotten from the rest of the world. The labor of my enslaved brothers and sisters is shared alongside their owners in the cacao farms and cattle ranching to provide the meat which is cooked by enslaved hands at the tables of the *panas* in town. I hear them discussing how without a cash plantation crop, they are unable to compete with the silver mines or sugar cane plantations of Brazil. Our numbers are relatively small and that is why several have been able to hire themselves out and, over time, eventually buy their freedom. I have seen Dakarai do it, seven years owned and working for all those extra

Sundays where he saved every *real*[4] until he could remove the bitterness of slavery from his tongue and become reunited with his daughter, Jendayi. Some, like myself, do not have the fortune of skills that they can manipulate towards freedom. I am a slave of the church and I know this is how I will die. With my one working eye and arm, it is much more difficult to do the work of cleaning, yet Jendayi delivers water to the church before attending school here with the other children who are free Blacks under Padre's guidance.

Costa Rica is nestled between two wide oceans, I am told. It does not offer much and so we are poor and huddled in the confines of the Orosi Valley, pretending that the Spaniards here are not forced to labor among their enslaved workers in order to pay the taxes to the Grand Audience in Guatemala. The details are hard to work out, but I know there is not enough money to create certain distances between those who are free and owned.

I waited an extra hour for her this morning. Jendayi cannot see me, but I can smell her youth, even after she has put the water down, making prints in the soft, slushy mud that has been made from the water she spilled. I only see out of one eye, so the world is concentrated in the other senses of my body. Creaks fill my ears as I straighten from the small kerosene stove which I have warmed my *café con leche* on. This

---

[4] Silver currency of the time period.

is my only weakness, as I do not always have access to milk. Normally, my coffee is rumbling brown and steaming hot. However, yesterday, Doña Elena came to the church to arrange for the baptism of her grandson with Padre and she brought offerings of milk and sugar. When Padre came out to my small shack, I thought he was coming for other things; things that go unsaid. Even in this old age, I do not have the freedom of my body. But Padre cleared his throat and handed me a tin cup filled with fresh milk through the partially opened crack in my door. As soon as he turned his back to go inside the church, I touched the cup to my lips and drank just a sip. Instantly, I was taken back to the time when my brother, Enrique, would milk the cows at the *hacienda* and bring some of it back to our mother. This is when I did not know the formal bonds of slavery; I was a child. Yet, I was smart enough to notice that my mother's back was like a crescent moon. She hardly looked up from her work and I have few memories of Mama ever looking at my face. I was left to play on my own and then eventually work on the *hacienda* until Don Domiques gave me to the church. I have seen three different Padres run this church. But this one is like the other bad one, who killed his brother in their sacred place, blood spilt on the altar where his spirit continues to moan at night, witness to my sleeplessness. However, this one is really the worst. He is young, perhaps forty, but already he has a stout body from all the rich food he finds at the tables of hospitable Spanish families. His straight brown hair often covers the meanness in his dark, narrow-set eyes. There is no kindness in him, though he pretends to be respectful to the wealthier patrons of the church to ensure his place at their Sunday dinner table.

Though I could be his mother, he expects things from me that no son should want. I think it is this church that makes his blood tainted. There is only death and sadness here, since the killing brothers. I have heard the tales, whispers, about the wandering soul whose voice I too have heard lamenting, as I clean the floors of the nave. I never fear him since his sorrows mirror my own. At times, these sounds provide company for me in a world that is so silent and cruel. The crimes of its current master scream louder than any dead man looking for redemption. In the daytime, Padre is the center of the community in Cartago and on Sundays he preaches the message of a vengeful God. When enraptured on the pulpit, the spittle from his mouth has often reached into the first pews, covering his parishioners like holy benediction. I can see, even with my one eye, that the Spanish people respect and fear him. He wears the brilliant robes I wash by hand and lay out in the sun to maintain their whiteness. If there is a stain from the wine when he performs Mass and I cannot get it completely out, he beats me.

After service, there is always a Cartago family who will invite Padre to their home for dinner. Usually, it is during this time that I am most afraid. He will return to the church, full of wine and talk and then when the night has turned down, he will come to me. Like a dog, he sniffs and grabs me with an unexplainable force. He is a holy man of their church and yet he climbs on me with a violent urgency that forces my spirit to sit at the hollow of my throat, deciding if it should finally escape this body called woman. This has been happening most Sundays for a year now and I want to rest. He never looks at me as he removes himself from my body. He always takes me from behind and though I used to hide in the corners, he forever captures me with such rage that now, I just sit at the door, expecting.

The first time he came, a year after he was installed in the church, I was so stunned that we fought. He climbed on me and I tried and tried to buck him off. When he was finishing, holding my face down into the earthen floor, I grabbed a candle nearby and swung my left arm wildly behind me. I caught him off guard and the flame grabbed the edge of his shirt and my dress. I could not move with his weight on my back and so by the time he got up to save himself from the flames, my dress was already on fire. He ran out, leaving me to scream as the flames ate my left arm and up my face to my left eye. All I have today are the external scars from a battle that I lost.

I am too old to bear a child. I have never been pregnant, and it is for the best. I cannot bring someone into this world that will have to face this life, especially if the child is a girl. Her status as slave is guaranteed because in the will of Don Domiques, he said that should I bear children, they too will be inherited by the church. My generations are imprinted with pain before their spirits even have a chance to enter this world. And so, I give thanks for the barrenness of my woman-body. Many times Padre has spilled his seed inside me, wiping himself on the coarse green edges of my tattered dress which I have worn day in and day out since that evening when my other dress burned. No life has ever resulted from this violence and this is my only redemption.

That Sunday night a year ago, I managed to stagger to the Cruz of Caravaca and someone in passing must have taken me to Dakarai's home, since it was the first on the road in *La Gotera.* I was not fully conscious but at times, I would awake to Petronila's cool hand on my face. She used aloe on my burns over the days it took for my body to decide to stay on this earth. Dakarai and Petronila have become my people, though I carry no memory of Africa beyond the sea as they do. I was born in this place. Only the two of them stand as witnesses to what Padre did to me and continues to do. I cannot voice it, but they can read it on my body and in my one eye.

Now, one night every other week when Padre visits a parish in the north which requires an overnight stay, I walk to the back of Dakarai's house and sit in the little work shed where he turns stone into language. In the corner, there is a clean sisal mat which I sit on and light a small candle. With very few words, I remove the small book I have sewn together from old parchment taken from Padre's desk and a piece of charcoal which Dakarai has whittled into a pencil for me. Here, with the respectful distance of a true son, he teaches me to read and write. I know that where he came from in Africa, he was a great, knowledgeable man. He told me that he can speak and read several languages.

Today, I can smell Jendayi's freedom. She has no idea that the soles of her feet can take her far away from this life. The *panas* call her Juana Maria, but I know she is Jendayi because I heard her father call her this name from when I entered their home a year ago. Jendayi has the carelessness of a child who has always had food in her stomach and people to protect her. She is a girl who dreams. I sleep in the hollow of darkness, always with an ear open to the night. She is the only child who has made me feel the emptiness of my arms. And so, I watch her from the shadows, and I hold the sadness on my left side.

When she delivers the water, I can tell sometimes that she wants to come and talk to me. She strains her eyes to see into the corners of my shack. But I always stand away. She does not know that her father is teaching me to read and write. I wrote a letter once to my older brother, Enrique. He died when disease came to the cattle on the *hacienda* and no one noticed him as all the Spaniards in the house were sick. No one cared about an enslaved African. I found him on his mat with our mother dropping water on his tongue as he could no longer swallow. He died in her arms. This is the only time in my life that I saw my mother cry. I did not utter a word, but I knew even then that I was saying goodbye to an entire life. Don Domiques was so distraught that his daughter, the same age as Enrique, had succumbed to the fever that he sold his *hacienda* and moved to Nicoya. This is when he left me to the church in Cartago. My mother died soon after my brother, and they are left in small, unmarked graves near the *hacienda*. I wrote Enrique a letter saying all the things I never said as a child when I watched him die. Today, this letter is my most prized possession, even at the age of fifty-one. I can never reveal the secret of my learning to Padre but whenever I clean, I read the letters that are on his desk and many times I have given the news to Dakarai to share with people in *La Gotera*. If I can help them be prepared, then I have done my job of mothering in this lifetime.

Dakarai

Same day, Dakarai's carpentry shop, Cartago

"Juan Carlos, there is a special commission I would like for you to undertake," Don Jimenez says without the courtesy of a greeting, as he enters the work shed. Dakarai looks up quickly, unhappy to have to respond to the name Juan Carlos when he still remembers his mother calling his true name. Putting down the wood he holds, he wipes his hands on the dark green apron around his waist and stands to give Don Jimenez, the town mayor, his full attention. Dakarai is one of a handful of free Africans who own carpentry workshops in Cartago. Though there are four other men who maintain the same livelihood, it is Dakarai's ability to carve delicate flowers into sturdy headboards and engrave names into baby bassinets that sets him apart from the others. For seven years, he worked for free as an enslaved man but over time, he had been able to rent out his labor, mostly carving at night, and he had eventually saved the 250 *pesos* in order to buy his freedom after years of backbreaking work on the cacao plantation.

In Costa Rica, the economy forces masters and the enslaved to work alongside each other in the fields, and so the challenges of maintaining the upkeep of another man are often too hard. Seasonal labor wherein enslaved men and women are hired on their one day-off a week to competing masters at harvest is a pattern many enslaved people take part in. Emancipation took years of focused work, but Dakarai had a vision of reuniting with his daughter and so the years turned into minutes and bated breath, until he was able to achieve his freedom papers. The irony of it all was that by then most of the Spanish families throughout Costa Rica slept on beds he had carved and ate at dining tables his hands had fashioned.

His daughter's freedom was never a question as she had been raised by Mama Petronila when he was sold all those years ago. When their ship had landed, after Towela's still-warm body was thrown into the tumultuous sea, Petronila had managed to hold onto his newborn, as those who survived were rounded into two groups. She also had her small daughter, Josefina, with her. Petronila was put into the group that was considered useless; too old or frail or sick to add to the labor economy, because of her bad limp. It seemed that word had come from the Portuguese governor, who had kept her for two years and fathered Josefina, that she was useless for work in the field and could no longer produce babies. Nonetheless, she had been added to the ship's cargo for a meager price. When no one purchased her, she was freed and made to fend for herself. She kept her freedom papers for all to see, though she could not read them herself. For Petronila, it was a moment of divine reprieve. Those who were not enslaved were sent to *La Gotera* to survive on their own. Eventually, some had managed to rent out their labor or sell their produce at the weekly Thursday market. Many just lived off the land and remained in *La Gotera*, happy not to engage with the Spaniards, yet always wary. Families had developed over time and many decided to stay as the terrain of Costa Rica was too treacherous to wander without the fear of being enslaved, if caught, and taken to the cacao plantations in the swampy and humid lowlands. *La Gotera* became the in-between space for those tentatively hanging onto the title of freedom.

Only those considered strong were sold quickly amongst the grasping hands of the Spanish elite at the impromptu auction in front of the church. Dakarai had just enough time to catch Petronila's eye as he was hauled away, his arms tied behind him while forced to walk to the house of Don Lindo, his new owner. It was only Petronila's kiss on the head of his fussy, days-old daughter that allowed him not to strangle the man who owned him. All those years, he had kept that moment like a painting in his mind as he toiled with the singular goal of being able to place a similar kiss on his daughter's head. He could not envision her beyond that newborn moment, could not envision the growing, gangly girl that he would eventually meet seven years from that moment of separation. It had taken some time to find the language to greet his daughter when he was finally reunited with her. Jendayi, who was identical to her mother, Towela, with the same lingering smile, always caused him to look twice.

It had taken time to develop his carpentry business, gaining the trust of the community, both Black and white. He felt great pride when his workshop was finally completed and he could generate income to feed his daughter. Though the shop was only a one-room wooden building that he built by hand, there were windows all around, looking out to the *campo santo* of the church to the west and the Volcano Irazú to the north. Every inch smelled of wood and dust with a hint of leather. Even though he swept daily, he could not conquer the wood shavings on the ground. All his work concentrated around the sturdy teak table in the center of the room, which was a workbench, eating space and occasional pillow to rest his head when his sleeplessness hit him. Near the door was a small square table and chair where customers could sit so business transactions could happen in a somewhat civilized manner. Several candles were placed strategically throughout the workshop for evening light. The outhouse behind the workshop brought occasional gusts of the rancid smell of urine through the windows, at times overpowering even Dakarai's seasoned nose. Most mornings, once setting down his lunch for the day, he would lean against the door frame and watch the world waking around him. Since he was on the central road into town, the noise, even in the early morning, was riotous as oxen saddled with fresh Orosi mountain coffee, fruit carts pulled by sturdy horses, barking dogs and food vendors all fought for another day. The church's bells divided the day for morning and evening prayers and it was this ritual of time that allowed Dakarai to mark his labor in Cartago. On a very busy day, a customer might come away with a mouthful of dust from the wood shavings flying under Dakarai's swift fingers. Although he was proud to own his own business and his time, there were no personal effects or decorations in the workshop, as Dakarai did not want to create any attachment there; it was simply a place of work.

Shaking his head, Dakarai attempts a half smile and faces Don Jimenez with a respectful, expectant half gaze.

Jimenez, seemingly agitated, remarks, "Doña Francesca de Ibarra is having an elaborate wedding for her son, Alvaro, who is now to inherit all their *haciendas* and cattle ranches in Cartago and Nicoya since his father has passed. However, Alvaro's bride-to-be, Isabella, has made it clear that she intends to snap his 'mother-strings' and has demanded a new house built with all new furniture. They are our wealthiest, most respected family here, and I have convinced Doña Francesca that she does not need to write to Spain for the furniture in the new bridal house. There is not enough time if they want an Easter wedding to have a ship sail with the goods. I believe that everything can be done here in Costa Rica. Doña Francesca has been in my ear about this problem as she worries that she will be sent to one of their remote *haciendas* should she anger this new daughter-in-law. So, I gave her another solution: She can hire you to make the bridal furniture. The house is already being built. The problem is that Isabella wants Italian tiles, stones and rare gems inlaid into the wooden furniture. The Spanish cedar and teak wood are plentiful here, so you do not have to worry over resources. As the mayor of

Cartago, I must do what I can to assuage our families and I am concerned because Doña Francesca is without a husband to help establish the authority in her family."

Dakarai is not expecting this and is instantly wary. Though not in a position to say no, he knows that by accepting this job, he risks being rushed to produce an entire house at the expense of other projects he has undertaken for several families. However, one quick glance at the desperation on Don Jimenez's face tells him that he is in a rare, and perhaps dangerous, position to negotiate. Dakarai straightens his back and watches the resentment tinge the corners of Jimenez's eyes. Yes, the irony is tangible as Jimenez stands facing an African man, once enslaved and now free with a viable business, who looks at him with a bare sliver of humility.

"Don Jimenez, this is an unexpected honor. As you must know, I have been commissioned for several other projects which need at least another month to complete. My concern is the limited time in which the furniture must be prepared, as based on your information I will only have six months until April to produce work which includes stones and tiles imported into the country. This is a weighty task."

"All those concerns can be managed. You know, this has never been done before, paying a *pardo* to build a new house's furniture, so understand that this is a once-in-a-lifetime opportunity. I cannot see what we must discuss further. You agree, correct?" Don Jimenez asks, drawing his pocket watch out of his waistcoat.

Dakarai walks over to a window facing the volcano. He already knows his answer, but he wants to give Jimenez a second to consider what a *no* could mean. Dakarai knows that the rumors are true. Jimenez wants to marry into the Ibarra family. He is clearly trying to gain favor with Doña Francesca, who is still a pretty widow within Spanish standards. Dakarai always felt she was too high in the heel, over powdered even on the hottest Cartago days and she never addressed him directly. She almost never spoke to any African in Cartago except the enslaved Micaela, who had been with her for years.

Clearing his throat, Dakarai replies, "Doña Francesca and her family are slave owners, Don Jimenez. You know my feelings on that."

Dakarai's words give Jimenez a start as he quickly states, "Slavery is legal in Costa Rica, Juan Carlos. You are not so far removed from that state that you should forget your tone with me. Freedom is a fleeting business."

Before making a response, Dakarai takes a deep breath at the clear insinuation that he should know his place. Freedom is precarious indeed. Taking a final risk, Dakarai stands taller in the fading evening light and softly says, "I am honored by this opportunity Don Jimenez; so yes, I will make the bridal furniture within the time period requested. However, my compensation is more valuable than a payment in cacao or *reals*. Doña Francesca owns three enslaved workers. My payment request is that she manumits them on the wedding day of Don Alvaro and Doña Isabella. If she wants them to continue with their service, they must be *paid* servants with the option to find their own homes outside of the *hacienda*. That is my price. And there is one more thing: I need to hire three additional workers to help complete the furniture, all who will be paid for their work."

Don Jimenez stares at Dakarai in outrage. His hand flicks by his side automatically as if he is itching to crack a whip. His body language makes it apparent the type of slave owner he is. Dakarai turns again to look out of the window, not wanting to watch Jimenez gain control of himself.

"Impossible. Who are you to negotiate the freedom of others who have no family claim on you? Why do they concern you? Those are not your people. What you ask is too great," Don Jimenez turns, as if already settling on the lies he will tell Francesca about why the African Juan Carlos cannot make her son's bridal furniture.

"Don Jimenez, I accept your feelings. I am not asking for the monetary payment of my labor. I was once enslaved and understand hard work without due compensation. My offer stands, and I am prepared to contact my other customers to seek permission to transfer their orders to Miguel and his brother Roberto, who do good work and sometimes are in my employ. However, maybe it is best for all of us, if you can go to them with Doña Francesca's request, as I am sure their price will not be so humanly high. Please give my regards to the Ibarra family," Dakarai offers with finality.

Don Jimenez stalks out the door to where his horse is tied. Dakarai understands that he has risked his entire business and the possibility of feeding his daughter with his demand because he can be blacklisted amongst the Spanish. But his gut tells him that Don Jimenez will return and accept his offer. He wants too badly to please Francesca as a way of ultimately tying her to him in debt and in marriage. Her dowry includes several vast *haciendas* that her son, Alvaro, cannot touch. Should he become her new husband, Jimenez will have the ultimate say, even in Alvaro's pockets. The Ibarra family stand out in their wealth, as very few Spanish had acquired such land and enslaved workers, barring the Catholic Church.

Three days later

The sun begins to set as Dakarai gathers his tools from the work bench. With more rain on the horizon, it is hard for him to take in the beauty of the Volcano Irazú. It has rained heavily all afternoon and his workday was somber as no customers appeared on his doorstep. However, the pause in the rain is a good indication that he should pack up and head home. With a start as he is not anticipating anyone, Dakarai turns to face Don Jimenez, who leans against the doorframe. Jimenez wipes his mud-caked boots against the threshold as he removes his riding gloves and clears his throat for attention.

"Good evening, Don Jimenez, I hope you and your family are well. Please come in and be comfortable," Dakarai offers with reservation, though he knows why Don Jimenez has returned so quickly. Rather than let him get right to the negotiations, Dakarai is all politeness, extending the pleasantries common amongst the Spaniards, even when they are lined with ill-intent.

"No, no, I am fine here, Juan Carlos. You know why I have come. We need to talk. Doña Francesca is now insisting on having you as the sole carpenter for this new house. She will not change her mind and she has placed her confidence in me that I will convince you to take on the work. She is prepared to make it very lucrative for you; you will be able to open a second shop in Nicoya or Guanacaste and hire additional apprentices because this job will not only make you wealthy, but much celebrated for the quality of your work," Jimenez explains in a gruff tone.

Dakarai takes this in silently. He is already appreciated for the quality of his work and his name is known, even in Panama. He has no need for additional shops or apprentices when he knows his daughter is the one who possesses the talent needed to pass on his craft. She was born with the hands of a carver. There are no advantages to Jimenez's offer and he instantly becomes distrustful. The *panas* are famous for their games of manipulation.

"Don Jimenez, I am humbled that you have returned with such interest from Doña Francesca. It would be a pleasure for me to do this work for her as a gesture of support for the new marriage in her family. As you know, I have more than enough work to last me until the next harvest. I am not looking to make more money when my farm in *La Gotera* feeds my family and manages to also take care of some of my elderly neighbors. I do not seek fame and fortune with this work, Don Jimenez. However, you know what I must say to you. The freeing of Doña Francesca's enslaved workers is the payment for the work that I will undertake over the next six months; much of it will be backbreaking and at the sacrifice of other jobs that I have already consigned. My position is the same as when we discussed it three days ago," Dakarai states, looking directly at Jimenez.

"Come now, Juan Carlos, you must consider the position that you are putting Doña Francesca and her family in. They are the leading family in Cartago and for them to suddenly release their slaves at the whim of a former slave, well, that is just unheard of," Jimenez scoffs.

Dakarai continues with a firm tone, "With respect, Don Jimenez, I have considered this very seriously. I do not feel that I am asking beyond the weight of my work for the freedom of three Africans. I know too well the price of slavery to take this lightly. What are Doña Francesca's thoughts?"

Don Jimenez straightens. Twilight has set and the breeze from the valley, indicating the coming rain, pushes gently through the door. The workshop is getting dark and Jendayi has his supper waiting at home. Going back and forth is useless. Dakarai knows he will never change his mind. Yet, he senses a battle within Jimenez.

"Don Jimenez?"

"Juan Carlos, I am sensitive to how much Doña Francesca wants this gift for her son and his future wife. I do not think you are considering the implications of this position for you, even as a representative of your people in *La Gotera*. Due to my steady influence as her advisor and friend, I have proposed, as a final option, that she indeed free the three slaves as a wedding gesture for Alvaro. She has agreed after much debate. If all goes well with your work, they will move into Alvaro's new house as paid servants, and she will undertake their compensation. However, she has made it clear that under no circumstance can it be known that this idea is at your behest," Jimenez wipes his brow with a starched handkerchief.

Taking a moment to put away the bristling white linen, Jimenez continues, "You will not receive a single *real* for your work and you are expected to complete all the furniture before the wedding date, with it installed properly in the house. Doña Francesca will be supervising some of the designs for the tiles and embedded stones throughout the house. I have heard that Isabella also has made very specific requests for her bedchamber and sitting room, but these will come in time. Juan Carlos, are you agreed?"

Giving a brief nod, Dakarai asks, "Don Jimenez, my request had another condition that you have yet to mention. I also asked to hire three additional workers who must be paid by Doña Francesca in order to finish within the time constraints. Six months is very little time and with three men working six days a week from sunup to sundown, we still may not complete the job in time. Has she agreed to this payment? I am asking for two *reals* per day per worker. It is not a lot, considering the work you are asking us to undertake."

"One *real* per day for six months, not a day over and only one additional worker. This person must be a *pardo*, no slaves will work on the property as I don't want them thinking that they too deserve pay when they are fed and clothed in our homes. This is my final offer. We have debated over this issue too long, Juan Carlos. State your position so I may go home to my dinner," Jimenez continues with an air of annoyance.

Dakarai looks in Don Jimenez's face. He has taken an immeasurable risk asking for the manumission of the three enslaved workers but in this moment he has won. Before his mind can wander to what this will mean for Micaela, Dakarai looks Jimenez squarely in the eye though Jimenez turns away quickly, not wanting to acknowledge that Dakarai is now an equal. Dakarai's acquiescence paves an easier road for Jimenez into Francesca's bed and pockets and there is an unspoken understanding in the air that Jimenez understands that he has been cornered.

In a moment of daring, Dakari extends his hand to shake on the deal. Jimenez reluctantly grazes his fingertips in response, pain etched across his face that he should find himself negotiating with an African. Fighting a sudden urge to escape the awkward handshake, Dakarai calls after Jimenez as he walks towards his horse, "Please express to Doña Francesca my gratitude. I will not disappoint. I should also like to visit the building site and lay the dimensions. We will require the specific details for the tiles and stones and what furniture should be included. If you could arrange for these lists to be brought to me by the end of the week, I would be very appreciative."

Jimenez's nod when he sits atop his horse is all Dakarai receives in response.

Esmeralda

The Church of Santiago Apostol, one week later

I cannot believe my ears. Without a doubt, I hear Don Jimenez tell Padre that Juan Carlos is demanding the freedom of the three Ibarra enslaved workers as payment for making the bridal house furniture for Alvaro and Isabella. Their hushed voices belie their anger about having to negotiate with an African. The townspeople will hear soon, and this could be a disaster as the tenuous relationships between the *panas* and the *pardos* could explode when they realize that Dakarai is an African man attempting to cross the line into power. I shake my head in disbelief. How can Dakarai make such a negotiation with the *panas*? I understand his position on slavery, but the risk is too great. Dakarai is like a son but nothing I'm hearing now explains his actions. I did not know this part of him, and it fills me with unease. Straining to catch more of the discussion, I hear Padre clear his throat and I know now that he is without counsel and stalling with advice for Jimenez. Most decisions about Cartago do not exist without Jimenez's involvement. As mayor, Jimenez walks with the care of a big man. But, deep down, I know that he too is a bad seed.

I saw him through the crack in my door, the day when Jimenez caught Padre unaware, just exiting my room while buttoning the front of his trousers, walking with the air of a man satiated. The smell on him must have told it all, and when Jimenez did not greet him with his customary hand-shake, both silently looked the other way while acknowledging what had happened. Jimenez pretended to ignore what he saw but it was a moment that forever shifted the balance of power between them. I know that no longer is Jimenez given so many Hail Marys at confession and no longer is Padre invited to his dinner table as often, and so remains the unspoken secret wrested upon my old back.

When both men stand up from the pew, I cautiously slip out the side door near the altar. My shoeless feet are used to the grooves in the tiled floor and my life speaks no shadows on it. For the first time in years, I know another type of fear, a feeling beyond the expectations of Padre's Sunday visits. This situation can cause a lot of trouble for Dakarai and the people of *La Gotera*. He is pushing too hard and it is inconceivable that he asked such a thing from the Spaniards who once sold him, as if a mango from a good harvest. Was it not possible for him to see that these *panas* could steal his labor and in the end, he could come away empty-handed, with nothing to feed his daughter? His shop could close, his business gone as the *panas* would see him as a man who needed to be put into his place. If this all went bad, he would lose everything, filling his belly and his daughter's only with convictions of freedom.

Could this be the same man who had treated my broken body with aloe leaves and boiled me lemongrass tea on that first night when Padre had climbed on me a year ago? Was this my Dakarai, a son, who taught me the curves of words and pushed in my hand the pencil of freedom? How could he be so reckless? What would have given proof that these people were trustworthy? I feel as if Dakarai is split into two men when I have always cherished one. These are the moments when the rumblings of slavery and its devastation to the mind became most apparent. Somewhere in the process between freedom, slavery and then freedom, Dakarai forgot. He did not hold onto the memory of his torment, and he had begun to dream as if he was indeed a free, educated man back in that place across the sea. Those days were gone and now this single act could cost them all.

I enter Dakarai's work shed at the back of his house. It is not a teaching night for Dakarai, so he is unprepared for my presence. From the shape of his shoulders, I can smell his tension.

"Son, I am here."

Dakarai jumps up, spilling a bit of his food from the bowl on his lap.

"Agogo[5] Esmeralda, I did not hear you enter. You are

____

[5] *Grandmother* in Shona.

welcome. Tonight, we are not expected to work, unless, unless, I have forgotten and made this plan with you?" Dakarai stammers.

"No, my son, I have not come to work. We have many things to talk about and there is little time. I come at a great risk because I will be punished if Padre notices I have left the church compound." I ease myself onto the corner mat which usually signaled that I, the pupil, was ready to begin lessons. Tonight, I feel the urgency in my body.

Dakarai turns his body towards me, rubbing his hands against his thighs in apprehension, and asks cautiously, "Agogo, how may I help you? Has Jendayi not been delivering the water on time to the church? I am beginning to worry about her; it is the age. I think she needs a woman to guide her, a mother. I am without hands as we turn this curve in her life."

"No, your daughter has been faithful in her job. She delivers the water and then goes to learn her lessons with Padre and the other children. She is becoming an excellent Spanish teacher to the little ones. They lean into her when she speaks, like small flowers bending to the sun. Her heart is pure. She is not why I am here, my son. Tonight, I come with a warning." I fold my hand gently into my lap and lift my head to look directly in Dakarai's eyes.

Reserved, he says, "So, you have heard."

"Yes, today in church, I overheard Jimenez and Padre discussing your situation. My son, all I can ask is why? Why do you think these people are trustworthy enough to follow through on their promises to a mere African man? I know that they are very disturbed by your demands and the fact that you feel you can negotiate with a Spaniard. My worry is that this will come at a cost that is bigger than we can foresee; they will try to make an example of you. Your freedom means nothing to them. I will . . ." I stop mid-sentence, startled by the light scratching at the door. Dakarai clears his throat and the door opens gently as a body emerges from the shadows.

Micaela, Doña Francesca's favorite slave, stands against the wall, with wide eyes, a covered wooden bowl in her hand. Saying nothing, she nods a greeting at me and remains standing. A woman just turned thirty with firm hips, plump, rounded breasts and skin the coco-brown color of morning chocolate, she is a beauty. Her hair is well oiled and plaited around the crown of her head, showing clearly the effort she had made to meet Dakarai. Without looking at either of them, I understand in an instant: lovers. It all makes sense now.

I get up with a swiftness which belies my age, "Ahhhh, my son, I see how the land lies. I am old and tired and must make my way back. My daughter, I wish you a good night." I am out the door and along the forested path towards Cartago in minutes. Though my body moves quickly, my heart is heavy.

"Micaela, sit," Dakarai says, indicating a space on the bench in the tiny work shed. "Tonight, I am weary and Agogo has brought some news that makes me distracted." Shadows dominate the space since only a few soft candles flicker near the windowsill. The air is punctuated with the occasional cicada call as leaves brush the clay-tiled roof of the shed. The on-and-off rain of the evening had helped Micaela ease through the shadows into *La Gotera*.

"I have made banana bread for you," Micaela places the bowl on the worktable and uncovers the cloth. The rich scent of bananas, cinnamon and vanilla hangs in the air. Though he has already eaten a late supper, Dakarai's stomach growls with anticipation and Micaela dips her head, pleased with his reaction.

Without a knife to cut into the circular bread, Micaela expertly pulls a small slice out with her fingers and hands it to Dakarai. As their hands brush, she gives him a knowing, familiar look. They have perfected their communication through the music in the touch of their skin. Dakarai, with the barest nod of thanks, takes the bread and eats in silence as she returns to her seat on the bench. They had become lovers over the past year and it was her place in his heart that motivated his spur-of-the-moment request from Jimenez to grant her freedom. To the Africans in Cartago and *La Gotera*, the man the Spanish call Juan Carlos the carpenter, is respected by all and completely unattainable to the Black and Brown women who admire his handsomeness. To have finally crossed into an intimacy with this man, once unreachable, is almost unfathomable to Micaela. To call him his true name of Dakarai, rather than his Spanish name of Juan Carlos, filled with the haunting memories of his enslavement, is indeed a gift.

As a slave for Doña Francesca, she is rarely allowed out of her sight. Yet, one day when Micaela was sent to offer Padre fresh flowers for the altar from Doña Francesca's garden, she saw Dakarai and smiled. She smiled because it was the first time in months that she had been able to walk alone to the church without Doña Francesca lamenting about her perceived laziness. So, Micaela strolled with her basket of flowers and enjoyed the hot sun on her head and the grinding rhythm of the stones under her light leather sandals, as she experienced a moment of timelessness. She did not even try to pretend that this was a life she could have but in that exact moment when she made eye contact with Dakarai as he was crossing the plaza, she had smiled with pure joy; one that made her beauty radiate. And he stopped and smiled back. Shocked, Micaela turned her head as she felt his look sting the blood inside her body. She ducked into the church, murmuring a greeting to Padre and handing him the flowers, while trying to ease the pace of her heart. Padre dismissed her with a disinterested blessing, distracted by the other parishioners coming for confession. With a mumbled directive to tell her mistress many thanks, Padre turned quickly and forgot Micaela's presence. Used to sliding into corners, Micaela quietly left the coolness of the church, all the while thinking of Dakarai. In those days, she too called him Juan Carlos. She did not expect that he would be waiting for her to emerge from the church.

He stood by a tree in the forest surrounding the plaza, shaded and alone. Nodding his head, he beckoned her to approach. Gazing around to see who was about, Micaela walked swiftly across the plaza to stand abruptly in front of him. As she drew up to him, his height and frame seemed imposing. She had never been this close to a free Black man before; she was only used to being near other enslaved Black men when they worked together, and even then, their interactions were limited. She smelled the sharp tang of lemongrass on him along with something else earthier as she inhaled deeply. Like many of the other Black women who whispered while working on the *haciendas* of the Spaniards, Micaela had once foolishly dreamed about being enfolded in the arms of this gorgeous man. Amused at herself for just noticing his newly grown beard, which covered his upper lip and chin in an elegant goatee, Micaela could tell that this was a man who took care of his looks. Rumor had it that he was forty-two, though his broad shoulders tapered into a trim waist and lean legs, giving him the look of a man half his age. Dakarai's dark chocolate skin had the ruddy burnish of being out in the sun for a bit too long. At that moment, Micaela could not think of any other in all of Costa Rica who was more beautiful than this man in front of her.

He looked her squarely in the eyes and said, "Micaela, I am sorry for disturbing your errands as I know the ways of Doña Francesca. You do not own your time, however, grant me a minute, there is something I would like to say," Dakarai leaned into Micaela, speaking softly so only she could hear. And Micaela stood there, a grown woman with lovely mahogany skin, tinged with pink from her walk in the day's sun, momentarily reduced to a teenager. She tucked her head into her chest, trying to still her pounding heart and then slowly looked up again into his eyes.

"You may speak freely, Juan Carlos. I can tell Doña Francesca that Padre was engaged, and I had to wait to give him the gift of flowers. I have a few moments to spare," Micaela whispered.

"Please, call me Dakarai, which is my real name. Juan Carlos is the slave name I was forced to carry and the *panas* are too unimaginative to believe I had a life, a name, and a history before I was their property. But, let me be straight with you, so that you see and hear me for who I am. I speak with the deepest respect for you. I am a man who dedicated a lifetime to the mother of my daughter. She is now gone fifteen years and during that time I have been both enslaved and free. I work and raise my daughter and have not thought too much of what the arms of a beautiful woman would feel like after all this time. Today, in seeing you, I have remembered what it means to be held and loved by a woman. And my need is now great. I would like to see you, Micaela. I understand what I am asking is a dangerous thing. I cannot offer you freedom, marriage, or a home. However, I can give of myself freely, if you will have me," Dakarai said as he pulled back slowly, shadowed by the tree which shaded them from the eyes of possible onlookers, though the plaza was empty.

Micaela felt words bubbling onto her tongue but could not find the right amount of air to say all that she wanted. She looked into his face and saw the lines of his story carved along his eyes. He was an exquisite specimen of a man, all muscle and pull, dark brown with a short afro and poignant, merciful eyes. She caught laughter in them as his mouth curled into a smile when she blushed, letting her know that he enjoyed her admiration of his strong, delicious body. She dared not look below his broad chest to his tapered waist and grounding legs, firmly planted in the earth and telling her that she was safe.

Trying to gain control of the color of her cheeks, all Micaela managed to get out was, "I will come late tomorrow night to your home in *La Gotera*." With those words, and a smile, she turned quickly and ran towards Doña Francesca's house, her heart slamming against her chest with Dakarai's ponderous offer. She also felt fearful of Doña Francesca's wrath if anyone had seen her chatting with him under the tree by the plaza.

A year has passed from that first meeting in the plaza. Their silence in the work shed no longer tells of that initial awkwardness, but of the familiar language they use with each other in love. Micaela watches him, conditioned to wait.

Dakarai

Dakarai too remembers that first meeting in the plaza as he chews the rich banana bread. It is still warm and the oil stains his hands. He thinks back to the first time he watched Micaela take off her dress in the flickering candlelight of his work shed, where he had created a makeshift bed. He can still feel the softness of her thighs as he rubbed her skin in anticipation. He can hear her soft cries as he moved steadily within her, careful, so careful not to spill his seed. She giggled when he reminded her to call him Dakarai, not Juan Carlos, because she earned the right to see and name him fully. But, most of all it is after, in the darkness, when he held her, and she sighed contentedly that he got the idea he must work towards her freedom. He keeps this thought inside all the times when she comes to him, bearing the risk of life and death in order to share these spaces of peace. He understands that she is a woman with no delusions. She is enslaved. He does not question her about her previous encounters with men, yet even as an enslaved woman who does not own her body, she lacks the trepidation of a woman forced into sex. What he cherishes most are their moments in the night's stillness when she offers some advice on how to raise a fifteen-year-old daughter. Micaela has raised Doña Francesca's twenty-two-year-old daughter, the surprise pregnancy at the onset of menopause, after just having her son, Alvaro, for years. Without being forceful, Micaela would recount stories of Lucia, the spoiled daughter and the bane of her existence in a house already fraught with drama and intrigue. But Dakarai always knew that each story was her roundabout way of sharing some suggestions about his Jendayi, without bruising his ego around fatherhood.

Tonight, he is too spirit-weary to make love to Micaela, though he is comforted by her presence. She is a woman who knows herself well, thinks Dakarai. She has been bearing the risk of these late-night meetings all alone at the expense of her life. Dakarai should not ask it of her anymore.

"Micaela, it is best for you to go back to Doña Francesca's. There will be more eyes on me now and I will not put you at any greater risk. I cannot offer you anything that you do not already have from me and so the only thing I can ask you to do is save your own life and not chance coming back for a while. I am hoping that in time this will change, but for now, I cannot say anymore. Please keep your eyes and ears open if you hear any talk about me and the work that I will be doing for Don Alvaro's bridal house," Dakarai shares softly, a sadness growing in his chest.

"Yes, I have been hearing some talk. They are not happy, but I cannot make out much of it, since they are keeping their secrets in quiet corners. That is the reason I also came this evening, I felt there was something going on and wanted to make certain that you are okay. I have been left alone with Lucia, who is ill as the Ibarra mother and son are attending a late-night dinner party. Lucia is fast asleep with laudanum that Dr. Margolis prescribed, so I was able to get away. But I take your meaning. It is best if I leave now as there is no moon tonight so I will not be seen. Dakarai, take care, please."

With those words and a brief caress of his cheek, Micaela eases out of the door and into the ink-blue night. Dakarai cannot hear her footsteps as she crosses the path between the work shed and the main house which turns out to the road. He continues to sit in the dark, timing the minutes until her estimated arrival at the Ibarra house. Minutes turn into hours as sleep grabs him on his stiff work shed bench.

"**D**on Jimenez, what a lovely surprise. Padre and I are just about to have a *cafecito*. Please, come join us," Francesca announces as she lifts her bejeweled hand in greeting from the gazebo in the garden when Jimenez appears at the side gate. Without waiting for the assistance of one of her male slaves, Jimenez lets himself in and walks towards where they are sitting in the shade. The air is fragrant as the morning rain has left flowers lush and open, heavy with drops of water. The heady smell of honeysuckle, strategically placed near the gazebo for guests to admire the flitting of hummingbirds that constantly seek its nectar, is overwhelming as the day has warmed since the morning's showers. The garden furniture is white, with several wicker chairs carefully placed around a delicately hewn table of wood and inlaid tiles. Set against the green of the ever-manicured garden and the fuchsia flowers of the hedges, the gazebo at once invites an air of respite. Jimenez almost smiles at himself since he knows that this space is more of a war room than a friendly place for local gossip.

Jimenez moves to sit in an empty wicker chair to Francesca's left. He greets them all cheerfully, not showing his surprise at seeing Padre visiting in the middle of a Tuesday afternoon. He has wondered about their whisperings while he was at the gate.

"Oh, Jimenez, I was just telling Padre that I am planning a pre-wedding party for Alvaro and will be inviting most of the local families. It would be an honor to have you attend. It will be in a fortnight," Francesca looks directly into his eyes with suggestion. She then dabs at her chin, which had been wet by a few drops of coffee she had been sipping. His nod indicates his acceptance as the invitation is a public formality in front of Padre. Jimenez has yet to bed Francesca, but he anticipates that the upcoming party's invitation finally offers entrance into her bedchamber, given the look she just gave him.

Francesca, on the late end of fifty-seven, is all flesh, pushed up to extraordinary heights by her restrictive corset. She is reminiscent of an over-painted debutante trying in vain to recapture her youth. Her skin is unnaturally white due to layers of face powder that her slave applies daily, and the most interesting part of her rotund body is her elegant profusion of black ringlets, which have yet to grey, a testimony of her easy lifestyle. Fastidiously religious, Francesca is famous for the daily covering of those flowing locks with her black Spanish-lace veil, as if she could fall any minute on her knees in supplication. Prone to gossip and having her nose in all town and church business, Francesca is inherently mean-spirited and takes little notice of anyone that does not serve her personal interests.

Micaela bends busily, arranging the coffee service. She respectfully places a cup and saucer in front of Jimenez but leaves the pouring to Francesca, who usually makes a fuss about her spilling the coffee. Micaela will not look into Jimenez's face because she feels her eyes will betray her need for information about Dakarai. She walks slowly back to the kitchen to get the small cakes and sandwiches that Cook Jenny has prepared, trying to ease her ears around their conversation.

Her removal from serving the coffee allows the three to speak more freely. Standing behind the frame of the kitchen door leading out to the garden, Micaela can easily hear Padre say with outrage that it was impossible for Juan Carlos to ask such a price for his work; the audacity of an African, barely free himself, to demand the freedom of the Ibarra slaves as his payment for the furniture work. As Micaela emerges from the house to place the food on the sky-blue-tiled table, the conversation stops as Doña Francesca clears her throat. Micaela is jittery. By accident, she knocks one of the small cakes off the silver serving tray and, mumbling a rapid apology, crouches to swiftly pick it up. Before Doña Francesca can scream at her, she excuses herself and runs back to the kitchen.

"Oh! What a clumsy, lazy girl. Padre, Jimenez, forgive me, Micaela is naturally slow-witted and my own cross to bear. She is lucky that I have not sold her to the next traveling merchant! It is only because Lucia has an affinity for her that I keep her on but really, she needs to be owned by a master with a firmer hand, I am simply too soft for her own good. I am sure Alvaro will know his expectations of her once she is in his household," Francesca states when both a breeze and her exaggerated movements cause the black Spanish lace veil to shift on her head, momentarily masking her face from her perplexed guests.

"Does Alvaro know that he will be inheriting your slaves?" Jimenez asks as he begrudgingly sips his lukewarm, over-sweetened coffee. Once he takes over this household, he will make sure that everyone knows that he has his coffee black and piping hot.

"No, no, he does not know about this whole fiasco. No one knows, and I am loath to tell Lucia that her beloved Micaela will also be leaving. I just cannot stand the tears. Lucia has her do everything for her; dress her, read to her, do her hair…" Francesca says with an exasperated air.

"Doña Francesca, surely you do not mean to tell me that your slave Micaela can read and write? How has this been allowed to happen?" Padre says with an air of consternation. "You know it is illegal. At best, they can be trained to recite the Holy Scriptures but nothing beyond. There are already too many free Blacks here who will not do our bidding but to have a learned slave in your own house, do you not feel the fear of God in your heart? What if she is plotting with others? What if…"

"My dear Padre, do not worry. Micaela was taught to read and write as a favor to my late husband. He was blind in his later years and she was trained alongside Lucia so that she could read to him when he could no longer read on his own. It was just too tiring an exercise for myself or Lucia; the sickroom is not a good place for women of our constitution. Micaela could bear it all. My husband said he found the reading helpful for his pain. But, alas, he is now with our Heavenly Father and Micaela has no use for reading or writing except when she must assist Lucia with a correspondence, which is hardly ever. I have never once seen her put charcoal to paper, so there is no need to worry. I find Micaela to be a very simple-minded girl; she keeps to herself and does not mix with the other slaves. She is harmless and Lucia will certainly miss her when she is off to Alvaro's house."

Sitting forward abruptly and placing her tea cup and saucer onto the table, Francesca announces suddenly, "You know, I am of the mind to keep her here with me. Juan Carlos will just have to accept this condition. My house cannot do without her. I refuse to bear Lucia's screeches when she hears that Micaela must go. Don Jimenez, you will tell him that I have changed my mind and will keep Micaela with us. The other two may go freely to Alvaro's house as paid servants, as was agreed." With this small speech, Francesca eases back into her chair and fans herself swiftly with her handkerchief. Her gold-plated rosary, tied limply on her wrist, jingles as she wipes the beads of sweat accumulating on her stout neck.

Before speaking, Jimenez gives Padre a look and then takes a sip of his now cold coffee. Francesca's dramatics are famous in Cartago amongst the Spanish elite, yet because of her stature as head of the wealthiest family in the country, most people overlook her exaggerations. Jimenez has also come to steel himself against her daily theatrics, but he is growing tired of it. What this woman needs is a firm hand from a man who, with a look, could send her back to her needlework and church charities and away from the everyday business of running a household and property, particularly the lucrative labor of slaves.

"My dear Padre, I am sure that Doña Francesca is correct in her assessment of Micaela. She is harmless. However, I will advise that any changes you may want to make, you keep to yourself. Let Juan Carlos think that he is getting the full deal of his bargain while he is building the furniture for the house. What happens after the work is complete, well…" Jimenez says with a wry shake of his head.

Clapping her hands together, Francesca calls Micaela from the house again, while addressing Jimenez, "Of course, you are correct, Jimenez. Micaela, girl, come here. Bring us some more hot coffee, this has gotten cold. And do not spill it. Look how clumsy you are. Has Lucia finished her bath? You must go up and instruct her to come down and greet our guests. Hurry now," Francesca marches out instructions in a rushed breath.

Micaela quickly replaces the cold coffee pot with a steaming one, makes a slight bow and runs inside to find

Lucia, her mind spinning. She has to speak to Dakarai. How has she warranted this risk from a man who had only loved her in the dark silences of his work shed? A feeling that she cannot name spreads over her stomach and causes her to pause on the staircase. So, this is love. She had not known.

Jendayi

Early November, end of the rainy season

The rumors about Dakarai's agreement to work for the Ibarra family spread like wildfire through *La Gotera*. With envious tongues, everyone whispers to each other as they gather water or walk towards Cartago for Thursday's market. Most envision baskets of silver *reales*[6] or bags of cacao for his payment. There are the elders who sit by and murmur over their *cafecito,* after a day in their gardens, that Dakarai has overstepped himself by working with the *panas*; he should have just remained in his place and not moved into their world. Dakarai is well-loved and respected in *La Gotera* and his bizarre actions left a general feeling of unease amongst his neighbors. However, people continue to greet him because he is naturally generous and rumors can be overlooked when shared work has to be

---

[6] The silver Real was the common and most important currency used throughout Costa Rica for everyday transactions, along with the barter/exchange system.

done. Jendayi notices strange looks but is not clear on what is happening. All conversations about her father end when she enters a space.

The late afternoon's heat remains fragrant in the air as Jendayi slices avocados. She has no idea how to respond to her neighbors' questioning glances, as she knows nothing of what is going on with her father, but she senses a new tension in the air. Her father has barely spoken ten words to her in the last two days beyond the hasty greetings at the beginning and end of each day. He disappeared into his work shed, with the candle sputtering out in the predawn light. For two nights, she noticed that he did not come into the house to sleep in his bed. Instead, he remained working and most likely fell asleep by his carving bench. She needs answers.

Josefina, perched on the wooden bench near the hearth, clears her throat as again Jendayi has drifted off into her own thoughts.

"Nicolas says that your father is closing his workshop in Cartago to go build a house for Doña Francesca and the *panas* are not happy that he has such a profitable opportunity. There is even some talk about the Ibarras paying him in gold for his work. I think this is all hearsay but your father better watch his back as he decides to make deals with these people. I hear that even Esmeralda, the church slave, has shared how upset the *panas* are about your father negotiating with them. He should just be happy for the work as a *pardo*, they say. How he can trust them, I do not know," Josefina states as she watches Jendayi make dinner.

She manages to mumble a few words to Josefina, giving the excuse that she is hot and tired and needs to finish boiling the *tamales* before her father arrives hungry from a long day of work in town, so she is not up for talking. She is grateful when Mama Petronila's voice wafts through the window in search of Josefina. Jendayi needs to be alone. Josefina waves quickly to her as she walks out the door. Jendayi knows that Josefina does not want her mother to come looking for her. Jendayi places the *tamales* alongside a small salad of avocado, tomato, and cucumber for her father. She is preoccupied with all the work that looms ahead because Thursday market is a day away and she has yet to gather the harvest from their farm, which runs along the Reventazon River. Nor has she gone into her father's work shed to clean and gather any sculptures he carved for selling. All this work makes Jendayi yearn to be away from the house.

Following a feeling in her gut, she quickly wipes her hands, lays a clean cloth over her father's plate, scribbles a note and leaves the kitchen, passing quickly in her room to gather a small clay pot used for personal washing. Filling it with water, she puts on her sandals and walks down the road into the twilight.

Esmeralda

I smell her before I see her. She approaches my door while my head is bent towards my lantern, preparing for the darkening night. I am caught unprepared. Nothing has warned me, not the shape of the clouds or the taste of my *cafecito* or Padre's tone, that she will come and linger on my doorstep today, clearly ignoring her father's orders to never trespass. Our roads were not meant to cross. She knocks, enters carefully and slowly puts the clay jug down near the entrance as an offering. She then stands still, waiting for me to say a word of welcome. She whispers a greeting, hesitant as she checks the shadows of my living. My pallet on the earth floor is neatly made with an old blanket my mother sewed on the *hacienda.* It was the only thing I kept from her, though her rosary was also a gift. I left that behind as I understood all too clearly the world I was entering as a slave to the church. I stand and turn slowly, the lantern drawing shapes around my ankles. I move to close the door firmly as she inches further into the room. I can tell that as her eyes adjust to the dim lighting, she is filled with fear, not just of me but of the answers I can possibly give. I can tell she has so many questions laced on her tongue that if she swallows, she would choke from the effort. I place my one wooden stool near the lantern, a reluctant invitation for her to join me. I sit on the edge of my bed. It is easier if I can see her with my good eye in the darker corner of the room. There are no windows in this shack. She sits quietly and waits.

"Speak, my child. You have taken a great risk in coming here. I may not have all the answers you want to receive," I command.

"I . . . I, uh, I am sorry to trouble you, Mama Esmeralda. I am happy to finally meet you. I know that the people in *La Gotera* have great respect for you, including my father. That is why he tells me never to bother you and that I must always be on time to deliver the water to the church so that you may clean the altar," Jendayi says, stumbling over herself.

She is rambling, trying to find a foothold to begin a conversation which she feels is difficult. Her youthful arrogance of assuming she should know the affairs of adults makes my heart soften towards her. I understand that my weakness for her can be the end of us all.

"What is it you have come here to ask me, young Jendayi?" I can see that I startle her with the use of her mother-name, rather than Juana Maria.

"My father . . . I feel my father is in some trouble and he will not speak of it with me. There is much talk in *La Gotera* about some transactions he has agreed to with the Ibarra family and Don Jimenez, but it is all confusing to me. I thought that maybe since you are at the church and hear many conversations amongst the Spaniards, you might know the truth. I just want to protect him," Jendayi can barely catch her breath as the words tumble out.

"My child, it is not my place to speak in the stead of your father. It is his right to inform you of what is happening around him. However, let me say this and you must take it deeply to your heart; your father has forgotten the time when he too was enslaved here, when he worked the cacao plantations, ever careful not to split his sculptor hands as his machete opened each cacao pod. His time was never easy, yet in seven years of newly-paid-for freedom in Costa Rica, he has decided to trust the people who once owned him. For this, we must all be afraid. Run home, my child, and warn your father to listen to his heart and remember all those who made the long trip across the sea. He must understand that the *panas'* words are never a bond to hold firmly with the integrity of man. He will end up doing all the work for them with no pay, alas, a slave once more. Mark my words. This is all I can say to you. Now go," I say, indicating the risk for me by her presence.

I stand swiftly, causing her to sway backwards on the stool. I go to the door and open it very softly to the young night's air. I can hear a few stray dogs and the cicadas filling the evening. When I back away, she stops in front of me on her way out the door, her essence filling my nose, and I long to just hold her to safety. But I steel myself and inch away before she has the chance to reach across history and touch my arm. It is almost too much to bear as I see her cautiously peer at the church and then take to the road towards *La Gotera*. I watch her moonless shadow until she has crossed La Cruz de Caravaca.

Exhaustion hits as I close the door softly and sit on the stool, still warm from her youth. If I was not so tired, I would cry, something which I have only done twice in the last thirty-five years of my life as a slave for the church; once on the day I was given to the church at sixteen and again on the day that my skin went up in flames after Padre climbed on me for the first time. Though tears do not come, I feel a mourning deep in my soul.

Cartago and its environs in the highlands are lush and misty. The vegetation, including the coffee bean, surrounds the area as all eyes focus on the north, looking up at the resplendent Volcano Irazú. The colonial houses, constructed by both the Spanish and their enslaved Africans, are traditional one-story adobe houses that have occasional blue stripes or orange-ocher to accentuate their whitewashed walls. Across the swath of the valley are traditional orange clay tile roofs. The evenings, even in the dry season, are chilly with drizzle, as the altitude is high. Yet, the lushness of the vegetation and the local flowers provide shelter on the warmest days, always accompanied by constant birdsong. By twilight, Cartago is a sleepy town where its inhabitants go to bed early to rise before the sun. The church's bells keep time for everyone, with its toll of dawn and midafternoon prayers. To keep the distinction clear between master and slave, most Spaniards ritually attend Mass, though none more faithfully than Francesca and her daughter. Very few Spanish women venture outside of Cartago, except when they accompany their men on annual farm inspections. Most of the rituals of life are performed within the confines of Cartago for the Spanish. Before the last star disappears from the night sky, the burning smell of smoke, horse as well as human excrement attack the senses as slaves and servants clean out chamber pots in the early mornings along the roadside ditches.

Every Thursday, the weekly market is the center of all activity, bringing countless people from the outskirts of the capital to display their wares, customs and languages. Most of the stalls are set up in the plaza before dawn. Every possible good is available in the market and new trinkets from Guatemala, Panama and Cartagena are added each week by traveling merchants. Clothing, religious items, jewelry, blankets, hats, woolen suits and English silver cutlery are all part of a hodgepodge of enticing goods that are painstakingly bargained over with the few silver *reales* that the Costa Rican Spaniards have. Locally made banana leaf mats, clay pottery, water gourds, leather shoes and bags, farming tools, soap and smelly tallow candles are usually found in the stalls that edge the plaza square. At the heart of the market are the stalls with piles of fruit and vegetables, in wondrous colors that rival the flowers perfuming the local gardens. Meat, poultry, fish, corn, wheat, beans, custard apple, soursop, papaya, granadilla, oranges, lemons, limes, blackberries, figs, quinces, root vegetables, palm hearts, ripe and green bananas, yucca, corn and herbs are displayed for all to see. Sometimes, to entice a potential customer, usually a Spanish *señora* with her slave walking behind with already too heavy baskets, *agua dulce* or aromatic *jícara* chocolates are offered to the weary shopper. For those who come early, stall owners place a tray of freshly baked sponge cakes with cheese atop their mountain of fruits and vegetables, so that the hungry will venture over first.

Francesca swats a fly near her face as she clutches her rosary, murmuring a set of the Mysteries as she leads a small procession of the devout into the plaza for Market Day. Marching behind are her three slaves, with Micaela walking next to Lucia, who is chattering away, eager to see the many things for sale and already clamoring for an *agua dulce*. Her mother looks at her with a stern eye, and crosses the main path flooded with stalls full of leather goods, wicker baskets, pottery, glistening fruit, and meat still fresh with blood amidst a cacophony of voices in Spanish, English and BriBri-tinged dialects.

Francesca is careful to pick her way through the profuse lumps of steaming horse manure that emerge like burnt pots of gold along the main road to the church. However, the caked mud on the bottom of her dark-burgundy dress causes Micaela to flinch as she understands the work that will have to go into cleaning it. Lucia, however, is careless with her hem as she drags all the savory, putrid smells of the public drains along with her into church. Amongst the impromptu stalls erected before sunup, enslaved people remain near their owners, while countless *pardos* energetically ply their wares before the normal four o'clock exodus from town.

As the sun begins to rise, Francesca walks with singular determination to the front of the church, inching past dogs, happy children and braying donkeys. She enters the solemn sanctuary as if she were the Holy Mother herself. Micaela quickly straightens the heavy lace veil over Lucia's head and passes her a chain of immaculate pearl rosary beads, which she had recently received as a twenty-second birthday present from her mother. With a scowl, Lucia takes the beads, and genuflects briefly in the aisle before taking her place in the pew next to her mother, who is already kneeling. The congregation, mostly women, has already begun the Rosary as Micaela exits the church. Slaves are not always expected to stay through the Mass, though they are to be available should their owner call. Most are given hasty instructions and a few coins to purchase goods at the market so they will be done and ready to return home once the service is over. Others are expected to hover near the door, always ready. For the brave ones, this time usually means a few moments of respite in the splendor of the Market or under a tree in the plaza. Micaela has clear instructions on the fruits she needs to purchase while the Ibarra mother and daughter pray for the forgiveness of their sins. The *panas* know there are too many eyes on them for slaves to attempt an escape and besides, most are resigned to their fates with the families who own them. Micaela knows that with all heads bent towards Padre, she can slip out to the Market and try to speak to Dakarai, using the excuse of needing to purchase fruits. She quickly walks down the stairs and into the mass of moving humans, goods, and animals.

Jendayi

"**B**aba, how do you know that woman who came to our stall today? She only bought a few papayas and a pineapple, yet your heads were together for a long time in whispers. Forgive me for asking, but I think she brings bad news," Jendayi asks as she busily dusts the few remaining sculptures her father has put out for sale. These pieces of art went faster than all the fruit and vegetables they brought from the farm. She does not investigate her father's face as she questions him, though the feeling she has in the pit of her stomach makes her alarmed as the silence grows. "She is Micaela, Doña Francesca's slave. And," Dakarai looks across the plaza, avoiding his daughter's face. "And, she is a friend, my friend, Jendayi. Do you take my meaning?" So, it has come to this. A chance meeting on Market Day and Dakarai's relationship with Micaela is easily exposed after a year of secret nights. Was it just his daughter's keen eye or had the entire Cartago seen their affection in those few minutes and deciphered his fate?

"I think I do, Baba. Is she to become my new mother?" Jendayi turns suddenly to face her father. Her shock is wrapped in her throat as she understands this woman to be her father's lover and possibly the true source of all the rumored problems between her father and the Ibarra family. Though this woman is lovely with her brown skin and gentle voice, Jendayi feels an instant dislike of her.

Facing his daughter, finally, Dakarai speaks gently, "She, Jendayi, is enslaved. And, no, she will not be your new mother. To me, that role can never be filled. In the face of great risk, Micaela has become my friend. I care for her and hate how she is treated in the Ibarra household. If you must know so that the rumors may stop here, I have traded my work to build the bridal furniture for Doña Francesca's son and his wife in exchange for her freedom."

"Baba, what do you mean? How can you make such a bargain with the Spaniards?" Angry, Jendayi mutters under her breath, "So, this is what Esmeralda meant."

Dakarai walks quickly to her side and grabs her upper arm, forcing Jendayi to turn with a start. "What do you know of Esmeralda? You were specifically told not to interfere with her. Jendayi, you are of an age now where you must understand and respect the lines I have placed for your safety. Leave Esmeralda to her world of the church. Your job is to get learning and help other children also acquire words and ideas so that they can dream of worlds where they will not just labor with their hands in Costa Rica." With a shake of his head, Dakarai releases her arm. Jendayi is surprised at the force of his feelings. Never has he been so angry at with her.

"All I do is walk around in your silence. There is so much going on around me and yet you wrap me up as if I am the *morpho* butterfly, brilliant blue but with a two-week life span. Baba, I have made it thus far, through birth, death, and separation from you for all those years when I was a child. But I am growing and cannot remain your baby forever. Open your eyes, see me. You have a whole life happening that I do not understand. You are taking risks not just for yourself and our family but for the people in *La Gotera* simply because you desire this woman? I always thought it was just going to be the two of us and the memory of my mother as the space binding us. This is all very confusing to me because I feel like the world knows what is going on before I see or hear things that directly affect me. It is not fair," Jendayi says all this in a loud whisper so as not to alert the people in the next stall of their disagreement. She does not realize that her hands are clenched at her side. She is shaking with the passion that has finally bubbled to the surface. Jendayi faces her father, both breathing hard, though trying to maintain a façade of decorum, lest they cause attention from a discerning eye in the crowd.

Defeated by his daughter's words and the depth of his own self-reflection, Dakarai turns away from Jendayi and says, "Go home. The day will be long, but I can manage by myself. I can bring the leftover goods back to the house. I will leave the carvings at my shop once I pack up. It is best that we talk about this later. But my daughter, know that I would never risk your life for desire or loneliness. My decisions are based on my feelings about slavery and I find myself in a position to negotiate with . . . no, let's leave it here. We will discuss this later when there are no ears leaning towards us."

Jendayi nods and without another word, picks up her basket and begins the walk to *La Gotera* alone.

Dakarai

January 1635, Cartago

The days move into months as Dakarai and Pedro, his assistant, begin making the bridal furniture for Alvaro and Isabella. The shop is closed in Cartago as they work at the building site, since the materials are closely guarded and accounted for by Doña Francesca. Dakarai speaks little beyond the formal greetings to the Spaniards at the beginning and end of each day. Francesca comes daily to the house, where glass windowpanes and candelabras, packed tightly in crates by hands in another country worlds away, are gently hoisted through open window frames and installed as they arrive bit-by-bit from the port in Guanacaste. Sometimes, Micaela is sent to the worksite to bring supplies or at times, if Francesca is feeling generous, some *tamales* left over from the Christmas holidays. Dakarai is always gracious with his thanks, looking Micaela in the eye with a round, half smile on his lips. However, both know that he will never eat the food prepared by Jenny, the Ibarra cook, who is famed for her fast tongue and deep hated of all things *negro.* Silently, he will wrap it in his satchel, filled with carving tools, never fully turning his back to Micaela but using the time to study the wondrous curve of her hips when she stands in front of him.

That Tuesday morning in January, the sun is at its zenith when Micaela comes into the compound. Dakarai and Pedro have constructed a small workshop of simple wood with slatted benches alongside the wall and a carved-out window for air in the dry summer heat of Cartago. The New Year has come and gone, marked by a simple meal with Jendayi and visiting with the neighbors in *La Gotera* on his one day off because of the holiday. The progress is incredible. The house is complete but the surrounding area of gardens and home farm alongside the stables have yet to be finished. Thick black earth is exposed around the house, with sections of mud for the landscaping everywhere. Micaela picks her way tenderly across the yard to stand outside the window of the workshop. Pedro sees her first and greets her quietly, then turns back to continue sawing the slabs of wood for the bottom frame of the wedding bed. Dakarai's last few days have been meticulously spent carving the headboard, slowly inlaying the stones and glass that Isabella ordered from Italy. Not wanting Pedro to notice favoritism toward Micaela, Dakarai nods and gives a short greeting before leaning his head back into his work. Though she does not attempt to enter the workspace, Micaela clears her throat, causing both men to look up at her again.

"My brothers, I greet you. I have brought a special stone from the main house. Juan Carlos, Doña Francesca says that you are to carve an icon of the Holy Mother and child which is to be placed in a niche of the headboard, so that the wedding bed will be blessed from the first day. She says that the stone is rare and is very costly. You are to be careful to not make any errors as there is no more to come by. I bring this to you because Doña Francesca has gone with Don Alvaro to Nicoya for three days, but she has left Lucia in my charge because she is unwell and unable to make the journey," Micaela rumbles forth, battling to keep the smile off her face. Brazenly, she looks Dakarai in the eye as she hands him the stone slab through the window. She startles as he winks at her; the anticipation in his eyes a surprising sign, since the first time he rubbed his callused hands along the side of Micaela's calf on their first night together, that he feels deeply for her. She doesn't look at his mouth, but already the blush is pushing beyond her cheeks on her brown skin. She nods a farewell and moves quickly out of the compound, away from the eyes of the builders who will have something to say if she lingers too long. Dakarai knows this is why she never enters the workshop, even when she is with Francesca. The woman is too shrewd, and Micaela cannot risk being found out. Already, Jendayi and Mama Esmeralda know about their time together and that is two people too many.

Dakarai stares into the darkness of the work shed, satiated as Micaela snores slightly in his arms. His thoughts are full. He has missed her and only now is he honest enough to realize how much. He does not move as she shifts against him, turning with a sigh in her sleep. He watches her, taking in the scent of heat, sweat and their joining. Underneath is the subtle smell of her rose oil, which she makes regularly for Lucia's baths. Whenever she comes to him, the roses announce themselves before she steps into his arms. In most cases, the smell suffices for the words of longing that they both have yet to share. But, tonight, after months of being without, they spoke. Timidly, in the heady rush of still being inside her, Dakarai stroked her cheek, called her name and said the things from his heart. Without catching himself, he talked of love. Easing out of her, he kept his arm under her so that as he rolled onto his back, she came gently on her side into his embrace. While he was true to his heart, Dakarai knew the foolish risk he was taking. Loving a woman enslaved. All the variables surrounding how this could turn out were bad at best. He knew he was promising a false dream, an unlikely future with freedom etched in it. Even if she did leave Doña Francesca's house, would Dakarai have a place for her amongst the memories that he and Jendayi had built these last seven years? Would Jendayi, a woman-child growing into her own, welcome Micaela or would she see her as the body trying to fill the empty space of her mother? These thoughts rumble in Dakarai's mind as Micaela sleeps with a noticeable ease.

True to her word, she arrived two nights in a row, happiness sealed into the baked banana bread and *tamales* she made by hand to ensure that Dakarai would eat them. Most worrying was that in Dakarai's need to fill himself with her, for the first time ever in being together, he was not careful and spilled his seed inside of her. This is when Dakarai knew that he loved her because even in the recesses of his mind, as he moved within her wetness, he knew she could mother his child, *their* child, if one should come. Taking her own pleasure, she did not immediately realize what Dakarai had done but when he remained inside of her after their hearts slowed, she looked at him and began to speak soft words. Dakarai slid his hands between her legs, listening as her voice hitched when his thumb rubbed across her swollen center. His desire for her was licked along the shell of her ear, a delicate balance of urgency and calm because though they were satiated, they needed more. The truths they formed, as the walls of his workshop stood as witnesses, brought forth a second, deeply embedded climax, unexpected by both of them.

And so now Micaela sleeps in Dakarai's arms and he is hesitant to let her leave though the first birds are soon to sing. As he finally moves to release her, she immediately awakens at his actions; fear tinges her skin. Dakarai can tell that she does not normally sleep with the peace that has been maintained in his arms. Tonight, both of them have let their defenses down and he suddenly worries about the consequences.

"I must go," Micaela states into the late-night air. Getting up and walking over to the small gourd of clean water on the worktable, she uses her handkerchief to clean herself. She wordlessly tucks her blouse into the waist of her skirt which she hurriedly steps into. She straightens, turning her back to Dakarai as she passes nervous hands over her shoulder-length braids, which less than an hour ago were splayed across her face as she took her pleasure from Dakarai. He slowly walks to her, pressing his chest against her back and using his left arm to hook around her waist. She stills, waiting for a word, his word on how to proceed. Yet, Dakarai is cowardly in the dawning light, so he kisses the nape of her neck, still salty from their time, and tells her to go safely. He knows Doña Francesca returns the next evening, so it is too risky for Micaela to venture out another night. What they have done and said to each other these two nights will have to be their food.

Dakarai

After Dakarai has cleaned up the work shed and put out the candle, he walks into his bedroom and eases into the bed. Exhaustion catches him in no time, and he is taken quickly into a world of dreams. He is on a bed in his old house near the Zambezi, rubbing his hands gently over Towela's firmly rounded belly. He feels butterfly movements as his palm holds firm to what must be a leg or an arm of the budding child. Towela's laugh rolls over his body as he continues to caress her stomach. Dakarai leans towards her, moving aside her wrapper to kiss her belly button. Even in his sleep, he longs for the smell of her sandalwood. As his lips connect with her skin, rose oil wafts into his nostrils and he reels back in shock, unwilling to look up at the woman lying beside him.

"Baba, Baba, wake up. You were shouting in your sleep. Please, Baba, the neighbors will come and think there is trouble." Dakarai hears Jendayi's voice as he slides between dream and wakefulness. The lingering taste of fear is on his tongue, sharp as lime. Jendayi is kneeling on the side of his bed, wide-eyed with concern.

"Jendayi, forgive me. I just had a bad dream. I am fine. Return to your bed, I promise, I am fine. These days have been exhausting and I have not had much rest. It is catching up to me. The morning will soon come. Go and rest," Dakarai says, patting her shoulder with a reassurance he does not feel inside.

Jendayi does not move, but remains with an insistence as she says, "Baba, you were shouting my mother's name as if you were saying goodbye all over again. Were you dreaming of her?"

Dakarai sits up in the bed; not sure how honest he wants to be. "Yes, I dreamt of your mother when she was pregnant with you. It has been a long time since I have seen her face in my dreams. I have missed her."

"Was it beautiful Baba when my mother had me inside of her? Was she happy? I have created scenes in my mind about that time when the two of you were carving sculptures, happy in your home. I want so much to see what that home was like, to know my mother's people, to find the family who belonged to you so that they can claim me as well, so they can show me how to behave in the ways of our people. I am just a girl growing as if I am never fully on land but in the hold of the bouncing slave ship where I was born. If you cannot teach me how to carve, then please, allow me the stories of your life, your real life before this one, so that I can sculpt a life for myself that is not just sadness," Jendayi says, a weeping tension caressing her tone.

Dakarai hesitates then moves forward so he is sitting properly along the edge of his bed. His feet touch the cool earthen floor. Passing Jendayi the extra blanket from his bed to wrap around her shoulders, he indicates that she should sit and listen. There is something in the early morning air that makes him feel like talking in order to remove the ghosts of his past.

"Daughter," he says, "I remember the first day I saw Towela. She was with her father, who was a famed scholar, and they had been traveling from a northern area called Kabwe to Mutare, which is where I was born. The slave trade had not touched our villages at that point and so our days were still bright with dreams. Your mother's father was invited to give a talk amongst the scholars who were discussing a new manuscript written in Arabic, which had been brought from the university at Timbuktu. I was there the day when they all gathered at the chief's compound. There was much pomp and circumstance because these visitors were highly respected and the information her father was bringing was especially anticipated. I was told that he had brought along his young son, who he was training as a scribe. However, when I sat amongst the elders in my village, including my father and grandfather, I stared right into the eyes of the most beautiful woman I had ever seen in my eighteen years. She was sitting to the right of her father on a small stool, I will never forget. Towela did not lower her eyes as people watched her, shocked that her father had put such trust in a girl-child. But the chief was gracious and there were many long evenings of discussion about the new manuscript and happy celebrations as the guests were feted. One day, towards the end of their stay, I noticed Towela walking from the well to the guest house in the chief's compound. I took my chances and went up to her with a solemn greeting, though I swear I was bewitched. She laughed at me, at my attempt to sound smart and older than my age. Jendayi, I promise you I had no say over my thoughts or my body when I looked into her eyes. And then we laughed together. It was at that moment that I knew this was the woman I wanted to spend my life with. The evening before she left, she came to my compound, softly asking one of the children to fetch me. I took her hands and promised my love to her. I told her that I would come and respectfully ask her people for her hand in marriage. I know the ways of the Tumbuka people. They do not usually marry outside of their group, but I was willing to take that chance to be with Towela. She leaned into me with her sandalwood scent and instead of kissing me, she pressed two *mkanda* beads, taken from the string around her waist, into my hands as her pledge to me."

"Baba, do you mean the beads you wear around your neck are my mother's waist beads?" Jendayi whispers in amazement.

"Yes, I do not take them off now, though when I was enslaved, I was not able to wear them around my neck, so I kept them in a small pouch under my mat. I never wanted to disrespect your mother's memory by wearing them. Only in freedom have I been able to press them to my skin. But I digress. If you want this story, here is your only chance as there are no witnesses except dawn's shadows."

Jendayi nods for him to continue.

"It was not long before I convinced my parents that we had to go north to present my case to Towela's people. Being Shona and from the South was not necessarily in my favor but I was earnest and that won out in the end. My uncle went ahead of my parents and I, bearing gifts for Towela's family. He sent word after several weeks that he had made headway with the negotiations and that we were to come to make the final suit. I arrived in Kabwe and the excitement was palpable. All I remember is the dust because it was the dry season. I presented Towela's father a sculpture I made. I remember kneeling in front of him and saying that the spirit released in the stone was a powerful one who would bestow blessings on his family for generations to come. Something in my address caused him pause because I think until that point, he had not really considered my petition seriously. What I did not know was that Towela was also a gifted sculptor and though she was an apprentice scribe for her father, her real joy was in carving. And so that was the beginning and the end. The marriage negotiations were completed, and we had our wedding with a ceremony that lasted one week. In the end, we were so exhausted that we barely managed to get to the house her uncle had given her near the Zambezi as a wedding gift. It was Shona custom that Towela also come and spend some time in my parents' house in the South, but they gave us a reprieve. With the blessings of both houses, this Shona man and that Tumbuka woman set up a life together. We carved and traded and had wealth. Your mother was a brilliant woman and she never let her beauty stand in her way, though many were stunned in her presence. All she wanted to do was learn. She read daily as she was accustomed to do with her father and there were times when he visited us with a request that Towela accompany him on short trips as his scribe. These were hard times for me. I would spend hours and hours carving because I had nothing else to do with my hands. She would come back and look at my mounds of sculptures, dirty clothes and unmade bed and she would just laugh and laugh, because she could read the misery I felt being separated from her, even for a day," Dakarai stops, frozen in time as he turns to finally see his daughter.

"More?" he asks Jendayi, though his soul is weary.

Jendayi nods readily, "Please, Baba, please, just a little more if you can manage it."

"I did not mind, you know, even after seven years had gone by and she still had no child in her belly. We were so well established at that point that we began a small apprentice school and would make the long trek into Mutare and Bulawayo to get the *rapoko* stone which we used for carving. Sometimes, we would send our young apprentices so that we would not have to go ourselves. Even I am not boasting to say that our work was in demand from mothers to chiefs to kings. Our names were called along the trade routes and many people came to visit our workshop, buying and asking for training. The days melted, and the years went by and we were happy. I only noticed in the later years how Towela began obsessively carving a mother and child figure. She would not let that one design go as if she was singing a mantra through her hands. Once a year, we would join the caravan that would take us northwest into the Benguela Kingdom on the Angolan coast. What wealth! I cannot explain what I felt the first time I entered their market. So many people from all over, trading, talking, fighting, laughing; just a vibrant mix of life and your mother and I enjoyed this time. We never stayed more than two weeks and less after we began to see the Portuguese men and started hearing about the *quintaloes,* the slave quarters. But we were oblivious to the trade of enslaved people then, so focused were we on our sculptures.

"We began dreaming of opening another small shop near my parents' home in Mutare. Towela talked of adopting one of my sister's children, as she already had six and we had more than enough wealth to ease the strain of feeding so many mouths. I think I finally woke up to the reality that Towela was unhappy because she could not bear a child. But I had never spent any real time thinking about this issue as the years grew because I was mostly content to spend my time carving and loving your mother. For me, it was a simple life. And then, without any announcement, five months before our annual pilgrimage to the Benguela market, Towela became pregnant with you. I was shocked at first because I thought she had gotten very ill, but then a midwife came and confirmed what Towela had already told me; our prayers had been answered. I didn't even know that I had been praying for a child. But Towela had been, with secret, deep devotion. In thinking back, I now recognize the grief she held so tightly to her chest.

"I know that she loved when I read to her in the evenings after we had eaten and cleared away our work tools. Sometimes, we would have visitors, but most evenings, we sat in our house, full of sculptures and simple furniture except the intricate wedding bed that I made for her when we first came to that house. We would talk into the nights, comparing ideas about what designs would work best at which markets until we slept from exhaustion. But suddenly, I began working alone as your mother was unwell in the early morning hours. Instead of reading, I spent hours rubbing her swollen feet. I could feel the fear in her sweat. I know she was terrified of anything happening to you, you, dream child of her prayers. And so, I encouraged her to spend more time resting and reading and sleeping early. This is how I learned to cook; during those months, I had to figure out how to put two and two together in order to feed us as the first three months of the pregnancy were so difficult. Her father visited us once during that time and what a celebration he hosted. Goats were slaughtered, and the entire village came to toast your future birth. I think Towela was uneasy about all this public fuss because she was worried that someone would wish us badly. And, my daughter, I think she was right. Every time I think back to our capture by the Portuguese, I ask, what did I do? Which ancestor did I betray or forget to get a life such as this? The only blessing in this story was that you made it here."

"Oh, Baba, I do not know what to say," Jendayi jumps up, the blanket falling at her feet as she walks near the window, looking out into the dawn, "Sometimes in my dreams, I can see my mother. We talk but I do not hear her words clearly. Recently, she comes to me as if she is trying to warn me about something. I can never make it out but there is fear in her voice. Maybe it is the fear that she carried in her body when I was forming inside of her that has transferred to my dreams? She now comes often, and most of the time it gives me peace, except when I cannot make out her messages to me."

"Jendayi, there is more to this story. The time of our capture and enslavement in the *terreiro publicos*[7] of Benguela; but those words cannot cross my lips this night. However, you are now fifteen and it is time that you know these things so that your hands are full of everything you need to judge the future in front of you. You come from a people and a place that is ancient. Look at my hands, Jendayi. Know that our stories are etched into the lines of these palms and I cannot and will not forget our people or where we come from. But, my child, I also know that I will never return there, not in this human form. One day, I will meet your mother again and remember the joy of my name."

Jendayi wipes her tears as she asks, "Does that woman, Micaela, bring you the same happiness that my mother did, Baba?"

---

[7] Slave castle holding cells.

Dakarai takes a deep breath and listens to his heart before he replies, "No, Jendayi. Micaela is very different from your mother. Both women have given me something to add courage to my skin and heart. They have shaped me with their actions and wisdom, and I honor both. But, no, Micaela finishes another need that had grown in me from living in this land of Costa Rica. She is made of firm earth and there are no dreams that we carve together. Yet, I value her life and yes, I love her. How this is to manifest, I do not know as I cannot see the future. Surely, if I was able to do so, I would not be standing on soil so far from where my people are buried. Now, I must honor the dead who we have buried here and continue to call their names along with our people from across the sea. Let me ask you, daughter, are you afraid of Micaela?"

"Yes. There is much to fear because she is enslaved and any interaction with her comes at great risk," Jendayi replies quickly.

"Well. I ask that you try and give her a space in your heart because you are the only one who can create a bridge," Dakarai looks over at his daughter who remains still, focusing on the starting day out the window. "Now, it is time to get a few more hours of rest before the sun is fully in the sky. I am sorry for waking you with my shouting, but our words tonight are important to share. I know now how grown up you are and am saddened that it has taken me this long to really see you. I am proud of you, my daughter. You are the center of my heart," Dakarai stands and slowly embraces Jendayi, whispering prayers over the crown of her head.

After a tight hug, Jendayi does not look back at her father as she moves out of the room into her own. Already the rooster in Mama Petronila's house is crowing as the night stars vanish. Never has she felt so tired. The idea of having to get up in a few hours to take the water to the church seems an agony as she wraps herself in a thin sheet and falls asleep.

Four evenings later, Dakarai's home work shed

Esmeralda looks up from her book, the pencil grasped tightly in her right hand, ready to write the words Dakarai spells slowly over and over for her. He stops mid-sentence and turns to sit on the workbench opposite her as he wipes his face with his hands.

Scratching his head of tight curls, etched with the faintest new patches of gray, he mumbles, "Agogo Esmeralda, I am at a crossroads and I cannot see my way forward. I am unable to focus on your lesson this evening; my heart is filled with worry. I am sorry."

Esmeralda puts down her book and pencil. She looks up expectantly as she says, "My son, if you so feel, please unburden your heart so that you can live. I have heard that you have taken two days away from the Ibarra housework and the *panas* are unhappy with you. They think that you are going to renege on finishing your work. But, in looking at you now, this does not seem to be the reason for your unhappiness. Am I correct? If so, my ears are yours."

Lifting his head, Dakarai faces the window near the door, careful not to catch Esmeralda's eye as he says, "Four nights ago, Jendayi woke me from my sleep because I had been screaming her dead mother's name. I had no choice but to finally give in and tell her some of the story of our past, of my time beyond the sea with her mother. But Agogo, I have not been kind to my daughter as I have framed a past that is only slightly colored with truth and mostly just my imagination. I refused to share with her the times of unhappiness. She does not know that Petronila, who also comes from my people's place in Mutare, is the only living witness to my true life. Only Petronila understands the weight of sorrow I carry because there are so many things left unsaid."

Dakarai stills suddenly, as if listening for footsteps at the door. He looks at Esmeralda, worried that she might feel burdened by his painful story, by his secrets. But he must speak about it. He sits back on the bench and says, "Agogo Esmeralda, please let me share my story with you tonight and forever we will go to our graves with it. Four nights ago, I watched my daughter leave my room, filled with ideas of a fantastic love affair between her mother and I, but all I felt was shame. See, I gave her a fraction of the truth because she wanted the story so desperately. I created a love story of how I met her mother and our perfect life as famed sculptors. I swore that it never troubled me that my wife, after seven years of loving together, never conceived my child. I told Jendayi how happy we were when she was finally conceived. But the words of truth stuck deeply inside my throat."

"How could I tell her of all those days when Towela went away with her father as his scribe that my mother's sister would visit, conveniently timing the long weeks when I would be alone. She would sit outside of my work shed at the door, shading her eyes as she greeted neighbors passing by. Only at night would Auntie begin to play with my mind, asking me how I could remain with a wife who spent her time in books and carving and not in the matter of making me a father, a true man. But I was young and ignored her when I could, except during the last time she visited. Petronila, then a young woman, was also visiting a neighbor and she and Auntie had come together from Mutare. On this side, she is my only witness to a time that I still fight with, begging the memories to remain untrue so I can continue to lie to myself. I saw when Auntie came with Lindiwe. She was to be my second wife; hand-selected and groomed by my parents. They had had enough of my barren Towela and began the wedding negotiations without my say. But, even from a distance that first time, I noticed Lindiwe's slow walk in a wrapper too tight for the curves of her thighs. My body reacted when she crossed the threshold of my house and the night was young when she slipped into my room and onto the sheets which still held Towela's sandalwood scent. She was delicious. All the resentment I felt towards Towela for leaving me useless except for a life that she dictated, that she dreamed and inspired, melted away each time I came between Lindiwe's legs. She never spoke much to me, but she was there every night for that entire week that Auntie visited. And so, she became my wife, my true wife in the Shona sense of family."

"My father was the one who eventually sent word that I was the father of Lindiwe's child. I had to pay *lobola* and complete the wedding rituals. All this went on with Towela slightly suspicious that something was amiss, yet I did not tell her. When the baby was born, named Omobamidele meaning 'Our child has come home,' I returned to my father's home in Mutare without Towela, full of anguish that I had now created a life that she had no idea about. But she must have known something was going on. I don't even remember the excuse I gave her about needing to visit my parents suddenly. We argued. This was the first time I ever remember thinking I wanted to be away from her. I wanted to see this child that I produced. Suddenly, it felt important to know that it was not my fault, that I was a man who could produce children. Though I loved Towela, I also felt lifeless with her at times. How was it that I could make love to my wife for years and no child could come yet a week of silly passion with a woman whose voice I cannot remember and suddenly my name is etched into the future? And so, I went and greeted my son, I paid *lobola* and named the child in a ceremony. My parents looked aside when people asked after

Towela, as they too understood that my job as first born, beyond all the material riches I achieved, was to produce the wealth only a child can bring. Lindiwe was the mother of my child, my occasional lover and functional in the world where children were the only honor feasible to witness. The *lobola* was to satisfy her people and give her ancestors respect but her job, as Auntie had seen to, was to maintain my line."

"So, now I sit, split in half, and wonder how I tell Jendayi that over the last three years before our capture, I would find strange and random reasons to visit with my parents alone and spend two weeks with Omobamidele and the two other sons I eventually created with Lindiwe."

First there was Akudzwe, which means 'Praise' and then little Anopa, who we named 'God Gives' because we did not think he would make it after a very difficult birth. Lindiwe was never without money or goods and nor were my sons ever hungry. They were raised near their grandparents and spoke Shona beautifully. But Agogo, I never said goodbye to my sons. Where are they? Have they too been taken into the trade? Have they managed to survive with the help of their mother and my parents? I can never speak that anguish. It tears my insides. Only Petronila has seen me with my sons, all three climbing on me one day when I arrived to greet them, sweets packed into the pockets of my pants. In my joy, I only noticed her once they were in my embrace. She passed, greeting me quietly with a surprised knowing. My reaction to the boys causes me great shame today, even some fifteen years later. How quickly I brushed them away, speaking harshly to Lindiwe to control them but it was too late. My life had unraveled with one false step," Dakari stands with those words. He is empty.

Esmeralda straightens, her soft voice floating into the air, "Dakarai, she is old enough to know this. Jendayi will never meet these brothers, but the truth is always the best way forward. Give her everything she needs to understand that life is a harsh place with few shelters. Let her be prepared for making choices. Have her understand what it is like to smell cruelty and be prepared to resist it. Don't paint her a picture of roses without carefully making her aware of the thorns and how deeply they draw blood. I have seen only what few can imagine and much of that shame is etched onto my back. She is a young woman, Dakarai, she must know how men and women behave. She will respect you for your truth."

Bending and taking Esmeralda's working right hand in his, Dakarai, whispers, "But, Mama, how do I tell Jendayi the surprise I felt when Towela's midwife confirmed that she was newly pregnant? As I rubbed her swollen feet, I counted all the months that had passed without making love. How do I tell my daughter that she is not the daughter of my blood, only of my heart? Towela told me with one look that I was to accept this child as my own. And I did, I do. But the textures of this story are too painful for Jendayi's spirit and it has taken me this long to say any of this to her because I am afraid of where I will slip, and the truth will fall like *rapoko* stone, splintering into all the slices of what my life has become."

Esmeralda releases Dakarai's hand slowly, and he realizes it has been a long time since they have touched, because he instinctively knows that Esmeralda does not usually like physical contact: but this felt like a good touch, an honest one. He needs holding up and for once, her hand instead of fighting, is a source of support. Her hand tells him that she is listening. But now, she stands and he also straightens in front of her. His height in the small workshop is not as overwhelming as the words he has just uttered. Despair laces his deep breath as he tries to gain control of his emotions. He looks at Esmeralda and thinks he sees fear staring back at him. What can she possibly offer him to ease his spirit?

Standing very still but drawing all the energy of the room towards her, Esmeralda finally says, "My son, you have shared words with me this evening that I never would have imagined coming from your mouth. I have nothing for you this evening, no balm for your wounds. Yet, I thank you for being brave enough to choose me as the one to help you across. But the waters are deep and treacherous and there are choices you will have to make that may alter your life path. Face them now before they overrun their course in your memory and you will have to spit them out. Tell your daughter the truth."

Defeated, Dakarai nods and answers in barely a voice, "Agogo, I have said too much this evening. Forgive me. I do not know how to go forward as the weight of my untruths with Jendayi and even Micaela drown me. If you can manage, please come another night for your lessons. I am tired."

"Yes, yes, it is time for me to greet the shadows along my way home. I say this in parting; you must know that Jendayi has already come to me with questions. She is feeling unsafe and suspicious of the adults around her. You cannot afford to be this person in her life; she must always be able to see you clearly in truth. There are many people who are willing to lie to her in this place where the lines between free and enslaved are thin, so it is your duty as her father to keep her eyes and ears open to who we are, people who have survived from the place across the sea," Esmeralda says, looking directly into Dakarai's face.

There is only silence as Esmeralda folds her small sisal mat and places the book and pencil on top of a small shelf. Dakarai follows her movement, taking in the shelf he built for her. He remembers the hesitant smile on her face the first time she saw it, how she asked if the tin cup he had placed there so she could enjoy *cafecito* during their lessons was also for her, and how she smiled for real when he confirmed it was. He had wanted her to know she was cherished. Esmeralda moves toward the exit, and with a wave of her hand, she opens the door into the night, letting the sounds of birds and barking dogs into the workroom.

Micaela passes her hand across the top sheet of Lucia's bed. The nausea bubbles in her throat and she straightens, pressing the back of hand against her mouth. Taking a deep breath to keep the bile down, she bends again to make the bed. Instantly, the nausea ripples across her belly and she clutches the side of the bed as cold sweat beads down her neck. Quickly, she takes a few leaves of mint from her apron pocket and sticks them in her mouth, chewing furiously.

"No one must know," she mumbles to herself as the mint distracts her body enough to finish making the bed. Out of the corner of her eye, she spots Lucia's bloody menstrual rags, strewn haphazardly across other soiled under-garments on a chair near the bed. Micaela stifles a sob at the reminder that she will not have her own bloody rags this month or the next six as she is certain that she is now carrying Dakarai's child. The fear of it racks her into a sudden panic and she lunges for the nearby chamber pot and releases her early morning *cafecito* and bread. Wiping her mouth quickly as well as her sweaty brow, Micaela grabs the pot and walks down the stairs to the latrine in the back, quickly washing away the vomit. Hesitating, she also dashes some of the cold water on her face and then with the chamber pot under her arm, she returns upstairs into Lucia's room to finish straightening up.

"Micaela, why have you taken so long today? I need you to come and brush my hair out in the sun so that it dries properly. I must attend Mama's dinner party tonight for Alvaro and Isabella and you know the fuss she will make if I am late. I can't wait to wear the new pink dress that was shipped all the way from Spain for this evening. Even if I do not have many friends, everyone will still admire me. Hurry already," Lucia says as she comes into the room and pushes away the soiled garments on the chair. Plopping down, Lucia stares expectantly at the woman in front of her.

Though the second-floor windows open onto the back garden and normally there are abundant breezes, even in the summer months, cold sweat continues to ease down Micaela's spine.

"Señorita Lucia, I was just straightening your bed and clearing your chamber pot. Let me put out the clothes for laundry and I will come straight down with the brush to prepare your hair. It will take but a minute," Micaela murmurs, never looking into Lucia's eyes.

Lucia chews her fingernails, then she laughs and says, "You are getting old Micaela, you move like molasses! Have you heard that the wedding house will almost be finished?

Mama said that *pardo* Juan Carlos has made the most exquisite furniture for Isabella. I just don't know why all the fuss is being made over that woman. I think Mama fears that Alvaro will send her to one of our cacao plantations and not let her stay in town if she does not listen to Isabella. That woman is so spoiled. You have no idea how much money she is forcing us to spend on her. Why, I was just looking at some of the expenses for the stones and jewels that Isabella shipped from abroad and..."

Micaela sucks her in breath and interrupts quickly, "Señorita! You have been strictly forbidden to enter Don Alvaro's study. Please do not look through his books. Those are not details for a young lady! You must study your lessons and practice your dancing if you want to please your mother and make a good match. You are one month into twenty-two and there is talk about you going to Spain with your mother..."

"Oh hush, Micaela, what do you know, you are only a slave. No one ever cares what I do or see and so it does not matter anyway. Mama is only concerned about this new house and showing off her wealth. She does not see that Don Jimenez is also trying his hand at her money. I have been watching them all because there is nothing to do in this God-forsaken country. I hate this place. Mama will never take me to Spain, so I may be presented at Court to Queen Isabella and King Philip. Perhaps she is trying to distract me by all the preparations going into tonight's party? All I know is that I am stuck in this back-water country where people are stupid enough to farm cacao and then use it as currency! You know, I could sell you for 200 *pesos* in cacao," Lucia laughs at herself as she continues to examine her hangnails.

Micaela turns abruptly, carrying the dirty laundry under one arm and strolls over to the enormous wooden dresser, grabs the hairbrush and the rose oil bottle, and walks out the room, leaving Lucia stunned. Never had she done such a thing when the rules were always to serve and melt into the background. Lucia's comments about selling her causes every hair to raise on her arms and again her thoughts go to her unborn child. Surely, Dakarai will care for the child. Maybe he can negotiate on her behalf, once she starts showing, with Doña Francesca. He can keep the child and raise it freely in *La Gotera,* even if she will not get to mother it. Her knees almost buckle under the terror of these thoughts.

Dumping the dirty laundry near the large zinc basin by the kitchen door, Micaela waves to Maria Gertrudis, a young Bribri servant who comes three days a week to do the laundry and iron the linens. Micaela ponders the fine line between the enslaved and a paid servant as Maria Gertrudis, who is given a pittance but paid nonetheless, has to scrub the bloody refuse from Lucia's rags while she as Lucia's personal property never has to do such menial work. As Maria Gertrudis approaches the washing area, Micaela lifts her skirts and proceeds to the shaded gazebo near the honeysuckle trees. Brush in her hand, she quickly goes to where Lucia is now sitting, fanning herself. Micaela apologizes for her hasty departure from the room. Lucia does nothing, except wave the thought away with her slight hand, already carrying three rings of precious jewels, like her mother. Relief floods Micaela as she has anticipated an outpouring of wrath for leaving without being dismissed but it seems Lucia is preoccupied, and this is an opportunity for her to put everything to rights. Quickly, Micaela undoes the loose, wet bun of Lucia's auburn hair and begins the methodical brushing ritual, gently drizzling drops of rose oil into Lucia's scalp and hair ends. Within fifteen minutes, Lucia's head tugs the brush as she drifts into sleep. With the urgent need to use the latrine, Micaela hopes that Lucia will remain asleep and she can quickly finish the braids so as to run and relieve herself. Never has she stopped mid-chore for a bathroom call but never have such circumstances presented themselves to her, she muses.

Slowly easing the brush from Lucia's hair and twining the remaining strands together, she wipes her hands awash with rose oil onto her apron and reaches out to put the brush on the table.

Praying silently that Lucia's snores will continue uninterrupted as her bladder cries, Micaela backs away from the gazebo and is half-way across the lawn when she hears Lucia's screech reach her ears.

"Micaela, Micaela, where are you going!? Return here immediately. I will have you whipped," Lucia screams, hands on hips and her newly braided hair uncoiled and streaming around her head.

Micaela stops in her tracks as the warm urine makes its descent towards her ankles. Fear, shame, and outrage gel on her tongue as she wants to lash out at Micaela, this barely-formed girl who has no humanity in her skin. The acid smell of her release assaults her senses as she forces her legs to return to Lucia, head bowed.

"Stupid girl, why did you go? You have ruined my hair and so you must stand here and do it all over again and I will surely tell Mama you are the reason I am late for the party," Lucia states, waving the brush in her hand as she retakes her seat at the wooden table of the gazebo.

Micaela takes a deep breath and moves slowly so the breeze will not pick up the scent of the urine, still drying against her legs. Her hands shake as she begins the process of re-combing each strand, though Lucia's hair is no longer wet and pliable.

"Ouch, stop! *Me matas*, you are killing me Micaela, you are pulling too hard on my hair. I am going to tell Mama. Stop this instant! I will get Gimena to twist my hair into a bun and put flowers in it, as you cannot even manage a simple braid. Anyway, you smell. Go this instant and wash in the latrines. I have no idea what has gotten into you but all week you have been acting very strange. Mama will be unhappy with your behavior and maybe she will sell you after all. Get away from me," Lucia pushes her chair back in anger. Grabbing the hairbrush from Micaela's hand, she swats her hard across the arm and stomps towards the house.

Never in the life she had with the Ibarras has Micaela been hit. The indignity of it combined with the stinging, dry urine caked against her thighs is almost too much. With a sob, she runs into the latrines where there is a make-shift bathing room installed with a small tin hip bath. Realizing that she does not have a change of clothes nor towel, Micaela goes around the side of the house to the laundry area where she finds Maria Gertrudis heaving dripping wet white linens onto a huge rock. Wiping her hair out of her eyes, Maria simply looks up to acknowledge Micaela again and then bends back to her task. Maria Gertrudis will not ask any questions, thinks Micaela, as she goes to the washing line and grabs one of her dresses which she had rinsed the day before along with a square linen cloth for drying. Without a word, she runs back to the bathing room, strips her clothes off as she pours cold water into the hip bath. If she is found out to be bathing in the middle of the morning, surely, she will be whipped. Worried, she steps into the tub and scrubs her legs with the crumbly bits of Spanish soap normally left over from Lucia's bath. Common to what is used amongst the Spanish elites, Micaela has learned to mix the wood ash and animal fat with drops of rose oil and at times lemongrass, which grow wildly on the Ibarra property. Now, the soap feels like sandpaper on her skin as the foam floats in the rapidly graying water. Micaela does not notice the cold of the water as every move is functional and quick. Not sure of what Lucia might do, she uses the linen cloth to dry her body, slip the dress over her neck and arms and bundles the dirty clothes into a ball to wash later. She will go to her room to get clean undergarments. Maria Gertrudis will not get the disrespect of her dirty clothes, though she had no choice with Lucia's. As she walks into the house and up the servant's staircase, Micaela prays that Lucia will be so busy with the evening's festivities that she will forget the events of the day.

Micaela is told to stand along the wall right outside the dining room, ready to hand the male slaves the elaborately decorated silver trays which they will carry into the formal dining room to serve the Ibarra guests. A solo harpist plays in a corner of the room, her melodies overcome by the clatter of silverware, the enlivened chatter and the chewing on the delicacies Cook Jenny has outdone herself with. Tray after tray of fish and fowl are brought in, though the seafood *paella* is the centerpiece of the meal. Tears fill the eyes of many of the Spanish guests when their most cherished dish from the motherland is placed in front of them. Don Pedro begins to sing an impromptu song about "*mi patria, España*" as he lifts his cup to toast a country he has not been in since he was a child. With more toasts to Francesca for her hospitality, and to Alvaro and Isabella on their upcoming nuptials, the room is silent when the twenty dinner guests begin eating the *paella*. Amidst gentle moans of pleasure, the heaping plate is soon diminished as coat jackets become unbuttoned and corsets are wiggled against. Male slaves refresh wine goblets as the room becomes warmer and the strictures of formal dining are loosened. Francesca reigns over the table, with Padre to her left and Jimenez to her right. Barely eating in order to keep a sharp eye on her guests as well as slaves, Francesca occasionally leans towards her closest dinner companions in conspiratorial whispers.

The only person who remains quiet all night is her future daughter-in-law, Isabella, whom Alvaro said four words to then turned to his dinner partner on his left and spent the entire evening speaking about hunting. Francesca decided to host an informal seating, which allowed the future bride and groom to sit together. Normally, in her more traditional dinner parties, she strategically places her guests next to others with similar interests and never puts a married couple together. That is how Isabella met Alvaro in the first place, at a dinner party she hosted two years back where the two had been seated next to each other. No one knows what was shared between them that evening, but it began a lengthy courtship that has brought both of them to this moment.

But Francesca has other things on her mind as she continuously sips her wine, which has yet to go to her head though she is feeling a bit of longing. She has decided to allow Jimenez into her bed this evening. It has been too long since a man has touched her and it is only after she has had a taste of what type of lover he will be, will she decide if she wants to pursue anything further with him. He has been obvious with his interests and intentions but she is the one to make the final decision. The trade-off for a warm bed partner against giving up some of the control over her estates seems feasible, if Jimenez has enough love-making skill. Her private property holdings and bank accounts in Spain are set in Lucia's name, which Jimenez can never touch, even if she marries him. Being a widow has many perks, including the discretion of taking a lover after such a long time. As the plates are removed for the desserts and tea before the dancing begins, Francesca slides her hand across Jimenez's left thigh and gives it a firm squeeze. Pleasantly surprised at its firmness as well as Jimenez's slight flinch at being touched so suggestively, she covers her mouth quickly, feigning a cough as she raises her glass in another round of "*saluds*."

Alvaro and Isabella open the dancing for the evening. The trio of musicians play the Spanish guitar and lute as a singer croons many of the traditional songs from the homeland. The guests find no embarrassment in taking to the ballroom floor that leads off to the verandah and back garden. Soon, the room is overcome by the sounds of clicking heels, in rhythm with the castanets that the singer has flourished. Without a doubt the evening is a success as the night winds down. Tired and not used to late evening hours, couples begin to leave. Francesca has seen Lucia on the dance floor several times through the evening and now, she is resting against a curved door frame near the verandah, flushed with exertion.

"My daughter, you look happy this evening," Francesca says as she stands alongside Lucia, who was still trying to catch her breath.

"Oh, Mama, it was a wonderful evening. I danced the heels off my slippers! These old things need to be replaced. I see that most of the guests are leaving and the musicians are starting to pack up, so I am going to say goodnight and see that Micaela helps me change my clothes for bed," Lucia said as she gives her mother a rare peck on the cheek.

"Good night, my dear. All in all, I believe this evening cannot be rivaled in terms of its success. I told Micaela that you will be up shortly so she is already turning down your sheets. Go and rest. I will close the house and then sleep, do not worry about me," Francesca says, startled by her daughter's sudden affection.

As she watches Lucia walk across the ballroom floor to the staircase, she overhears Alvaro behind her, calling out his own good nights. He has walked Isabella home and returned exhausted. He too follows Lucia up the stairs to his room, one which he will sleep in for just three more weeks.

Francesca smiles and says goodnight to the last remaining guests in the foyer while instructing the slaves to blow out the candles and clean the kitchen, and then, as arranged, she walks out to the gazebo, where she has invited Jimenez to wait for her.

"Look, Micaela, I brought two sweet cakes for you," Lucia says as she unwraps the white linen cloth in her hand. Inside are two *pan de elote*, made from the condensed milk and fresh yellow corn that most Spanish families loved and had as an after-dinner staple.

Michela looks up in surprise. She has come upstairs to pull back Lucia's bedclothes as Doña Francesca had instructed her. Only Lucia knows that the *pan de elote* is her secret favorite food. Once, when they were smaller, Lucia had convinced her to steal a corner of the newly baked sweet from Cook Jenny's worktable. Bravely, she had grabbed a big enough chunk for both herself and Lucia. While she was running back to their hiding place behind the stables, she had managed to gobble a few succulent pieces of corn and sweet milk. It was the grease stains on the corner of her mouth and hands which had given her away and Lucia had shrieked so loudly that she had eaten all her cake that Cook Jenny had eventually found them, evidence all over their hands and dresses. Surprisingly, both girls had been scolded, not just Micaela for Lucia's transgressions, which was the normal course of action. There had been a moment, where both of them, eight years apart but growing like sisters as children, had giggled behind their hands when they were sent to nap as punishment instead of being able to run around outside. Thinking back to that moment, as the years passed and Lucia created the formal distance between slave and owner, makes her work sometimes a bit more bearable. She remembers laughing, their friendship, their adventures in the garden and the small stream that bordered the property and sometimes the monotony of her life is almost manageable. Of course, this is until she found Dakarai. Then, the concept of living began to actually make sense, even for one who is enslaved.

"Señorita Lucia, thank you. You remember my fondness for the *pan de elote* from our childhood. I thought you had forgotten. Why don't you share a piece with me?" Micaela says with feeling as she accepts a piece of Lucia's gift. She knows she has been forgiven for the day's transgression.

Lucia holds a chunk of the moist bread, full of corn, and takes a huge bite, humming a song from the party as she sits on the chair next to the bed. Micaela continues to stand at a distance as she gingerly places a morsel into her mouth, allowing for the mix of corn and sugar and dough to hit her all at once. She has been craving just this. Without thought, she closes her eyes and moans softly. Lucia's giggle forces her eyes to open quickly, embarrassed that she lost herself in the moment. Looking into Lucia's face, for a split second she sees her childhood friend whom she gorged herself with behind the stable walls until caught by Cook Jenny all those years ago. Micaela feels the laugh in her belly before she can control herself and it erupts like sand over her skin, filling the room. Lucia laughs so hard that the tears stream down her face as both gasp for air.

They do not say much to each other after the food is gone and Micaela gives Lucia a lavender-water scented cloth to wipe her hands and face. Lucia seems to be locked in her own world, twirling to the music in her head and enjoying being a girl who has been the center of attention at a party. Micaela has not seen this part of Lucia in years and she has almost forgotten her. Now, she is grateful to be reminded that indeed, deep down, Lucia's heart is wide open.

Lucia uses the chamber pot after stepping out of her evening clothes and undergarments which Micaela rush to gather so that they can be aired out and washed in the morning. Climbing into bed, Lucia's snores quickly punctuate the air as Micaela tidies up the wash basin and puts the dirty laundry in a pile for the next day. Before blowing out the bedside candle, Micaela looks down into Lucia's face and for a second, a great sense of loss sweeps over her without explanation. Trying to make as little noise as possible, Micaela makes her way into the adjoining room; a repurposed closet for her so that she can be available for any of Lucia's needs, day or night. She does not need candlelight to conduct her ablutions and change into her night dress, since the routine is etched in her body. Lowering onto the pallet on the floor, the cool of the evening makes Micaela shiver as she pulls the folded blanket at the bottom of the bed over her. In the darkness, she ponders how long it has been since she laughed like that. As sleep takes her, a far-off banging sound interrupts the air, as if a bed is being slammed against the wall. Too tired to listen further, Micaela drifts off knowing she has only a few hours of sleep before she must be up to prepare Lucia's breakfast for her in bed.

"**P**adre, a word please," Francesca says softly, leaning towards him as the congregation files out the church after the special evening prayers for St. Perpetua. In the twilight, the prominent Spanish families are marching ants against the deepening shadows. When Padre nods to her as he gives benedictions to his parishioners, she stands by his side, grasping her gem-encrusted rosary beads, her breath rapidly moving the black veil covering her head.

With a nod to Lucia, Alvaro and her three slaves, Francesca indicates that they should walk ahead of her to the house. She allows Padre to escort her to a seat in the last pew of the church. The breeze carries the scents of roses and honeysuckle along the aisle of the church. These are the moments she enjoys the most; the calm after a special evening mass when only she remains with Padre, to savor the blessings for her sacrifice of remaining in Costa Rica after her husband died.

"Doña Francesca, are you in need of confession?" Padre asks with a frown. Francesca is infamous for her thirty-minute confessions and his dinner already awaits him in the parish house.

Instantly, she blushes, thinking back to the night she had with Jimenez after her dinner party.

"Oh no, Padre, I will come for that on Friday as is my practice. There is no sin so heavy on my heart that I need forgiveness mid-week! I am here because of a concern that has been circulating amongst some of our families. I want to make sure that I know exactly what is going on. I have heard that the Grand Audience in Guatemala has decreed that all *pardos* in Costa Rica must live in a proper *pueblo* outside the city. *La Gotera* will no longer be a hodgepodge of people but a small *pueblo* onto its own. Is this correct? Is it true that they are also requesting a census in order to increase the taxes and tributes we already pay for our slaves and hired hands? How does this decree affect our slaves, Padre?" Francesca makes sure to emphasize the collective understanding that they are both slave owners and thus no different from each other in the end.

"Doña Francesca, you must have gotten the message on the wings of a bird. It is astonishing that news so secret has circulated so quickly. But, yes, you are correct. Don Jimenez has been directed from the Church headquarters in Guatemala that he must turn *La Gotera* into a formal settlement where only *pardos* can reside. *La Gotera* is a mess of people living with each other, many poor Spaniards also live there, and they are to be moved into Cartago proper. A census will be taken amongst those who live in *La Gotera*. Those who own slaves or hire *pardos* for seasonal work will have additional taxes. The Cruz de Caravaca will demarcate formally the entrance and exit of this new *Puebla de los Pardos*. This will all take time; years, I suppose, but we must follow the ordinances of the *Capitania General de Guatemala*. We are already neglected, so far removed from them, but it is wise to be prepared as I expect a delegation will be upon us soon enough."

Padre continues, not looking into Francesca's face but at the altar in the rising moonlight.

"It will inconvenience many of our families as we now have to pay more for our slaves but what can we do? Their lives within our households bring them closer to our Godly light and we provide what they would never get in the pagan wilds of Africa," Padre says into the night air, his voice echoing off the sparkling tile floors of the church.

They discuss the few details which Padre had gotten from his earlier meeting with Don Jimenez, and with a stifled yawn, Padre suggests that he escort Francesca to her door as the night air is fresh and no slave has remained behind to take her home. They walk in silence, which is unusual as normally Francesca has much to say. Padre wonders how she has come across the information so quickly when the few written decrees have been across his desk only this week. It must have been Jimenez, though the documents had been safely locked away in his desk since he first received them the previous Monday morning. When he had spoken to him quickly before the evening's mass, Jimenez had seemed genuinely surprised at hearing about the missives from Guatemala. Yet, Jimenez is the only one who knew about the census so it must have been what he was whispering in Francesca's ear before Mass.

As the silence grows uncomfortable, Padre speaks about the mundane, commenting on the impending rains and the upcoming marriage of Francesca's son. Surprised that she does not take the bait of speaking about the wedding, Padre remains silent, thankful that they only have to turn the corner to enter the Ibarra *hacienda.* As he opens the wooden fence for her, he raises his hand in a slight blessing over her head and before she can say more than a good night, he turns and is already on his way back to the parish house. Francesca stands at the gate as Micaela comes to the door with a candle, calling her name softly to enter the house because if not, she will catch a cold.

Jendayi

The next day

Jendayi does not hear Padre as he enters the schoolroom. She is intent on figuring out a math problem that he left on her slate before he was called away by Don Jimenez. Jendayi senses there may be some trouble, but she keeps her fear at bay while she starts dividing her numbers for the third time. How she wishes math would come as easily as language. The numbers stare back at her while words create songs in her ears, and she is able to sing back to them.

A few of the other children are sitting in the front row. The eldest ones like Jendayi instantly straighten their backs and keep their heads focused on the slates in front of them. The schoolroom is an old cooking space that had been built at the back of the Parish House which Padre had converted. It is the space which has had the least amount of work done to it since the earthquake. Jendayi knows Padre is only interested in teaching the Catechism so that they can receive First Communion. Every child in the room, about sixteen of mixed ages between seven and seventeen, are *pardos*. Some, like Jendayi, were born free but the majority had been enslaved at birth and then their freedom had come through purchase or manumission.

"Juana Maria, please step forward and review the vocabulary words. I must attend a meeting in town and will not be able to return to the lessons today. I trust that you will be able to complete the remaining work and help the little ones finish their addition. The rest of you may be dismissed once the vocabulary words have been written three times on your slates. Javier and Oscar, make sure you stay behind with Juana Maria to sweep the classroom. The slates must be washed and stack the benches against the wall so that Esmeralda may come and wash the floors."

"*Bendiciones,*" Padre says as he raises his hand in the sign of the Cross and quickly walks out to the sacristy.

Annoyed at having to take over Padre's job when she needs more time to concentrate on her math, Jendayi goes over the spelling words, carefully sounding them out so that the students have the time to write them on their slates but also practice the words on their tongues. Thinking ahead to what is left of her day, she knows that once back in *La Gotera*, she has to spend another hour teaching Spanish to Mama Petronila's charges and prepare dinner before her father gets home. Fighting the urge to leave the class, Jendayi walks between the benches and looks at the slates, noting which students continue to struggle with their writing. She adjusts a piece of chalk in several little hands until finally, dusting off her own chalky-white palms, she tells everyone that they are free to go for the day. An instant cheer erupts as the students gather their small satchels and head through the door and onto the dusty path leading to *La Gotera*. Freedom is calling, all the possibilities of *futbol* and mango tree climbing ahead instead of a day spent copying words from the Bible and rumbling numbers around trying to make sense of 2+2.

"I heard that they are moving us all out of *La Gotera* so that they can use the land for farming," Oscar says, once the other children have gone. He wants to finish his chores quickly and so he grabs the straw broom propped behind the door. Winding his way around the benches that Javier has yet to move, he pushes the dirt on the floor into a neat pile by the front door.

"No, that is not true. Padre said that only people who are not *pardos* have to move, that is what he said to Don Jimenez and I overheard them," Javier says, leaning against the window frame.

Jendayi begins cleaning the slates with the damp cloth Esmeralda has left by Padre's small wooden desk. Without turning to the boys, Jendayi says, "I think that before you both start rumors in *La Gotera,* you better get your facts straight. I will ask my father and he will know the truth."

"Your father is one of them; he thinks he is a *pana,* though his skin is blacker than mine. He will probably be the one driving the cart which carries the things out of our homes and into the street. Why should we trust him? He is no *pardo*, he is a slave to the *panas* and forgets who his people are," Javier says with a sneer, never moving from his lounging position against the window.

Out of the corner of Jendayi's eye, she sees Esmeralda passing the door quickly. Clearly, she has been eavesdropping. The venom from Javier's response about her father sticks in Jendayi's throat and she cannot dislodge it. Not bothering to respond to Javier or look deeply into Oscar's wary eyes, she packs up her satchel, places the damp, dirty cloth into the small orange-clay bowl and walks out the door.

Tempted to stand outside and listen to the boys talk about her once she is gone, Jendayi forces herself to walk swiftly to Esmeralda's door. With a small tap, she pushes the half-opened wooden door and is instantly swallowed by the darkness. It is the first time that she notices the room is windowless. The night lives there without restrictions. The shack is simply that; a tiny wooden structure that looks more like a shed for tools than living quarters. The wooden slats have gaps that allow light and wind and rain to filter in. Inside the shack, the floor is dirt yet it is packed tightly and Esmeralda has kept it clean. There is a pallet on the floor to the back right and a simple wooden stool where Esmeralda has a small cooking stove. She uses this to warm meals, usually beans and rice and whatever leftover the servants prepare for Padre in the parish house that she is given. She has several clay pots on the floor to the left side of the room where she keeps various herbs for teas and for clean water. The room is smokey, dense, dark, and gloomy. There is always a chill, even on the warmest days. If one looks closely, the bigger slats in the wood have been stuffed with leaves in order to keep the Cartago cold out. Beyond the smoke, there is a smell of lemongrass which elevates some of the gloom. Esmeralda makes lemongrass tea so often that its sharp, tangy smell sits permanently in the air.

As Jendayi's eyes acclimate to the dark, she notices that Esmeralda is sitting on the low stool near the door, which has been ajar, bent over a garment that she was mending. Not startled by Jendayi's presence this time, Esmeralda simply nods in the direction of her pallet. Jendayi hesitates. After mumbling her greeting, she sinks onto the straw pallet, her satchel of books clanking noisily by her ankles onto the smooth dirt floor.

Esmeralda does not look at her when she says, "Jendayi, this is the second time you have disobeyed your father and crossed my door. You have now made me guilty in complying with your wishes, not his. Speak quickly child, as I must finish mending these pants while I have the light. Sewing with one good eye in the dark is dangerous work."

"Well, why don't you just use candles or your kerosene lamp or go sew outside. I am sure Padre will allow it," Jendayi says defensively.

Esmeralda chuckles in resignation, "Only a person who is free and well-fed talks about material possessions like candles and the freedom to sit in the sun, as if it is of no significance. My child, these are not things I possess, especially my freedom. I am relegated to these four walls and then within the shadows of the church to clean and prepare the altar. I do the washing and mending for Padre, but he has his own servants at the Parish House. I am not allowed outside the perimeters of the church property at the risk of my life. I have been a slave of this church for thirty-five years and I will die that way."

Quickly, Jendayi calls out, "Forgive me Mama Esmeralda for my careless tongue. I do not mean to give offense. My world is also limited. Daily, I am hit from behind with ideas and thoughts that are being kept from me, but they affect my life. Who is to protect me but myself? I am still shocked to find out that many of our people think my father has forgotten himself and has become an ear and eye for the Spaniards. This is not who my father is! When did people start thinking this way about him? Is this why people have stopped buying our products at the Thursday market? We have been giving fruit away at the end of the day when normally our cart is empty, and we have heavy sacks of *pesos* to count on the way home. What is happening?"

"Jendayi, the air is thick. People are apprehensive about the lines between Black and white because in the world the *panas* know, there is no balance, only Black slave and white master. But they need us, and this is their problem. In our world of Costa Rica, slowly this has changed as there are now *pardos* roaming freely. From what I hear, the Church in Guatemala has ordered that *La Gotera* be turned into a formal town for only Africans who are *pardos*. There will be much moving and mixing and re-defining of people's identities and the real ideas about freedom and slavery will be put to the test. Many feel that when your father took on the work for the Ibarra family, he went into a secret deal with them and became their "ears," but we both know that is not the real reason your father took on the work. However, he will never expose Micaela to prove his loyalty to the people in *La Gotera*. It is a terrible situation and I have no idea how this can be fixed. It will come to a head soon enough. We must all be prepared. Ignore those boys out there; they are simply gathering nonsense overheard through fearful parent whisperings."

So, she had heard the boys' comments in the schoolroom and she knew about Micaela. Jendayi smiles to herself. At least she had never second guessed her feeling that Esmeralda is an ally.

"I must go, Mama Esmeralda. As always, thank you for your wise words. Forgive me for putting you in a position that you had little control over as I barged in your door. But I am grateful that you have taken the time to speak to me. That is all I ever want," Jendayi smiles, clutches her satchel and pushes her way out of the low door frame, not looking back into the darkness.

One week before the Ibarra wedding

On the Saturday before Palm Sunday in the last week of March, Jimenez, with Padre and a few other Spaniards, appear in *La Gotera*. They stop door to door, inquiring after the name of each resident and demanding their freedom papers, all while writing them down in a large black book.

"I wonder what he is going to say about Sebastian when he finds him," Josefina says, as she leans out the kitchen window, trying to document Jimenez's progress.

"Hush. Sebastian left last night with his family because word had already arrived that the *panas* were coming to start census taking today. He figured that as long as they make it to Nicoya, there will be work on the cacao plantations and not too many *panas* to check his status," Petronila states, never lifting her head from the dough that she is kneading with her thick fingers. Every now and again, she shifts in her seat, indicating the hip pain that creases her days. Lifting a hand to point at the rice to be cleaned, she starts to order Josefina to stop daydreaming and get to work. However, before she can speak, Jendayi, who has been sitting silently in a corner of the kitchen, picks up the flat, braided basket filled with rice and returns to her corner, quietly sifting the grains away from the stones.

Dakarai had asked Jendayi to stay with Petronila and not alone in their house once the word came from Esmeralda that the Spaniards were visiting *La Gotera.* The people know this will be a long process, but most prefer to stay at home, on the watch. Many of the *pardos* feel secure with their status as free Blacks, yet any involvement with the Spaniards from Cartago is fear-inspiring. One knows not to trust them, and it is warned that with a tricky word or shaky story, one's status can be changed from free to enslaved overnight. Sebastian, a man without freedom papers, had been given just enough time to pack a few things and slip away under the cover of night. Without a doubt, a few more people of *La Gotera* would end up missing over the next few days as the counting continued.

"What do they want anyway?" Jendayi asks, head bent over her task.

"They are here to make sure that each person is noted for the Grand Council and we will all be taxed for the church's tributes. There will be no escaping now and what is worse is that we give up the money that we struggle to make and then there is no guarantee that the money is sent to Guatemala. We are forced to trust the people that have enslaved our brothers and sisters and so our hands are tied. Sometimes, I think freedom is meaningless," Petronila says.

FINDING LA NEGRITA

Startled by her proclamation, both Jendayi and Josefina speak in a rush, tumbling over each other with words, begging Petronila not to say such a thing. With one look, she silences both girls from continuing with their pleas.

"You are both old enough to see what is in front of you. Why should I pretend that this is not the way of the world? I remember the days when I held laughter inside, afraid that I would burst because of happiness. I knew the simple things of my mother's hugs and my father's special tea. I enjoyed the times when I could go visiting with neighbors over long weeks away from home, but safe as I was protected, fed, and cared for. I never once doubted my freedom or that my life would not provide me with a family of loving children and a husband to share a home with. Now, I am old and have become grandmother to the many small children of *La Gotera* though my body-memory craves the ones I left behind. You, Josefina, are the only one who now fills my arms and for that I am grateful, but I am not meant to stay here long. I am always looking back into my past, retasting the dust on my tongue from long walks during the dry season at home beyond the sea. My two small daughters, the ones I left behind, will never get the answers they need about their mother who went on a trip to the north and never returned. What stories were they told to ease their worries, my twins? There is not a day that goes by where I do not long to give them the rest of the story; to tell them that their old mother survived but would I be lying to say that? Is this living? My own child, I do not know how to protect your body from the *panas*. I could not protect myself and look at my body, broken and disjointed at the whim of a Portuguese governor who beat me so badly because I refused to lay with him so soon after your birth, that he broke my hip not three weeks after I had given birth. I will never be able to walk properly again and no amount of liniment will cease the pain and so I am forced daily to remember him and that time. Why should we pretend that there is safety and power in our arms, when we know that any day, we are theirs to take and possess? I am done, *m'jias.*"

Jendayi remains with her head bent over the rice but she feels as Josefina gets up and embraces her mother. Silence fills the air as the women refocus on the cooking tasks in front of them. Jendayi is stunned to imagine that Petronila has left her twin girls behind. She will never see or hear their voices again. Wanting to finally ask questions about her father's life in the village that he shared with Petronila, Jendayi clears her throat but then swallows the words as she looks up to see Petronila staring at her. She can see that in her eyes, there are many stories that will never spill onto Jendayi's head and heart.

"Mama Petronella, I am done with the rice," Jendayi says. She places the cleaned rice basket on the center table as she starts for the door.

Petronila blocks Jendayi from leaving, and firmly states, "No, your father explicitly said that you are not to be left alone while the *panas* are here doing the census. I agreed because who is to say what will happen to a growing girl found alone? It is their word against yours and even if your body speaks the truth, no one will hear it. Take my warnings carefully daughter, I tell you this because this was the life I led from the moment those Portuguese bastards took me into the *quintaloes*. They like having the power over our bodies. For two years, I was a concubine for one of the Portuguese governors, his bedroom directly over the women's slave pens. Though it seemed like I had a better life than the others, it was torture listening to my sisters and brothers scream for mercy, day and night and worse when they were taken onto the canoes into the oceans, facing their fate on these slave ships. But, within a month, I was pregnant and once the child kicked inside of me, there was nothing I would not do to stay alive and to ensure the baby did as well. When he was angry with me or wanted another girl, he would send me back into the slave dungeons, belly swollen with his child, as a lesson to me. But he always brought me back. I never expected anything more or less from those people. But then he beat me when I refused him, my body still bleeding from childbirth and he broke my body. When Josefina was two, he replaced me full time and sold me to the first ship captain heading away from those shores. Miraculously, that ship held your mother and father, Jendayi, and for that I am forever grateful. I understand it was a mercy. If I was to die, then I would do so among kin who could whisper the prayers of the dead over my head before being thrown overboard."

Taking a deep breath, Petronila continues, "Josefina is the one I chose to keep as I knew she would be the last to form inside me and I need someone to bury me when it is my time to go home. I was given my freedom along with Josefina's because no one would buy us at auction, most turned away when they saw my deformed hip and shortened leg. I knew no more babies were coming from my womb. No baby deserves the life of a slave; worse a concubine for these dirty *panas* who never wash their mouths or their asses. The Portuguese and the Spaniards are twins, interchangeable in their behavior. Listen carefully because I have never said these words to you before, but Josefina knows them well. I have had to train her on how to protect her body and that means mixing the herbs we grow in our small garden. Don't be afraid, Jendayi. You have no mother whose medicine can protect you and your father does not understand how these things can be done. He is still too amazed at the possibility of life that he would never consider ending one; not willingly."

"But Padre says that it is a mortal sin to kill a baby in the womb. It is a gift from God and as mothers, it is our job to protect it and continue bearing children as God so sees. Is he wrong?" Jendayi asks carefully.

Cursing under her breath, Petronila says, "Padre is a man; very much a man who also desires power. Be careful with him. He does not know the limits of what he can and cannot have, because he believes that he has divine exemption. He does not. No mother wants to end a life in her womb yet when the child is placed there through perpetual violence, over and over again, only to be born to face a life of despair; then it is an act of mercy, of the divine that enables her to swallow the medicine that will let the baby sleep for good."

Still unsure, Jendayi presses on, "Do you mean that Padre thinks he is untouchable and cannot be judged because he is God's servant?"

Petronila shouts, "God's servant, ha! Esmeralda is God's servant, my dear, and she is a slave of the church passed from one *pana* to another as if she were a loaf of bread. Padre is simply a man hiding in white cloaks, talking their religion and then eating, drinking, and carousing with the rest of the *panas*; then running back to the church to ask for his God's forgiveness. And most importantly, he has been unkind to Esmeralda. She has suffered greatly under him. He is the reason she sustained such burns on her body. But, no more of this today. Jendayi, mark my words; there is no redemption for that man in this world."

"Should I be afraid of him? He has always been very nice to me. He does assign me a lot of the teaching work that I think he should still be doing, but I don't mind, mostly. I never thought to fear him," Jendayi asks tentatively.

"You must not fear him because then he can catch you unawares. All I am saying is that you are no longer a child and you must be able to watch the world around you to survive. You are here in front of my daughter and I must give you the words that I have shared with her. These are my only gifts to you, as an auntie from the place of your people. I can track the dust on your father's feet and remember the tears of your mother as she gave birth to you and held you in her arms with her dying breath," Petronila says this while still facing Jendayi, a look of worry creasing her brow.

Jendayi just nods and wipes her hands slowly on her dress. The thin fabric stretches under her anxious hands. There is just so much to think about. She wants a chance to get away and walk along *La Gotera* so that she could process Petronila's words carefully.

"Mama Petronila, thank you for your warning. It is true that I am motherless and have no one to guide me in this world of men. But it is late, and Baba forgot his lunch today, so I must walk over to the Ibarra house and give it to him before darkness falls. Remember, he has given me permission to be outside of *La Gotera* as long as I am not alone in our house. I know if I am late, he will be angry," Jendayi lies, hoping that if she does not catch Petronila's eye, she will not be able to get away.

"He forgot his lunch? How odd. Okay, you may go, as the days are long and your father works until the sun is down. But here, take this fresh meat pie that I have baked. Let Josefina go with you. Go and collect the food and then both of you must return quickly, as I have given your father my word that you would remain with me today." Petronila wraps one of the warm pies that she had taken out of the clay oven near the hearth and hands it to Jendayi. The heat of the crust and the pressure of Petronila's hands as she places the food into Jendayi's almost makes her cry. As she mumbles a word of thanks, Jendayi turns and tilts her head, indicating that Josefina should follow her across the backyard path that joins their two houses. The sun is high in the sky and the winds are building, causing the birds and trees to dance in unison.

Jendayi

"You lied to her," Josefina says as soon as they enter Jendayi's backdoor into her kitchen. The bright yellow embroidery cloth that she has recently made hangs on the wall. It is a new favorite and Jendayi smiles to herself as she looks at the wildflowers sitting in a clay cup at the center of their table, framed nicely against the warmth of the cloth's colors. Rushing to pack some food items together, Jendayi whispers, "Be quiet! How else was I supposed to get out of there? I cannot hold so much information in my head. I felt like I was going to explode. Why did she tell me all that? Why have you not told me any of those things?"

"Twin sisters left behind? Padre as an abuser?" Jendayi continues with her back turned to Josefina. Petronila must have known that she was lying because she sent Josefina along. Now, the real trouble was trying to convince her father that she needed to be there giving him this food when he had already taken the lunch she had prepared early in the morning.

Also speaking softly, Josefina admits, "Sorry. I did not know about Padre. I always thought it was just about the cursed brothers in the Santiago Apostol Church that made Mama insist I stay away. But I feel it, Jendayi; the things that Mama says about him are correct. I do not trust any of those *panas*. I see how they look at me when I go to Thursday market. Nicolas gets so angry but there is nothing that he or I can do. How can they want me while they have their slaves and their wives to entertain them? Is it never enough?"

"Padre is supposed to be a man above that. He is not to marry or have a family. This is what the Catholic Church mandates. To think that he is the cause of Esmeralda's suffering is frightening. There are no rules here that I understand, Josi," Jendayi says with deep sadness.

As they let themselves out of the house and silently walk on the dirt path towards the Cruz de Caravaca, they watch Jimenez and his group exit yet another one of their neighbor's houses. Rather than catch their attention, they walk quickly out of *La Gotera*. The distance is not far once they pass the church and Francesca Ibarra's house. The new compound is six minutes walking from the house that Alvaro has grown up in. It is far enough not to have his mother in his business every day and close enough to still have the resources of the main house accessible to him if need be.

"Look, isn't that Doña Francesca's slave nearing Don Pedro's stall? Doesn't she look like she is getting thick around the middle? I wonder if Alvaro finally got at her! Jendayi, don't stare. She will suspect that we are talking about her," Josefina whispers as they pass the small market stalls haphazardly built near the compound to profit from the workers as they spent months building the new house and installing the surrounding gardens. Jendayi's eyes widen as she glances over at Micaela, who has not noticed them in the process of picking out eggs from Don Pedro's stall. As she leans over to pick up each egg for inspection, the apron around her normally trim waist gives way to a small, round thickening.

Panicked, Jendayi diverts Josefina's attention to another stall as she picks up her pace, navigating past the market to arrive at the wooden fence demarcating the new Ibarra property. Trying to sound as casual as possible, Jendayi retorts, "You are talking nonsense, Josi. She looks like they finally gave her some food to eat in that house. I heard that Doña Francesca has been going with Alvaro to their Nicoya farm because there has been some unrest with the workers. Micaela must be at home with that lazy Lucia, eating chocolates and doing no work. Though she is a slave, I heard that she does not do any cleaning. She combs Lucia's hair and reads the Bible to her in the afternoon. I even heard Padre say one day that Micaela writes and does sums better than Lucia. I think they will sell her when Lucia goes to Spain for her 'come out'."

Sucking her teeth, Josefina jokingly replies, "Lucia is never going to Spain. Nicolas told me that Doña Francesca has used some of Lucia's dowry to pay for the final pieces of furniture for the new house. Due to the labor unrest, they have lost a lot of money from their farms in Nicoya. Alvaro is lazy, and he never followed up on the work of his father and so now, the consequences are clear."

"What do you mean?" Jendayi asks as she enters the new Ibarra compound. From any angle, the house is awe-inspiring in its dimensions. Shining glass windows twinkle from the first floor while latticed terraces wrap around the entire second floor, allowing for French doors to open out from each of the upper bedrooms. The grounds are expansive, though the ornamental gardens are still being planted. Already, it rivals Francesca's perfectly manicured lawns with their precision mapped to mimic the famed new Palace of Versailles in France, which had been completed the previous year. Sketches of the palace and surrounding grounds had found their way across the ocean as letters arrived from abroad. It was Isabella who instructed the master gardener to copy the design so that she could enjoy it from her bedroom window. What already had been created is beyond the imagination in splendor, color, and beauty.

Moving ahead, Josefina calls behind her, "Come on Jendayi. We must find your father. I heard that when Alvaro and Doña Francesca got to their *finca*, they found only seven of their fifteen slaves living there. And bags and bags of cacao have vanished. So, they are feeling it now. I think that Doña Francesca does not want to admit that she may no longer be the wealthiest woman in Cartago."

"But what will happen to their farm? Don't they need more workers once the harvest comes?" Jendayi lowers her voice while asking Josefina. They are nearing her father's workshop and she does not want to chance him overhearing them.

Before Josefina can respond, Dakarai exits the workshop with his back to them, hands full of the teak wood that is famous in Costa Rica.

"Baba," Jendayi calls out timidly.

Dakarai turns abruptly, bending slightly to catch the wood as it careens out of his hands.

"Jendayi, Josefina, your presence surprises me. Is there a problem in *La Gotera*? Are you okay? Have Jimenez's men come to do the census?" Dakarai stands stock-still, waiting for the two girls in front of him to calm his suddenly agitated heart.

"Baba, all is well. Don't worry. I…I could not remember if you had taken your lunch with you, so I brought some food from Mama Petronila. She made a special meat pie for you. See, it is still warm. These are the final days here and you have been working past sundown. I wanted to make sure that you were okay," Jendayi says, looking past her father's shoulder as she replies to him.

"I see," Dakarai continues to look at both girls. He reaches out and takes the covered dish from Jendayi's hand after placing the slabs of wood on the ground next to his feet. Their hands touch briefly; the sweat from Jendayi's palm has dampened the light blue cloth the food has been wrapped in.

"*Tio* Dakarai, please do not be angry at Jendayi. She has been helping us cook all day to avoid Don Jimenez and his census people. There is much disruption in *La Gotera*, and people are unsure where they will be living tomorrow. Many have fled. We were concerned that you would be out here working without any food. And so, my mother sent us," Josefina states earnestly, staring into his face.

He cracks a weary smile and replies with a thank-you. He asks them for help carrying the wooden slabs to the house since he now holds the food. Jendayi and Josefina are both surprised that he does not send them straight back home. Happy to be his helpers, they are even more surprised when he invites them to see the inside of the house.

The smell is the first thing which hits Jendayi as she crosses the threshold. The afternoon sun sprinkles sunbeams through every window in the entry hall and throughout the spacious, high-ceiling rooms. Intricately designed furniture fills each space, built with the balsam, Spanish cedar and teak woods brought from the rainforests on the coast. She is so proud of her father's work. Jendayi can see the details on the dining table which seats twelve from where she stands at the entrance, still struggling with the wood slabs she carries.

"This table is made with *cedro español* and I carved it with fifteen *colibri*. This was Alvaro's request as he says his wife-to-be loves hummingbirds. It is a sign of good fortune to see the *colibri* with its long beak and fast wings. I once met a BriBri man who told me the *batsu*, which is the *colibri* in their language, flies to the sun and brings down love to each person and flower it meets. He also told me that if you see a *batsu*, it is a message from the ancestors saying that they are well," Dakarai says as he takes the wood pieces from the girls and lays them behind the front door. He leads them into the kitchen.

"Look at the new cast iron stove they sent to Panama for. It took four horses to bring it from the port," Dakarai says, mostly to himself as he runs his hand over its black top in admiration. Jendayi is not interested in the kitchen. She keeps looking towards the opulent staircase leading to the upper floor. "Baba, may I go upstairs quickly to see the rooms. Please?"

"I don't want Doña Francesca to know that I have brought you here. You may go up quickly, but I am preparing to go back to work now that the wood has been brought inside. I will give you three minutes and then you must leave, and Jendayi…" Dakarai says with a firm tone.

"Yes," Jendayi said, already moving towards the stairs.

"Do not touch anything. You must promise me this," Dakarai insists.

"Sure Baba, of course. Josi, are you coming?" Jendayi asks as she takes the stairs two at a time.

"No, I will stay here, I am not interested in the bedrooms of those *panas*," Josefina says with a haughty stare.

"I am going to the workshop. Three minutes, Jendayi, and you and Josefina must be at my work shed to say goodbye. Both of you make sure no one sees you leave. Close the front door firmly behind you," Dakarai gives them both a final look and walks outside.

"Josi, you don't know what you are missing," yells Jendayi as she reaches the landing of the curved staircase, her voice echoing against the polished wooden floors.

Jendayi does not wait for Josefina's response as she looks at the closed doors all around her. Tentatively, she walks to the second door on her left and turns the knob on a door made of *roble coral español*, a special wood that her father had spoken about at length for its rarity. She knows it by its reddish color, and she rubs her hands against the frame as she pushes the door open. What she sees inside quickens her breath. Following her gut, her first choice had been the correct one; the master bedroom. The room is dwarfed by the bed in its middle. There is a huge mattress and four bed posts which hold heavy brocaded green curtains. They are securely tied to each post by gold cords. But it is not the beauty of the cloth that makes Jendayi speechless; it is the headboard which her father has carved. There, towering above the mattress is a wonderland of hummingbirds, butterflies, squirrels, and other small land creatures. Their world is framed with fragments of glass, tile and gems which glitter from eyes, wings, and feet. As Jendayi gets closer, longing to touch the headboard, she notices an indented niche at the center. Leaning closer to see the detail, when she reaches out to touch the wood, she accidently knocks a piece of tile off the depressed ledge.

"Oh mother! What have I done?" Jendayi says to herself in a panic. Trying not to disturb anything else, she climbs onto the mattress and leans her slim arm down the crease between the mattress fabric and the wooden headboard. She fishes around for the object, silently cursing. With a bit of a twist, she pulls it up as she sits back firmly on the bed. Looking down at her hands, Jendayi feels her heart skip a beat. It was not a piece of tile but a carved sculpture of a mother and child, like the Shona pieces her father made for her as a child.

In the middle of the small black stone, there is a small crack on the Mother's hand where she holds the child. Jendayi begins to tremble.

"Jendayi, it's been more than three minutes. Your father is going to be furious. Let us go," Josefina shouts from the bottom of the staircase.

Jendayi looks around wildly. What should she do? Maybe it would be best if she takes it home and asks her father to work on the crack and then he can return it with no one knowing? Wrapping the carving into her handkerchief, she tucks it into the waistband of her new brown skirt, thanking the heavens that Mama Petronila had sewn it for her three weeks before. The elastic allowed for the figure to sit snugly against her skin as she runs down the stairs with the sound of the bedroom door slamming behind her.

"What is it? You look like you have seen a ghost. Jendayi, slow down, what is happening?" Josefina says as Jendayi barrels to a stop in front of where she has been sitting on the bottom staircase step.

"No ghost," Jendayi says, breathing quickly, "it's late and I have taken too long, I am fine. Let's go." Grabbing Josefina's arm, Jendayi leads her out of the house, making sure to close the door behind them. Then without saying a word, they both run across the cobblestone entrance towards Dakarai's temporary workshop.

Jendayi

The week of the Ibarra wedding

The days of the week go by with the same rhythm. Alvaro's house and grounds are near completion with the wedding just days away. Dakarai barely comes home as he finishes the final details on the furniture. Rumors flew around Cartago and *La Gotera* that Dakarai's work has even surpassed the expectations of Doña Francesca. Many of the Spaniards grumble about the amount of praise given to Dakarai, hoping to limit any public elevation of a *pardo* when there are many still enslaved throughout the country. It is too dangerous for slaves to witness one of their own feel the envy of the Spaniards.

Jendayi sleeps with the carving under her pillow, promising herself daily that she will give it to her father to fix and return. But, every time she tries, she is unable to admit what happened. The carving reminds her of her mother and the life that her father had spoken about from the place beyond the sea. She has now taken it as a sign from her mother, reassuring her after she has seen Micaela's growing stomach. The aching fear of what it means forces Jendayi further under her sheets, her hand slowly caressing the stone as she falls into yet another fretful night of dreaming.

The next morning, Jendayi delivers the water to the church, attends school for only two hours with a very distracted Padre and then returns to *La Gotera* to sing songs in Spanish with Mama Petronila's small charges. Four of them happily dance around her as they chant,

Ting Marin
Me Dos
Me Fue
Ticara Mackara
Ticara Fue[8]

As they collapse into a pile around her, Jendayi's laugh stops mid-breath as she sees her father enter the yard. The shock of his presence and the instant terror that he has come for the carving leaves her panting on the grass with the children still singing their song, unaware of the impending moment between father and daughter.

Gathering her skirt quickly around her, she stands up and dusts herself off. "Baba," she says in a rumble of arm movements, words, and breath, "It was a mistake. I have been meaning to give it to you, but I have not had the chance. I will get it for you quickly if you . . ."

---

[8] A popular childhood song in Costa Rica

Dakarai scratches his head and replies, "Daughter, slow down. What are you speaking of? I have come to warn you. Jendayi, you must not go back to the plaza in Cartago this afternoon. I have heard that they have smuggled some enslaved Africans off the Caribbean coast from Panama, and they are bringing them to auction at 3:00 today. I will not be able to come back to *La Gotera* this evening as this is our final day and we must work through the night to place all the furniture in the house and dismantle the work shed. I asked the others to let me leave quickly as I did not want to send a messenger. I need you to look into my eyes, Jendayi, and promise me that you will not go to the plaza. It is very dangerous and not suitable for a young girl. When the lust for wealth has filled the blood, there is very little discernment about who is free and who can be purchased. I don't ever want that mistake made about you."

"Yes, Baba, I have heard you," Jendayi murmurs, promising very little. She is able to lie to her father for the first time in her life without feeling a sense of crippling guilt. This surprises her and she is unable to look into his eyes. Knowing herself very well, she will not be able to remain at home during a slave auction. She needs to witness the faces of all those who have come from the place across the sea before they are sent to the corners of Costa Rica. It is her turn to be brave.

"Fine. I must return to the work site. Should you need anything, please ask Mama Petronila. I will be back tomorrow. And Jendayi," Dakarai says sternly, "you must heed my words. I have no reason to doubt you as you have always been an obedient child. However, I warn you, do not bring trouble into *La Gotera.*" With one more quick look at his daughter and a rushed blessing, he walks out of the compound toward Cartago. The children who had been singing around Jendayi's feet took one look at her serious father and quickly abandoned their games to sit near the house, allowing them a few moments of privacy.

Jendayi smiles at the children and says goodbye. She waves to Mama Petronila who is at her kitchen window, explaining that she is heading home to complete some work that her father has asked her to do. She crosses the dust path into the back of her small house. Once inside, she quickly puts down her satchel, washes her hands and prepares a simple meal of leftover rice and beans. She eats without focus and the heat of the beans burns her tongue as she gobbles the food. Once finished, she rinses her dish and cup and then rushes to straighten her clothes as she double-checks the fire in the cooking hearth to make sure it is completely out before she exits the house.

The late afternoon air has warmed considerably. Jendayi notices that the birds are cacophonous in their conversations. There is nothing foreboding as Jendayi walks along the path to the plaza, trying to remain unnoticed by her neighbors in *La Gotera.* So focused is she on getting to the auction, that she is not instantly aware that there are no others walking along the normally busy path. Clearly, the message has already spread in *La Gotera* about the buying of enslaved Africans and it is now a ghost town. A few stray dogs sniff each other, and a donkey brays, but otherwise Jendayi is alone. The noise from the plaza reaches her ears before she can see the crowd of Spaniards who have amassed, eager to see the new bounty. Jendayi scans the area and walks into a dense copse of trees on the north side of the plaza where she can hide. Using her slim legs and strong arms, she quickly climbs into a tree, happy that the crowd has a singular focus that does not include her. While climbing up, she snags a sheet of parchment that has been nailed against the bark. Once seated on a high branch, trying to take in her surroundings, Jendayi glances at the missive in hand. It is a public announcement of a slave sale: *Doña Margarita de Morales is selling to Capitan Juan de Luque, resident of Cartago and neighbor of Granda (Nicaragua) a slave called Juana Josefa, of the* pardo *color, 20 years old, in good health, round face and good disposition, good countenance, mortgaged, or subject to any obligation of the issuing debt without having committed any crime; healthy all public and no secret disease, ill at heart, gout, buboes; clear eyes, without being either fugitive or thief, drunk nor any other defect or blemish that prevents serve well. Price 300* pesos.[9] The shock of the words causes Jendayi to gasp, forcing her to hold tightly to the tree branch as she inches up another limb to be completely out of sight. Juana Josefa regularly visited her stall at the Thursday

---

[9] Meléndez, Carlos and Quince Duncan. *El Negro in Costa Rica.* San Jose: Editorial Costa Rica, 2012. p. 41. Translation by author.

market to buy fruits and vegetables when she worked in Doña Margarita's house. She was kind to Jendayi, always making silly jokes about the boys near the plaza, which caused her to laugh and break the monotony of the market day. Sadly, the captain was known for his cruelty. Jendayi's heart hurts for Juana Josefa because she knows the captain will eventually leave Costa Rica, taking her with him.

Trying to steady herself, Jendayi realizes that she is both terrified about being caught while filled with the anticipation of the auction. She has no idea what she will see but with all the men milling below, she catches snatches of different conversations. The air holds a tension beyond the normal bustle of Thursday's market. There is a sense of hunger as numerous Spaniards gather around a small holding pen just to the west of the church which has been marked by braided twigs and palm fronds. She can barely make out the top of the heads of several brown bodies huddled together on the packed, dirt floor. Words drift past her ears, *casta mina, casta arara,* and *casta congos* as potential buyers pace near the auctioneer, speculating where these Africans have come from. Many seem heartened at their good fortune, and they joke with each other as if sharing in a thanksgiving feast. Most enslaved peoples are sold for prices way above Costa Rican pockets in the fashionable markets of Portobello in Panama. To find a small cargo of slaves directly from Africa, not yet sold and resold on the coastal markets, is a small miracle. They could be molded into the ways of Cartago life easily since they have yet to experience other masters.

Jendayi feels a lump in her throat thicken as fear permeates her skin, a thin sheen of sweat and doubt wrapping itself around her. Just as she decides to slide down the tree and rush home as quickly as possible, she sees Padre and Jimenez lean closely against the tree next to her and begin to speak in loud whispers.

"You must buy two, Padre, Esmeralda cannot do all the work as she ages and with the eventual extension of the school hours, you will need additional labor. Plus, the church has money for such things," Jimenez prods.

"Ah, my son, the church is not as wealthy as you believe. It is you who should be vying for a few slaves for your Nicoya plantation. I hear The Giant will accept our *zurron*[10] as payment and not expect silver *reales*. This is a bonus for us as a blessing from our Lord and Savior. Why else would these brutes find their way to Cartago? They are out of temptation's path in the markets of Portobello and Cartagena. They are meant to be saved from their heathen ways and will easily see our wisdom as they serve us. I am sure anything is better than the barracoon," Padre states, clearly not moved by Jimenez's tinted jeer.

"No, I am not personally purchasing anyone today. I am here on behalf of Doña Francesca as she has asked me to procure some slaves for her farm in Nicoya. There has been

---

[10] A *zurron* was a 97 kilogram/214-pound leather bag of cacao worth twenty-five *pesos* (Lohse, 2014, p, 84).

unrest and many of her slaves have run away. I have made clear to her that I will assist in the training and management of these new slaves so that escape will never be an option for them," Jimenez replies sternly.

"I see. You are much trusted to take such a direct role in the Ibarra household and management. Should I offer my congratulations? Are there to be two Ibarra weddings this year?" Padre asks with a mocking smile.

"Padre, I am fortunate indeed for the friendship I have with Doña Francesca but no, there will not be any double weddings in the foreseeable future," Jimenez says awkwardly, thinking about that lackluster night in Francesca's bed. Once naked and wrapped in the sheets, he had been instantly turned off by her body odor of caked powder, sweat and arm-pit musk which she had tried to cover with too much *eau de toilette*. However, her ardor was so strong and focused that he eventually was able to do the job, pounding away until they both found their pleasure. When she had wanted him to stay the night, he insisted that it would not be proper if they were caught. Dressing in the dark and leaning over to kiss her hand, he whispered a few sweet nothings in her ear and tiptoed from the bedroom, down the stairs and out the front door with the most haste he had employed in years. The next day he had insisted on a bath being drawn for him, though this went against his singular midweek washing ritual. He must have gained her approval because this morning at Mass, she had personally asked him to take over the purchasing of new slaves instead of Alvaro. Confident that he would run the Ibarra family in the end, Jimenez snuck a quick kiss on Francesca's pink lips as a confirmation of their understanding. He had not waited around to see how she responded.

Jendayi waits patiently, every muscle on edge so as not to cause a leaf to stir. One sound and she will be caught and there is no way she can conjure up an explanation for her presence. Luck is on her side as The Giant, the infamous auctioneer, with his greasy, balding head and hulking frame, begins calling out, drawing the attention of the Spanish men who are present. Padre and Jimenez quickly join the others near the pen. There are no Spanish women in sight. The only brown skins are those tied together in the pen. Jendayi counts eight in total; five men, two women and a small boy of about four, who is clinging so tightly to his mother, it is as if her skin will rip. Feeling his vulnerability, Jendayi again thinks about escaping her perch because everyone's focus is on the sale. The Giant's assistant, a man of questionable origins with his pale skin and curly, jet-black afro, leads the male captives out of the pen, tugging hard against their roped arms. This causes a few to stumble against each other. The men are connected by their wrists and have individual leg chains. Jendayi decides this is the moment for her to run home. Yet, the auctioneer's voice compels her to keep her peace, at the risk of it all.

Leaning a bit further along the branch to get a better view, Jendayi notices that each slave had been branded with the sign of the Royal *Asiento*. So, they have been to at least one other market along the way. These were stolen cargo. But the *panas* will turn a blind eye and see these enslaved Africans as their good fortune, never questioning who they belonged to or where they have come from. She has seen the brand too many times from her neighbors in *La Gotera* who tried their best to wear long sleeves to cover the scars which marked their identity as slaves, even for those few who had made it across the line to freedom. The men stand awkwardly in front of the gaping crowd. The silence is palpable, except for a lonely cry which comes from the small child, wild-eyed with fear. What he must have gone through to get to this point, Jendayi cannot imagine but it tears at her heart.

The bark of The Giant's voice startles her and her stomach muscles clench. In broken Spanish, she hears him start the bidding process. The wrist ropes are not removed as prospective buyers walk slowly to each man, inspecting with their German-made bow spectacles, perched timidly on bulbous noses as they circle their prey. The enslaved, exhausted from their journey from the port of *La Caldera*, follow instructions mechanically by bending, lifting their legs, opening their mouths only by aping what the Spaniards did themselves. Finally, a *ladino,* a Spanish-speaking African, is summoned by The Giant. Given brisk instructions, the man begins to speak in what must have been the language of the congos or minas because it was the first time the enslaved turn their eyes with focus towards someone other than their own. However, their wariness is abundant.

Jimenez stands alongside the *ladino* and asks him to say where each man hails from and what their ages are. The men slowly respond, some confused by the questions. The situation leaves most speechless. Frustrated, Jimenez gives up on documenting the slaves and nods for The Giant to begin again with the auction process. The men, finally examined in all ways inhumane, are returned to the pen as the two women are dragged out. Jendayi tightens her jaw as she sees how the Spaniards pinch their breasts while trailing their fingers along the buttocks of these women, barely clad. She flinches, along with the women, instinctually pulling her shoulders up around her ears as if to protect her own body. But there is no one to protect the bodies or the lives of these women. Wishing they will be bought by someone in Cartago, rather than sent off to the hinterlands of Matina or Nicoya, Jendayi bites hard on her tongue as she notices that one of the men put back in the pen is trying to slip his hands out of the wrist ties. Fashioned by thick rope rather than the same chains which strangled his feet, the blood from the constant chafing freely spreads over the fibers and drips along the base of his hands. Slowly, he had twisted a loop loose, shredding the skin of his wrist in the process. Chewing her bottom lip, Jendayi watches, fascinated at such bravery. How is it that no one notices what he is doing? However, all attention is towards The Giant as he begins naming his prices while the women are paraded again in front of the salivating *panas*. As hands go up and shouts share offers, the women are to be sold first. Jendayi breathes a sigh of relief when she sees that the little boy has been sold with his mother for a combined price of 350 *pesos*. As their new owner makes loud plans to have the fourteen bags of *zurron* delivered to The Giant, Jendayi keeps a keen eye on the man who is working through his ropes. He is probably just a few years older than her, his broad chest testifying to his youth and strength. Despite the travails of the slave route, he is a beautiful man and instantly, Jendayi closes her eyes in prayer, "Please, let him escape this terrible life. Give him freedom, dear ancestors, so that his life will be more than just empty labor for a slave master who will never see his value." Steadfast in her thoughts, Jendayi takes a deep breath and opens her eyes as she shifts on the branch, her entire body stiff with the anxiety of staying in place.

What she sees before her eyes is beyond belief. The young man has managed to free his hands, grab his foot chains and begin a fast shuffle behind the men in the pen. She can see that he is panting hard from his efforts and the look of terror of being shot on sight is reflected on his face. Jendayi knows he needs help. Sliding down the back of the tree and scraping her chin against the bark, Jendayi uses the foliage to hide herself. She gives thanks that the area is lush with dense bushes and trees, cleared only for the opening of the plaza and church. Crouching low, she hurries between the trees in a complete circle until she is directly behind the pen. She whistles softly, trying to get the young man's ear over the commotion of the women's auction. He stops instantly, his body sharply taking in the sounds around him. The second woman is being haggled over for a longer time because she is in her prime and her firm breasts are an added incentive as the Spaniards add *peso* upon *peso* for her purchase. Jendayi knows a way out but it must be fast. She walks closer to the pen, crouching low, and whistles one more time. He turns and sees her. No sounds, wide eyes, only a gesture to follow. Almost on his knees, he grabs his foot chains and backs out of the pen, knocking over a palm frond in the process. Instantly, Jendayi notices the smells: human waste, despair, pain, and sweat. She is so close to the pen that she can see that the other men are much older than the young man in front of her. There is no time for pretense, as the only thing that saves them are the *panas'* lustful greed and the dense forest behind them. She puts her hand on his shoulder, right above his brand where the skin has collected into a seeping blister, and mouths "come." He does not hesitate. They edge their way around the plaza, with him shuffling then resting then shuffling, until they are far enough amongst the trees that the voices no longer cause their hair to stand on end.

Jendayi finally stops, her heart about to leave her body. What has she done? Leaning against a tree, Jendayi looks up at her new friend. Remembering her Shona, she utters a few words of greeting. He looks at her with no recognition, the impossibility of the entire situation right in front of them. She points up, as the challenge now is to climb the tree in front of them and wait out the evening until she can take him further to freedom. Understanding what she wants him to do, he drops the chains and with his long arms, blood lacing the wrists, he pulls up on the lowest branch, lifting his body with him. Not high enough for his own safety, he climbs branch after branch, dragging his lower body, heavy with chains, up alongside him until he is fully hidden in the leaves. Jendayi takes a deep breath again, knowing that her life is fully at risk for this stranger. As she turns around to take one last look up into the leaves, she hears a light whistle and understands its meaning.

"You are welcome. I will be back." She mumbles under her breath as she begins a rapid return to *La Gotera*.

Jendayi

Her mother must be walking alongside her as a guardian angel because Jendayi manages to get back to her house, slipping past her few neighbors who barely notice her, until she closes the front door with a soft thud. The pounding in her ears makes standing straight impossible and she sinks onto her haunches, leaning gently against the closed door. What has she done? What if she risks going back there and he is long gone, caught, and killed because of the audacity of her actions? She has not remained long enough to hear their reactions when they realize that one slave has escaped. What she does know is that those men are so greedy with this illegal parcel of Africans that they were tripping over themselves for the few that were there. Their covetousness over the women clouded their ability to safeguard the others and Jendayi is secretly glad. Jendayi is not happy that the women will likely suffer in the hands of their owners, but she is glad that at least one person took the chance at freedom. She is also proud of herself for surviving such an act when she had never done anything like this before.

The moon is full and carries Jendayi's shadow as she creeps along the outskirts of *La Gotera* into the plaza. The stars must be in alignment for her father to have to spend this one single night at the work site rather than at home. Trying to orient herself in the moonlight, she notices that the holding pen has been left erect, a ghostly home, to the west of the church. Using that as a marker, she moves swiftly, weaving between the trees, careful not to drop the still-warm *tamales* she has wrapped in cloth.

As she approaches the area where she thinks that she has left the stranger, she gives a low whistle and leans into a tree. Nothing moves except a few birds deep in sleep, shuffling their wings and dreaming of the morning call. Again, she whistles, and she faintly hears a reply. Pressing her ears into the night, she moves towards the sound. She whistles one last time and jumps back in fright as the young man swings down from a tree a few feet from where she is standing. They look at each other, barely outlined forms in the dark with only the moon as their light. Jendayi waves, and then seeking to be brave, she walks over to him and sticks out her hands with the food. He looks at her, standing still. She unwraps the cloth with the *tamales* and makes a show of putting her hands to her mouth in a gesture of eating. He nods and slowly stretches his hands to accept the food. As their hands touch, his smell overwhelms Jendayi and she tries not to gag. He sees her actions and shuffles back with the food in his hands, his head lowered in apology.

Jendayi is ashamed of herself. The last thing she wants is to make him feel bad when he has been so brave. She has no idea of his story but surely, he has one. Her father has told her that everyone is a mother's child and they come with their own unique story.

Without waiting for her any longer, the young man drops to his haunches and carefully places piece after piece of *tamale* into his mouth. Jendayi tries not to watch but it is the effort he is making which causes her pause. His wrists! Jendayi remembers the aloe salve she had made into a paste and tied into a banana leaf which she placed in her dress pocket. It does not take long for him to finish the food and Jendayi is instantly sorry that she could not bring him water but carrying a gourd was too much of a risk if she needed to run. He leans against the tree awkwardly, trying to straighten his legs held by the chains.

Jendayi goes over timidly and sits down a few feet from him. She sucks in her breath, trying not to swoon from the stench of his skin and fragmented clothes. Taking the aloe out of her pocket, she imitates the action of putting the salve on her own wrist, so he can see what her intentions are. He nods after two tries and she pushes the salve towards him, hoping he will apply the paste to his wrists. He reaches to take it and drops it once in his hands. Jendayi realizes that he is shaking all over and without thinking, she grabs the salve and takes his left hand in hers. He jumps at her first touch but otherwise remains immobile and she slathers the rich paste, tempered with lavender oil, around his wrists, forearms, and hands. The fresh scent causes a distraction from his stink and Jendayi works steadily until she finishes both arms. Just as she is wrapping the remaining salve, she hears a dog bark in the distance and her body tenses. With eyes having adjusted to the night light, Jendayi puts a finger to her mouth for him not to utter a sound and stands swiftly; taking the empty *tamale* leaves and wrapping it back into her dress pocket, alongside the aloe so that not a trace of them will be left. She holds out her hands to help him up and then she points to the church as she begins to move, hoping that he will understand her and follow along.

Several more dogs suddenly begin to bark, disturbing the night. Something is happening. They must move fast. The young man shuffles behind her, but he is painfully slow. Jendayi knows he is probably beyond exhaustion, but the entire day will be for naught if she cannot take him a step further. Once she hears shouts joining the dogs' barking in the distance, she knows that they have to run. She turns toward the stranger and indicates that he has to move. He rocks forward on his feet, trying to create bigger steps with the chains that bind him so tightly. Jendayi can see that the Parish House light is on so late in the night. Trouble. She wonders if the dogs have picked up their scents. Impulsively, they weave in and out of the trees until they finally reach the tiny copse near Esmeralda's shack. Terrified that she will be turned away, she bravely knocks against the door, trying to flatten her shadow as well as the stranger's, who instinctively knows to remain crouched low. The moon is both a blessing and curse. When no sound comes from behind the door, Jendayi simply pushes it open, fear and need trapped in her throat as she pulls the young man inside the shade of darkness. Everything else happens in slow motion as both turn to see Esmeralda stop abruptly from her ablutions in the dim candlelight, her faded dress hanging precariously over narrow hips, small breasts bared at the onslaught at her door. Struggling to cover herself with her working right hand, Esmeralda walks towards her bed and picks up a light blanket and puts it around her shoulders.

"Why?" Esmeralda's whisper ricochets off Jendayi's skin.

Timidly, she whispers in return, "Mama Esmeralda, I come only at the risk of death. My brother here escaped the slave market this afternoon and I can now hear the dogs after him. I cannot think of any place else to go. His feet are chained; if they were not, he would be gone. Please forgive me, forgive me," Jendayi weeps; the enormity of the situation in front of her is too big for the fifteen years she has already lived. She, unwillingly, has put all their lives at risk. She cannot even communicate with this stranger. Consumed with her own worry, she does not instantly notice when Esmeralda begins speaking quietly to the young man. He responds eagerly, a sense of relief tinges his voice as he gulps through his story. In the distance, Jendayi can hear dogs and voices. With relief, she notices that they are not getting closer to the church, so maybe they can buy some time.

"He is called Gwelo and he is *casta* Angola. I know the Benguela language because my mother was *casta* Angola and so I can understand the basics," Esmeralda says over her shoulder as she leads Gwelo to the corner and helps him ease down to the mat. She blows out the candle and without its light, they are just voices. Gwelo's smell consumes the air and Jendayi takes puffs of breath to keep focused.

"How will we get the chains off him? He cannot remain here long. I am so sorry that I brought him here, but we have nowhere else to go because he cannot walk quickly," Jendayi says into the air.

Esmeralda works fast, mainly ignoring Jendayi's persistent voice as she gathers a cloth and her clay basin and begins the work of bathing Gwelo. The water, laced with lemongrass, eases the air and Jendayi can hear Esmeralda murmuring softly. Slowly, Jendayi can make out their shapes in the dark as she notices the moonlight through slits in the wooden shack.

"Jendayi, go to the back of the church near the schoolroom. There are two gourds of water. There is also a small basin of lye next to the wash bowl. Take the lye carefully and pour it into one of the gourds, then quickly spread the water over the path you have just taken to get here from the plaza. This will distract the dogs from your smell and give us some time as we figure out how to remove these chains," Esmeralda says firmly.

Jendayi stands rock still.

"Go," Esmeralda hisses.

With a nod more to herself than Esmeralda, Jendayi moves out of the room and into the night air. The dogs continue to bark, but seemingly on the other side of town. However, Jendayi knows that it can all change in an instant. Gathering her bearings, Jendayi follows Esmeralda's instructions, grateful that she knows the ins-and-outs of the church. Mixing the lye and water, she carefully tries not to let the stench overpower her or the liquid burn her fingers as she backtracks and tosses the mixture onto the dirt. She moves through the forest and to the side of the plaza where Gwelo had climbed the tree, careful to protect every last drop so that she can cover all their tracks. Thinking it will be best to divert the dogs as far away as possible, she trails the water towards the other side of town, near Doña Francesca's house. She does all this holding her breath, sweat dripping under her armpits. The light in the Parish House is still on and once she gets closer, she can hear Padre and Don Jimenez's voices from the window. They are up at this hour, nearing two a.m., for only one reason.

Circling the church from the side of the Parish House once again, Jendayi slides against the cool brick surface while holding tightly to the empty gourd until she reaches the back of the schoolroom and re-deposits it. Cursing herself, she realizes that she will have to make two trips for water in the morning because she emptied this tonight.

Lightly tapping Esmeralda's door, she pushes her way into the darkness again.

"Mama Esmeralda, I have done what you have asked. What can I do now?" Jendayi asks into the silent, dark space.

Esmeralda stands from the small stool she is sitting on and Jendayi jumps in fright, surprised in the dark that she is so close. Thinking Jendayi is going to scream, Esmeralda grabs her arm firmly and urges her to hush. In the same way that she pulls her, she releases her as fast; this touch a lifetime without words.

"Go home. There is nothing more for you to do here. Tomorrow, bring the water as normal and then help your father prepare for Market Day. I am sure there will be a commotion, but no one will check here. He is safe for one more day as we figure out what the next step is. After you leave the water, stand by my door and I will give you instructions. Do not come in and make sure that no one sees you standing over here. Move slowly and do not attract attention. Everyone will be tense. The Ibarra wedding is on Saturday and now the slave auction has caused a problem. The Spaniards will be angry. This is what they get for their greed," With these words, Esmeralda walks over to the door and opens it a crack. The moonlight allows Jendayi to see Gwelo slumped in the corner of Esmeralda's mat, fast asleep, soft snores bristling the air. Jendayi does not need any more instructions. She eases out of the doorway and runs swiftly to her empty house, giving thanks again that her father remained at the Ibarra compound for his final night of work and clean up.

Jendayi

The Wednesday morning before the Ibarra wedding

"Why are you still sleeping?" Josefina asks, leaning into Jendayi's face. Startled, Jendayi jumps up, a haphazard arrangement of thoughts and words littering her brain as she stumbles to stand upright. The sun is shining brightly through the window and Jendayi moans. She has overslept again and may have already messed things up.

"What time is it?" Jendayi croaks.

"7:30 and your father has already returned and is in the kitchen wondering what can be taking you so long. He sent me in here to get you up. Come on lazy bones, this is not like you." Well, if Jendayi had had more than four hours of sleep, she could think clearly but now Josefina is an annoying reminder that she is late. Washing and dressing quickly, she asks Josefina to help her carry the bigger gourds of water to the church once she has prepared breakfast. Josefina reluctantly agrees and promises to be back in fifteen minutes.

"Good morning, Baba. Sorry for sleeping so late. I was not feeling well and drank some *manzanillo* tea last night. It always makes me sleep later than usual," Jendayi says, never looking directly towards her father as she busies herself with cracking some eggs into a clay bowl.

"Good morning, daughter. I am relieved to see you. There has been a great uproar in town because of a male slave runaway. There is even talk of postponing the Ibarra wedding until he is found but that will take us into the rainy season, and I am sure that Doña Francesca wants everything perfect for the outdoor banquet," Dakarai says while sipping his coffee.

"Baba, I did not hear of any of this. How did he escape? What will they do to him if they catch him?" Jendayi asks quickly, wanting to know more about Gwelo's situation. At least she knows that he has not been found.

Dakarai smiles as he says, "You are eager for information this morning, but I do not have any answers for you, except they think that he was stolen by one of The Giant's men as they were inspecting the other enslaved men. No man could have escaped that pen on his own. They had the dogs out last night. The *panas* are determined to find him and make an example of him. Yet, these are not our worries. They have decided that there will not be a Market Day tomorrow, so I will go to the farm myself as I have the day off. The work is done, finally. You are to go give the water to the church and return immediately. Do not delay in town, Jendayi. There will be no school for you this week until this matter has cooled down. Come Saturday with the wedding festivities, they will soon forget this once they are deep in drink and food."

In order to assuage her anxiety about Gwelo, Jendayi changes the subject with her father, asking him to detail the Ibarra house and all its riches. She still has the tiny mother and child icon under her bed but no longer feels the need to return it. This is her lucky charm; a gift from her mother and she has decided she will not part with it unless her father asks her directly. No one has noticed that it is missing and so Jendayi remains silent.

After breakfast, when she barely pushes the food past her lips, Jendayi cleans the dishes outside in a clay basin. She returns to the house, taking the iron kettle off the hearth and pours her father another steaming mug of coffee. She notices that he has settled in his chair, calm for the first time in months. The strain of working non-stop lines his face but as he sips his coffee, his restfulness belies the fact that he must not have discovered Micaela's growing belly. Well, that is not her story to tell, though the thought of it all makes her nauseous. Gwelo's face rises in her mind and she knows there are more pressing dangers that await her and for the first time, she feels her childhood slip away. Asking gently to be excused so that she can take the water to the church, Jendayi watches as her father waves to her and then starts to doze, the coffee mug still in his hand. Removing the mug with little protest, she takes one more look at him, wondering if his face will be as peaceful the next time they meet.

Impulsively, Jendayi goes to her bedroom and takes out the mother and child icon from under her pillow, carefully wrapping it into a small cloth and tucking it into the pocket of her dress. She needs as much guidance she can get and by simply touching it, she feels a sense of purpose. Gathering two of the bigger empty gourds while waiting for Josefina on the dirt path, Jendayi is preoccupied. She wants to turn back and get some of the warm bread Mama Petronila sent over with Josefina, which her father has eaten along with his eggs. Since she had not been hungry, she had left her piece aside and now with the rumbles of her stomach along with her nerves causing havoc within her, she longs for the comfort of home. Surely Gwelo would want the bread but it is too risky to go back and chance waking her father, though she cannot imagine where Esmeralda will get enough food to feed a runaway. Gwelo; she runs the word over her mouth, sucking in the sound around her tongue and tucking it gently into her throat for her own heart song. Gwelo.

Confident that Josefina will not come near the church, Jendayi manages to fill their walk with empty chatter to distract herself. Josefina does not notice. She speaks dreamily about the Ibarra wedding and has no interest in the whereabouts of a runaway. Doña Francesca has promised to set a few tables out near the kitchen for a few *pardo* families so that they too can partake in the wedding festivities if they exchange their hands for work. Arriving at the church, Jendayi thanks Josefina for her help with the large gourd. She then balances both on her shoulders and makes her way to the back of the church. Leaning down, she places them in their normal spot and then she stands up, listening carefully for any voices inside the church. It is unusually quiet. With school being canceled, the missing sounds of children cannot hide her panting breath. Slowly, she creeps along the wall to the entrance of Esmeralda's shack, looking at the church in case Padre makes a sudden appearance. She does not have much time because if her father wakes and notices she has delayed, he may come looking for her. Brushing her hand slowly against the tin shed door, Jendayi crouches down as if to tie her sandal, preparing a *tableau* in case she is seen. After a few seconds, the door creaks open.

Softly, a bodiless voice comes through the crack.

"You must retrieve some tools from your father's work shed so that we can remove the chains. There is little time. They have decided to keep the wedding as planned for tomorrow, so it will be a good chance for him to go, as everyone will be focused on the Ibarras. But they will hold him in the back of their minds and so I am not trusting that we will be problem-free. It is certain that they will not come to me, but I cannot hold him much longer. There is not enough food. He also needs clothes. If you can spare some from your father, then I can mend them quickly for him. Return tonight and do not fail, daughter." With these instructions, Esmeralda disappears into the darkness of her shack, the door closing as if by a ghost.

A few birds chirp and Jendayi looks up at the sky for the first time in what seems like forever. There are dark clouds overhead. Finally, the rains will come after the long summer months. A few scattered drops catch her as she makes her way back to *La Gotera*. Too worried to care about the sudden rain shower, she moves steadily while others run with laughter past her once she crosses the Cruz de Caravaca. Children dance in the mud, filling empty coconut shells then tossing the rainwater at each other. Jendayi watches them; envy over their innocence creeps inside her. Her thoughts go back to Esmeralda's instructions and her body tingles with anxiety. Luckily, she knows her father's work shed like the back of her hand. The trick is to make sure he does not start carving this evening. She has to convince him to rest. For the wedding, he will be expected to help erect the tables and carry the heavy baskets and trays for the women in the kitchen, since he was hired for day labor.

Shaking out her sodden dress as she enters the house, she finds her father snoring in the chair near the hearth just as she left him. Sighing with relief, Jendayi tiptoes to her room, removing her leather sandals so as not to squish across the floor. Pulling off her dress and putting on a blue skirt and green shirt, she almost throws the soaked garment to the floor when she realizes that the icon is still in the pocket. Gently, she removes it and tucks it under her bed mat. She will need to wash her dress so if the sun returns in the late afternoon, it will dry, and she can put it back on tomorrow.

Peeking her head out to make sure that her father is still dozing, she walks into his small bedroom. He barely sleeps these days, and the room feels empty. In a corner, neatly folded onto the only chair in the room are a few shirts and pants she has painstakingly mended over the years. No matter the number of holes or the haphazard pattern of her stitches, her father always praises her work and confirms that he is the cleanest and neatest African man in *La Gotera*. As she got older, her sewing became stronger and she could straighten out a few pant hems and eventually, she made a shirt for him that he only wears at home in his work shed. The soft patterns and simple neckline reminded him of the clothes he once wore at home beyond the sea, he told her proudly on the day she presented her gift to him. Knowing that her father rarely wears that shirt and will hardly notice if it goes missing, she searches for it at the bottom of the pile and pulls out a worn pair of pants that she has mended too many times. Loathe to throw anything away, her father has kept these as testaments more to her child-like mending rather than as actual clothing that he will wear to work. She fingers the cloth, thinking of Gwelo in them, and a warm rush of heat comes to her cheeks.

"Jendayi, what are you doing in here? I was calling you from the kitchen," Dakarai asks from the doorway, an expectant look in his eyes.

"Ah, oh Baba. You frightened me. I was looking for your clothes to mend since the rains are here and I cannot go outside. I wanted to see to the clothes that you will wear to the wedding," Jendayi replies hastily, turning back to the pile of clothes to gather a few more items. Bundling them all to her chest, she moves rapidly around her father, smiling as she walks towards her room.

"Don't worry about making me fancy now, I am just hauling wood and bringing tables to the garden," Dakarai laughs gently.

"Of course, Baba. No matter what, I am sure you will be the handsomest man there," Jendayi says with real happiness. It has been so long since the natural ease of their relationship has felt like this. If only this moment can stand forever.

Pulling on an old sweater hung on a nail by his bed, Dakarai says, "The rain has started to ease so I will go to the farm and bring back some fruit. I hear that Nicolaasa Mina has been sick for a week and no one knows what to do for her. I must ask Esmeralda to make a special lung tea for her. I will bring some of the *guanabana* to make juice tomorrow. Please take it to her while I am at the wedding. I know you do not like the sickroom, Jendayi. I can see it all over your face, but Nicolaasa Mina helped raise you when I was away in Nicoya all those years. It is my turn to repay her. Maybe you can do some mending for her while you are there. I am not asking much, my daughter."

Jendayi stands motionless with the clothes pressed firmly against her chest. Words of dismay collect in her throat and she coughs, trying to press them down. On Saturday, she was supposed to go to Gwelo and Esmeralda, not sit with a sick woman who will spend the afternoon telling useless stories. Stricken by her father's plan, Jendayi nods in agreement and returns to her room. Sitting on the bed, she pulls out the icon and rubs it, wishing away the frustration rumbling across her skin. Feeling the smooth surface and the tiny ridges her father had etched eventually brings her a sense of peace as the beauty of it sits in a corner of her heart. Resolved, she decides that tonight will have to be her farewell to Gwelo.

Once her father has left the house, Jendayi is able to look around his work shed, gathering the tools needs and moving items around so they will not be readily missed. Adding them to the clothing bundle she has taken for Gwelo, she prepares food and gathers extra candles, as a gift for Esmeralda. She then mixes coconut, rosemary, and lavender oils in a small clay pot as ointment for Gwelo's skin and hair. Hiding everything in her room, Jendayi anxiously awaits the night to come so she can sneak away.

Dakarai

Walking towards the farm near the river, Dakarai whistles. He feels a huge sense of relief now that the Ibarra project is completed; it has been done better than even he has expected of himself. Now, bone-weary, he is grateful to put it behind him. With the wedding in the morning, only one more day stands between him and any further relationship with the Ibarras. He agreed to the day labor at the wedding because he wants to witness the freeing of Doña Francesca's slaves, as they have agreed. Feeling hopeful, he tosses around the idea of asking Micaela to eventually move in with them in *La Gotera*. He had not seen her for almost twelve weeks, but he knows that she is working every second under the dictates of Doña Francesca in preparation for the wedding. He admits to himself how much he has missed her; he wants to rest in her arms.

As he crosses the path to his land, he sees that it had lain fallow for too long. He curses himself for neglecting the weeding and harvesting as he has not encouraged Jendayi in the last few months to set up their stall in the Thursday market by herself. It has been weeks since he has come to check the land. He sets upon pulling weeds from the earth before he goes to the small copse of trees which hold budding mangos and papayas. With his hard work, he welcomes the combination of sun, wet earth, and plump produce. Pulling the squash and melon from the vines in the earth along with tomatoes and green beans, Dakarai fills his sack with the harvest that is salvageable. Jendayi will be able to make a good soup for Nicolaasa Mina on the morrow along with a tea if he can get word to Esmeralda. Maybe he can go to her in the evening, with apologies since he has not given her lessons in several months. After that fateful night when Micaela had crossed his doorstep as Esmeralda had come to warn him about the rumors in town, Esmeralda had only returned that one last time where he had spilled his secrets. He is ashamed that he has used the excuse of the Ibarra project to avoid facing her. The look on Esmeralda's face during their last time together told him everything and he knows that he is holding back from going and explaining his case.

Stopping occasionally on the way back to greet his neighbors in *La Gotera*, Dakarai shares a fruit or two from his sack and it lightens considerably by the time he nears his home path. The news about Nicolaasa Mina's health is startling. Everyone seems to think that she has caught a disease from the *panas* and if she dies, there will be no one to look after her four children, the youngest being a babe at her breast. Her husband only returns from the Matina plantations twice a year with his meager earnings; long enough to plant another seed inside of her and then return to his futile existence amongst the cacao pods. This is not the life of freedom. Dakarai makes a mental note to ask Petronila to find a wet nurse for Nicolaasa Mina's baby because it seems unlikely that she can continue to produce sustenance for the child without eventually fading away. Esmeralda can make the teas needed to aid her lungs and give strength to her body. These thoughts preoccupy Dakarai and he almost walks past his own house, so focused is he on getting to Esmeralda's that evening. He knows he has to be cautious with the rumblings about the runaway still on the tongues of the Spaniards, who are not yet drunk from the pre-wedding punch Doña Francesca's enslaved workers have set up on the back lawn for the early wedding guests. Many have started to arrive from *encomiendas*[11] far and wide across Costa Rica. He is ready to see the entire event put behind him and longs for the regularity of his workshop in town.

Coming around the back of the house, he puts his sandals near the kitchen door and washes his muddy feet be-

---

[11] An *encomienda* was a legal system used by the Spanish Crown during its colonization of Latin America in order to regulate indigenous labor. The Spanish Crown granted a Spanish colonizer a specified number of Indigenous people who they were responsible for. In exchange for their protection. These Indigenous people were at the mercy of their "protectors" and were forced to not only work in virtual slavery but were also forced to pay tribute to the Crown in the form of labor, gold or produce. They were also forced into Catholicism and had to learn the Spanish language.

fore entering. As he sloshes his toes, gently kneading the dirt away, he can hear Jendayi humming to herself inside. The innocence of it all chokes him and for a second, he almost screams, wishing that the truth lay between them and not a past full of half-lies decorated so bright as to blind.

Dinner is plentiful with the vegetables from their land and is eaten in a companionable silence, except when Dakarai expresses his concern over Nicolaasa Mina's health. He does not mention his plan to visit Esmeralda in the evening since he does not want to pique Jendayi's attention about her. She is not aware that he has been teaching Esmeralda her letters. One day, he promises himself, one day soon she will know everything and there will no longer be secrets in this house. After clearing the plates together, Dakarai wishes his daughter *husiku hwakanaka*, a good rest, and walks into his work shed, hoping to whittle the evening away instead of sleeping. It is best to leave after midnight, so he has a few hours ahead to sit inside his head.

Jendayi

The Friday night before the Ibarra wedding

Jendayi closes her eyes in frustration. Why, oh why, is her father going to his work shed now? Can't he just sleep? He barely rested in the morning and then went out to the farm and now Jendayi has banked on him going to bed early, in preparation for the wedding day ahead. She will have to be very careful as she slips out the house. Maybe he will fall asleep at his work bench but there is no way of checking unless she goes to see him, and she does not want to raise his attention. Instead of changing into her nightgown, she lays on her bed with her day dress and sandals close by the foot of the bed. She keeps rubbing the icon to ease her agitation, but it feels useless. She eyes the clothes wrapped around the tools along with the other supplies on the chair next to her door. The sparseness of the room fills her with a sudden sense of longing; she dreams that she can make her own carvings to fill the shelves her father has lovingly added to the wall alongside the single window in her room. A tiny mirror and a few sprigs of lavender cover the shelves now.

Jolting awake, Jendayi realizes that she has dozed off. By the stillness around her, she wagers that it is now late enough to leave the house. Blowing out the candle near her bed, she hurriedly slips into her sandals, tossing the icon into her skirt pocket as she grabs the bundle from the chair and makes for the door. Stopping to listen for her father, she decides to turn back to her bed and put an extra blanket under the bedclothes so that it appears she is fast asleep, should her father peek in her door. Hoping that the door will not creak, Jendayi tiptoes out the front. There is a small, flickering light from the work shed and her heart quickens as she realizes that he may still be awake. There is no movement from within as far as she can tell but she does not have time to ascertain further as she begins to run towards Cartago. A few dogs bark, but there is no one about.

Reaching the church feels like time travel; Jendayi's feet caress the road by heart, turning the corners without seeing. The bundle has little weight and does not obstruct her movement. At Esmeralda's door, she hesitates and for the first time ever, she hears a slight noise inside the shack. Leaning her head slightly towards the sound, she realizes that Gwelo has shifted his chains somehow and the clank of the metal is not muffled. Grateful that no one else is around, Jendayi scratches her hand softly against the door, alerting them to her presence. The door is opened a crack, and she slips inside but does not walk further into the space; the dark pushes against her skin in a deep breath. It is cloudy and the moon has been hidden. There are no stars to guide her and the dank smell of unwashed bodies and airless space compresses the urgency of her mission.

"Greetings," Jendayi says in a whisper. "I have brought the things that you have asked, Mama Esmeralda." Extending her arms, Jendayi pushes them in front of her. She can feel Esmeralda's presence as she carefully takes the bundle with her working right arm. A sudden burning smell fills the air as Esmeralda strikes a teak wood stick bundled with sulfur to light one of the candles Jendayi has gifted her. If she is moved by the gesture, it does not register. In the furthest back corner of the room, Gwelo leans against the wall, his chained feet in front of him. Jendayi cannot help herself as she smiles into his face. He is beautiful. He looks at her calmly then mutters a soft word, which she assumes is a greeting. Esmeralda watches the interaction with caution, turning slowly to study each face in the dim light. She has already smelt the thing that is growing like wildfire between them; the man-woman thing which, once lit, must live its own life until it wears itself out.

Wasting no time, Esmeralda busily carries a clay bowl of water and a square of cloth and places it on the floor next to Gwelo. Heaving off his dirty shirt, Gwelo grunts as it rubs the edges of his raw wrists. Jendayi struggles with clearing her throat as she witnesses the broad expanse of muscle and brown skin. A sigh escapes her lip and, embarrassed, she hunches down near the door, trying to avert her head. Nothing she can say to herself allows her to turn away fully. She must look at him. Jendayi leans into the contours of his man-body, the smells no longer offensive as sharp lemongrass in Esmeralda's water attests to his new bathing routine. The rough clanking of his ankle chains pulls Jendayi out of her reverie. The dancing candlelight reflects Gwelo's eyes as they catch each other. She focuses on his chains to distract herself from sucking in his form. With an entire life in front of her, even at fifteen, Jendayi knows that she wants him for herself. Yet, she will have to release him into freedom. The longing already sits as a tiny knot in her throat.

Esmeralda moves the candle closer to Gwelo's legs, lining up the tools Jendayi has brought alongside his ankles. Quickly, she picks each one up, unsure of which to use first. Jendayi realizes her confusion and without a second thought, she walks over to them, crosses her legs, sits next to Esmeralda, and begins to whisper instructions on which tool to use. She has seen her father use each one again and again over the years so that she could describe its function with her eyes closed.

She bends closer to look at the heavy chains, flinching at the charred skin around Gwelo's ankles. Though it looks as if aloe has been rubbed over them, the rawness of the cuts remains apparent. She tentatively puts her hand out and touches the top of his toes. When he jerks back, she looks up to see his half-smile. He mumbles something that causes Esmeralda to click her tongue as if annoyed.

"What is he saying, Mama Esmeralda?" Jendayi mutters.

"This foolish boy is admiring your beauty. He should be helping me saw these leg chains off. I only have one arm! If we start now, by tomorrow night we will be done, but we must work without rest. Our only advantage is that tomorrow, the *panas* will be at the wedding so we can work without interruption," Esmeralda explains without looking up.

"May I also return the compliment, Mama Esmeralda?" Jendayi's heart is pounding fiercely in her chest and she looks at Gwelo while her words are directed to Esmeralda.

"Daughter, this will never work. Leave it now. You have done your job here; do not give your heart as it is unlikely to be given back. You have brought the clothes and the tools; you have given Gwelo his real freedom," Esmeralda quips, already bent over the chains with what looks like a small crude hand saw. For a few minutes there is no sound beyond the zig-zag scrape against the metal.

"But it is too late," Jendayi finally says. She reaches for a small wooden pick, scoots over to the other ankle, and begins to feel around for the latch. Maybe rather than saw a piece off, she can break the lock.

"Oh, I forgot, I have also brought food and coconut oil to help his skin. It is in the banana leaves under the clothes," Jendayi says as she gets up from her work to retrieve the bundle. The tiny clay pot of ointment she leaves by Gwelo's feet, but the food she unwraps herself and hands tentatively to him. He does not hesitate, but takes it from her hands eagerly, his apprehension gone about her intentions towards him.

As Gwelo focuses on his food, Jendayi turns to Esmeralda and says kindly, "I have brought enough for you too, Mama Esmeralda. I also have several more candle sticks for you to use as I was so selfish last time to assume you had them in plenty. Please accept my small tokens." Esmeralda just nods as she bends back to work by the wavering candlelight. Gwelo is immobile as both women now focus on his chains. Jendayi peeks at him occasionally. Thinking he had dozed off, she blushes when he suddenly returns her stare and smiles deeply, filling the inside of her lungs with heat. He then returns to his meditation, shifting his wrists which are thickly coated with aloe.

Maybe six feet tall, Gwelo is all lean muscle captured in tangerine brown warmness. His brow creases while his eyes close; his spine betrays his alertness and caution. His fingers are what catches Jendayi's attention the most. Long, tapered with round nails; hands that were meant for scribes, royalty, and pampered sons; not for men running from the slave pens. Tired of bending over the lock, Jendayi straightens and finds herself almost hip-to-hip with Gwelo on the packed dirt floor. He turns his head slightly and opens his right palm. She slides her left hand neatly into its fold; letting the words flow between them.

In her right hand, Jendayi fishes out her icon and begins to rub it. Without words, Gwelo gestures for her to share her treasure and she does.

"Mama Esmeralda, can you please explain to Gwelo that this is my father's carving of the mother and child, a very famous sculpture from our home beyond the sea. Tell him that my parents were famous carvers known throughout Southern Africa. This is my mother's most famous piece; the mother and child icon that my father has replicated. It is now my good luck charm because I feel like she is with me whenever I hold it in my hands. Can you tell him all this, Mama Esmeralda?"

Esmeralda looks up with faint interest in Jendayi's icon. She can see that it is made of black stone and fits into the palm of her hand when Gwelo hands it back to her. Unable to see the details of the actual carving, Esmeralda mumbles a translation of Jendayi's story and then bends her head to work. However, in an uncharacteristic moment, she thinks again and stretches out her hand to Jendayi, asking to see the icon. Jendayi bends forward, her left hand still clasped in Gwelo's, and places it in Esmeralda's right hand. The icon is warm from being held by both Gwelo and Jendayi. Instantly, it fills Esmeralda with a deep sense of peace, that is at once disconcerting and gentle. Continually amazed by Jendayi, Esmeralda gives the icon back to her and refocuses on her work, though a simple calm covers her spine.

Times stands still as Esmeralda works. Intermittently, she tips her ear to the wind, body stilled by the sounds outside her door. Though it is just past midnight, Padre and the choir are busy in the church intoning songs for the wedding mass in the morning as a final rehearsal. Having so much activity around makes Esmeralda more nervous than usual, though she is glad that the wedding preparations have diverted Padre's Sunday attentions from her. By instinct, her body curves in on itself a bit more as if to protect her heart from what cannot cover her body. Gwelo coughs lightly as she accidentally scrapes his ankle, disturbing the raw skin. She quickly apologizes. Esmeralda does not fail to notice that Jendayi's hand remains casually in Gwelo's, with her head tipped along the side of his shoulder, dozing. After what seems like an hour of incessant sawing, she has managed to get a portion of the manacle open. Dragging the chain around will be burdensome, noisy, and too dangerous to risk, but if she continues to work through the night, he should be free by mid-afternoon tomorrow. Standing and walking towards her small gourd of water, she bends and scoops out some for him to drink.

"Drink and rest, my son; over the next few days, it will be unlikely that you get to close your eyes," Esmeralda speaks firmly in the language they share. Her tongue pushes the words out of the recesses in her brain with force since she is devoted to holding onto this last link from home.

Grateful, Gwelo takes the water with his left hand, trying his best not to wake Jendayi as he gulps its freshness until drops slide down his chin. In a moment unlike any other, Esmeralda finds herself smiling at his youthfulness. He is truly an innocent and a life of slavery will age him within seconds. His search for freedom inspires her to feel something that is a first: hope. It is a concept that she moves around and around in her spirit, rubs between her ears and she has yet to fully understand this thing, but she knows he has it and as does Jendayi, yet it is not something her life can fully allow inside.

The coded knock on her door stops everyone mid-breath, except Jendayi whose light snores punctuate the darkness. Esmeralda knows that only Dakarai can be at her door with that signal, and panic fills her stomach. Quickly placing her finger over her lips and nodding to Gwelo to wake Jendayi so that she will not speak in an outburst, Esmeralda blows out the candle and slowly shuffles to the door. She can hear light murmurs as Jendayi wakes and the soothing of Gwelo's voice increases her panic and she can only foresee destruction.

Finally getting to the door, she slips it open a crack, barely allowing the evening air to enter as she whispers a greeting to Dakarai. All is now quiet in the church. On the few occasions which warranted a visit, she normally invites Dakarai into her space; though he never takes advantage of his right to be welcomed in. Now as she greets him and feigns sleepiness, Esmeralda can see the look of expectation on Da-karai's face as he glances over her head, waiting for her to widen the door and not speak in-between the shadows. But tonight, she will not let him in, and it makes both uneasy. He, instantly thinking that she has not forgiven him for the offense of Micaela and neglecting her teaching, shrinks back with apologies for disturbing her at such a late hour. She, straining her ears to the movements of Gwelo and Jendayi crouched in darkness against her back wall, is distracted. Both manage a few more words of greeting and then when Dakarai fully realizes she is not allowing him in, he very quickly gets to his request for her special lung tea for Nicolaasa Mina. He explains that if she can prepare it in the early morning, he can collect it and give it to Jendayi for delivery before he goes on to the wedding preparations. With a quick sigh of relief, Esmeralda agrees, knowing that she already has enough tea to give him but she does not want to move from her sentry post at the door. Pretending exhaustion, she whispers that she will prepare the mixture by first light and leave it wrapped in a banana leaf outside her door so that he can take it without notice. Dakarai thanks her and says he will return in the early morning. As he leaves, he turns back only once, looking in the direction of the darkened church.

Once Jendayi reaches the house she stops, listening for her father's movements but all remains still, except her heart. The thud vibrates across her shoulders as she takes deep breaths, trying to calm down. Her father's presence at Esmeralda's has shaken her to the core and the resentment she feels towards him frightens her. She did not want to leave Gwelo's side, the warmth of his skin still measuring the length of her palm. But all that is no longer as Jendayi creeps around the back to the kitchen, hoping she can slip in without a creak of the door. As she eases her sandals off and turns the knob, she hears shuffling within and ducks back outside. Her father is still awake and there is a very good chance that he knows she is not in bed. Trying to conjure up a story in her head, Jendayi leans against the door frame in the dark, hoping to wait him out. Reaching for the remedy of her icon to ease her nerves, she cannot find it in her pocket. For one entire second, her heart stops in complete and absolute fear. Has she truly lost the icon? Is this a message from her mother that she is in too deep over her head? In trying to retrace her steps while catching her breath, Jendayi realizes that she must have dropped it at Esmeralda's in her rushed exit after her father departed. She estimated the time it would take for him to get home and then followed shortly after. Exhaustion hits her, and she slides down the wall onto her haunches.

Josefina's new puppy wakes her up as he pushes his paws onto her lap while eagerly licking her cheek in greeting.

"*Vayase Picante!* Naughty dog!" Jendayi grumbles as she pushes the dog away, reluctantly rubbing his head as she struggles to stand. Falling asleep outside is not clever and every bone aches as she stretches her arms above her head. Peering up at the budding sun, she realized that the day is still young. Taking a chance, she opens the kitchen door, peers in, confirms that her father is not there, then walks into the room, sandals in hand. Looking around, Jendayi notices her father's coffee mug and an uncovered half loaf of bread on the table near the hearth. Happily, she hears his snoring and quickly changes her clothes once in her room and snuggles into bed, bereft at the loss of her icon as sleep claims her.

Later, Saturday morning, Jendayi wakes to find propped against a candlestick on her table, a folded piece of paper with her name on it. Walking quickly across the small room, Jendayi reaches for the note from her father.

Jendayi,

I have gotten the lung tea tonic from Esmeralda before going to prepare for the wedding. I will come in very late tonight and will not wake you. Today, I will let you sleep in, so I have made my own cafecito. Please take the vegetables and fruit I have collected in the basket near the hearth to Nicolaasa Mina first thing this morning. I also placed the tea tonic in the basket. Please give my regards to her and assure her that we will take care of her needs. Go well, my daughter.

Love,
Baba

Safe! He did not realize her absence after all. Breathing a deep sigh of relief, Jendayi goes back into her room to grab clean clothes. She then prepares for a bath, mechanically going back and forth with gourds of water heated on the hearth to the tin hip bath she places in her room. She splashes a few drops of lavender oil into the water and eases her body into the steaming heat. Leaning her head back, she can hear the world of *La Gotera*; Picante barking next door, laughter from further away and the endless birdsong that fills their days. Maybe this will all work out in the end, Jendayi thinks as she sits up and scrubs her elbows.

After cleaning up her bath and putting on a clean striped-green dress, Jendayi lays across her bed, feeling suddenly weary though the sun is already in the sky indicating mid-morning. Not having her icon makes her feel disconnected from her mother. She has gotten used to rubbing the smooth stone and sharing her thoughts; imagining her mother's answers filled with gentle wisdom.

"Ah, *Negrita*. What is going to happen to Gwelo? I am so afraid. I know that Baba senses something. Esmeralda's actions last night must have alerted him that something is off," Jendayi mutters aloud to herself, half expecting to hear her mother's voice in the air. She finally drifts off into sleep again, worry filling her belly.

Saturday, April 7, 1635, the Ibarra Wedding

Micaela feels the tiny fluttering inside her belly, confirming the life inside her. Ever grateful for her shapeless house dress, large white apron, and lack of appetite over the last few months, the budding baby inside her has not been noticed. The fervor of the wedding has allowed her to slip around corners and carry out her work with Lucia, who rarely notices when she is in the room once her wishes are fulfilled. Rubbing her stomach slowly with her left hand, she looks at the small box in her right. Why did Alvaro delay her, asking her to give Lucia the wedding rings to bring to the church? She prefers to be out of sight from any Ibarra family member. All she wants is a chance to sneak into the kitchen to speak with Dakarai as the work of the wedding preparations are carried out. It has been over three months since she has seen him, much less enfolded herself into the contours of his embrace. Everything she has missed; his smell, the momentary safety and taste of possibility but mostly the immediate pleasure of his body filling hers. Closing her eyes, she remembers his sigh as she troubled his full bottom lip with her teeth in a kiss. His simple moan had almost brought her to climax, the tension running from her jaw to the base of her spine; awed at the ability to gift this man satisfaction when he was so committed to making sure she always took her pleasure first. Joy mixed with trepidation causes her to rapidly blink back tears as she opens her eyes and moves into the world surrounding her. She has to tell him about their child growing inside of her.

Clasping the ring box, she exits her sparse room next to Lucia's. There are no personal items other than a few books near the base of her pallet where her dark brown blanket is folded. It makes no sense to claim objects and hold them close since she understands too greatly the power of having items bought and sold without thought. Taking the servant staircase towards the back of the house down to the kitchen, Micaela tentatively enters the fray of steaming pots, a yelling Cook Jenny, assorted flowers, barking dogs at the hearth and Doña Francesca, fully dressed with a head full of paper curlers, screeching at the top of her lungs with instructions. Before she can back out unseen, Francesca spots Micaela and points, trying to catch her breath in order to say her name amidst the chaos.

"You! Where have you been? Lucia is in tears in my room, unable to finish dressing because you have abandoned your duties! You will be punished for this behavior, my girl. Consider yourself warned. Go immediately to my room and help Lucia get ready," Francesca states as the room stills. Even the dogs cower at the force of her voice. Rather than attempt an explanation about Alvaro placing the wedding bands with her for safekeeping while Lucia dresses, Micaela bows her head and runs back up the stairs, wiping the tears off her cheeks as she gains the top step.

Taking a deep breath, she knocks softly on the bedroom door and enters before Lucia calls her in. At the window sits Lucia, leisurely smoking a cigarette as she takes in the scene below of the servants setting up the reception in the garden. At the sound of the opened door, she tries to put the cigarette out but stops mid-air as she sees that it is only Micaela.

"Señorita," gags Micaela, "what are you doing? Your mother will beat you if she finds out that you are smoking those things, as they are so unladylike. Put that out quickly for both our sakes, please."

"Oh, relax *mujer*," Lucia says with a deep inhale. "Where do you think I found these? In my mother's bottom drawer! I never even knew that she smoked but if she does then I can, and she cannot say a word to me."

"Please, I beg of you, put it out so that you do not get in trouble and cause your mother any extra worry as the wedding is within the hour. We must finish dressing in your room. Forgive me for being late, your brother had a task which delayed me," Micaela pleads.

"Fine, let's go. We are supposed to be at the church already. I don't know what my mother is screaming about downstairs," Lucia throws the cigarette on the floor and mashes it slightly with her foot, before leaving in haste.

Micaela looks back briefly, hoping that the curtains and breeze will erase the smoky air. She will sweep the room later and remove the cigarette.

They are now officially late, and she can again hear Francesca screaming Lucia's name, imploring her to get a move on things. Rushing into Lucia's room, Micaela picks up the dress that she has meticulously prepared and begs her charge to hurry and step into it. The intricate baby blue lace collar and ivory buttons on the sleeves take long to arrange but finally after fastening the last hook, putting the hairbrush down and pinching Lucia's already pink cheeks for rouge, Micaela turns her towards the full-length mirror. Smiling with approval, Lucia picks up her parasol and egg-shell blue gloves. Without a word of thanks, Lucia rushes out of her room, already assuring her mother, who is at the bottom of the staircase, that she is ready. Remembering her church veil and the box with wedding rings, Micaela runs back into the room, grabbing them both, and rushes down the stairs, placing them hastily in Lucia's hands as she exits the front door.

A faintly smoky smell fills the upper hallway, but Micaela does not think about this as she closes her eyes because of her spinning head and slowly reclimbs the staircase. Thankful to finally see the family off to the church and relieved that the housework for the wedding lunch needs all serving hands and does not force her to attend the ceremony, Micaela leans heavily against the balustrade, trying to catch her breath. She sniffs cautiously again as the smell of burnt wood catches in her throat. Thick clouds of smoke meet her at the landing. These last weeks of pregnancy have made her sensitive to smells and now her internal alarms surround her. What can be burning? Before moving towards the master bedroom, Micaela hears shouts from below. Holding the railing at the landing, she sees two male slaves running into the foyer below with gourds of water.

"Whaaaat is it?" Micaela shouts as more smoke consumes the passageway.

"Fire! The outside of the house is burning under Doña Francesca's bedroom. You must come away at once," Salvador shouts, tumbling halfway up the stairs.

"Micaela, move. You must go outside before the entire house goes up in flames. There is no time to save anything," Antonio says as he runs up the stairs, pushing past Salvador to reach across the landing and grab Micaela's arm.

Micaela's head is reeling. Overcome, the dark smoke fills every inch of her body and her knees start to give when arms like timber pick her up and carry her down the steps. Just as she loses consciousness, she smells Dakarai's familiar lemongrass scent caress her cheek.

Dakarai

Dakarai paces the small space in front of him. Fragments of the day float in his head as he waits for one of the servants he has begged to return with the doctor's report on Micaela. He had seen the flames from outside the house as he and the Ibarra enslaved males were moving chairs onto the lawn from the central dining room. He rushed in behind Antonio, heart seizing as he watched the men try to convince Micaela to leave the house. He had just made the top landing in the smoky haze when she had collapsed. Instinctively, she curled into his arms before passing out and he was unsure if the public intimacy was noted by the others who were trying to put out the fire.

In the end, the fire had been managed before much of the house was damaged. The smoke was the worst part along with the remains of Francesca's bedroom. The master bedroom would need to be gutted and the years of precious mementos which she kept had vanished in minutes.

There was no major structural damage beyond the inside of the room. The smoke would eventually dissipate with the approaching rainy season. Beyond Micaela's limp body in his arms and the panic tight in his chest, the worst moment was sending Antonio to the church to alert the Ibarra family of the fire. Luckily, the wedding vows had been completed and the final blessings were being offered when Antonio crept along the Vestry to Francesca's front pew, sooty hat in hand and indicated that he had a message for her. The Cook's scrawled letters about the fire and the ruined master bedroom caused Francesca to scream as the Benediction was starting, stilling the entire congregation. With a mumbled apology, Doña Francesca whispered a few words in Antonio's ear, sending him scurrying away as eyebrows began to rise. After the couple was given the final blessing as husband and wife, Doña Francesca stood in her pew and announced loudly that there had been a slight change in plans and the wedding lunch was now going to be held in Alvaro's new house's garden with a three-hour delay to the festivities. Alvaro turned sharply at the announcement, surprised that the entire Spanish community would show up at his new home without him having slept a night in it.

And so, the Ibarra servants, slaves and day workers did just that; they moved every pot and table, every cloth and candelabra, every glass and chair to the newlywed's garden before the guests began arriving in plenty. It was only when Doña Francesca came to gape at the burnt hole below her bedroom window, that Dakarai approached her about getting a doctor to see Micaela. Already distraught and trying not to seem out of control, Francesca agreed to send someone to get the doctor before Lucia found out about Micaela and started fussing.

Dr. Abadia, disgruntled that he has to delay his arrival at the wedding feast to treat a spoiled slave, examines Micaela near the pantry on a makeshift table used for cleaning vegetables and drying herbs. Dakarai maintains his pacing outside as he cannot justify why he needs to be near the examination. Yet, he cannot leave to his duties until he knows that she will survive. Lost in his thoughts, Dakarai does not hear Carmen, the Cook's assistant, call his name.

"Forgive me Juan Carlos. You asked for a report about Micaela and now that the doctor is leaving for the wedding party, I thought it would be a good time to find you. The doctor, sir, he is saying that there is nothing he can do for her. He just checked her nose and ears and then said that the smoke filled her lungs. If she wakes, we will be lucky. But maybe it is best this way; if she does not wake, I mean," Carmen says as she looks over her shoulder, hoping not to be seen by Cook Jenny.

"What? Why would you say these words?" Dakarai growls in fright and anger.

"They are blaming her for the fire. They said she was careless with a candle this morning and if she wakes, she will be given twenty lashes in the plaza for all to see. And sold. So maybe it is best that she sleeps forever because what awaits her is only hell," Carmen, forest-brown and barely fourteen, runs away on her thin legs, trying to catch up with the others leaving the house towards Alvaro's.

"Oh, mother father god," Dakarai slouches on his haunches outside the latrines, where he had settled to wait for the news. He needs to get her away from here; but what can he really do for her except create more empty promises? Never will she taste freedom; his dreams of a life together slither down his throat and into the pit of his belly. Tears unexpectedly fill his eyes as hopelessness careens to a stop in front of him.

Warily looking around so that he is not noticed, he slides along the back wall of the house, all the while the smell of charred wood fills his nostrils. Using his handkerchief to cover his face, he approaches the kitchen, waiting to see who has remained behind as the Cook has taken her small army of workers to the new Ibarra grounds. Reassured that there is no one left, he does a double-take at Micaela, who has been haphazardly moved to a pantry table, with pots, spices, herbs, cloths and chicken feathers all scattered around her in someone's haste to lay her down. Angry that no one else had bothered to keep watch with her, he eases up to the table, never taking his eyes off her slumbering body. Noticing that her legs are crossing each other, causing her dress and apron to rise above her knees, he instinctively goes to adjust her clothes, aware of her natural modesty. Straightening her legs, he tugs the fabric down, yet the cloth remains snug, so he goes to her hips to lift the back of the dress which has gathered behind her. In the silence of the pantry, he reaches across her hip, accidently rubbing the tiny, firm mound in the center of her belly, hidden by the large white uniform apron she wears. In sheer terror, he jumps back, colliding with a basket of potatoes as he already knows how his life will play out in front of him.

A baby. His baby. A dying mother. Oh, what cruelty this life's hand has dealt him.

Weeping silently, he looks around for something to make a pallet for Micaela, unable to leave her so exposed on the table, squashed amongst fruit and herbs. He knew that this is how she is viewed as one who is enslaved; just another item to be consumed. But he will not stand for it; not with his child growing in her belly. He is tired of this story; wishing the ending away, he runs outside to gather blankets near the stables and crushes them against his chest as he returns to the kitchen. Folding the coarse cloth, thick with horse, he clears a corner of the kitchen closer to the hearth and busily moves Micaela from her perch on the table to the floor. If Cook Jenny enters the space, she will notice Micaela without having to be disturbed from her myriad of tasks on this day. Dakarai looks down at her sleeping form, amazed that she feels so light when he had lifted her. Her beauty chokes him. She has soot smudged across her nose, mouth, and cheeks. Quickly surveying the kitchen, he spots a gourd of water and searches for a clean rag before pouring it into a smaller bowl which looks clean. He then proceeds to wipe her face gently, clearing the edges of her nose. He smiles to himself, a first on this day, when he realizes that Jendayi would advise him to use eucalyptus or lemongrass essence in the water to help Micaela breathe. But he has none of those things in this house which he has only visited one other time in all his years in Costa Rica. With a clean face, Micaela looks years younger, yet his body still responds with the truth and wisdom of her age.

Suddenly, as he is clearing the water and dirty rag, he hears steps approaching the pantry. Moving away quickly from the hearth, he busies himself with the basket of potatoes that had spilled earlier in his shock at feeling Micaela's belly.

"What are you doing here, Juan Carlos? You have been asked for at the wedding feast. We need your hands as the work is overwhelming," Cook Jenny says sharply, surveying the scene in front of her.

"Cook Jenny, I was asked to bring a few items back to the wedding from the pantry, yet I have mistakenly knocked this basket over when I saw the girl laying there on the table. She was in the way of my work, so I moved her near the hearth. If you will excuse me, I have the items needed and will return," Dakarai replies, never looking Jenny in the eye. Her muttered curse indicates her suspicions.

“A nd I am clear, as soon as that girl is well again, I am selling her at Portobello. She has ruined it all, my house! On such an auspicious day, I tell you. It is only because my dear husband is buried in this country that I do not return to Spain. Ah, such cruelty," Francesca hiccups to her semi-attentive companion, Padre. Already deep in their cups with the flowing champagne and sweet white wine from Chile, many guests are slow-dancing on the makeshift dance floor as the four-piece band croons the romantic *zarzuela* with two guitars accompanying the main operatic singer.

"Doña Francesca, never fear. The day went off without a hitch in the end. Look at the newlyweds, they are happy and have no knowledge of the fire. Lucia is also unaware; see how she giggles with the other girls around her. I am sure Juan Carlos can come and re-build the bedroom and make sure the structure is secure in no time. But I do agree with you that it is time Micaela is sold. She has always seemed unappreciative of the good life you have bestowed on her. Indeed, the markets in Portobello will offer you a good price as she is in her childbearing prime and the money can compensate for the house repairs. Do not despair any longer. Come, let us greet the Barrantes family; they have an eligible son who has significant holdings in Spain. We should consider them carefully for our Lucia," Padre says, all the while surveying the teeming party in front of him.

The alcohol, rich food, and heavy sun eased the formality out of the guests as they begin leaning into each other, outside the rules of propriety. Caked powder, starch, rose water and body odor mingles in the air as guests walk by, nodding their head at Padre as if in confession. Francesca has insisted that he sit next to her in the shade, claiming a desire for a kind ear to her laments. Watching the dancers, he too feels a spring in his loins and his thoughts wander to the release he will get tomorrow evening in the dark shed outside the church.

Bolstered by the flowing wine, he escorts Francesca to the table where the Barrantes family sits, noting Juan Carlos's brusque greeting as he almost falls into him while walking across the lawn to deposit what seems like a basket of raw potatoes near the make-shift outdoor kitchen Cook Jenny commands.

"Isn't that Juan Carlos now, Padre? I have been looking for him all afternoon after he requested the doctor for Micaela. I sent Jimenez to run the kitchen and organize with Cook Jenny as I need to be hostess. He was supposed to bring Juan Carlos to me," Francesca whimpers into his ear.

Reassuring her, Padre explains that Juan Carlos was one of the men primarily responsible for putting out the fire and then transporting the furniture so he was entirely too busy to stop and chat. They will certainly speak to him later about selling Micaela. Surely, he can be in the group that will take her to market. But these discussions are for after the wedding celebrations.

Dakarai

Almost bumping into Padre turns out to be a lifesaver for Dakarai as he edges out of the Ibarra compound and circles back to Francesca's house. He has made his presence clear, all while planning how to eventually disappear Micaela before she is gone from him forever. The plan is coming together in pieces as he tries to still his heavy breath. Every muscle is alert and on edge and he cannot lose control of himself. The implications of it all threatens to crash him to his knees.

Once at Francesca's house, Dakarai goes straight for the stables. He will need a horse to transport Micaela out of Cartago and away to Nicoya or Matina near the cacao plantations. How will he reconcile this leaving with Jendayi? She will have to forgive him; he will secure Micaela and stay until the baby is born to ensure that Francesca has not sent out a bounty hunter for her capture and sale. He will have to live two lives. But maybe it is all too risky? How can he do this and keep everyone safe and alive? The only person he can think of to help him during this time is Esmeralda. Without too much explanation, she will understand the situation and give him advice, maybe even keep Micaela hidden for a few days without raising suspicions that he has been involved in her leaving. Hope springs faintly inside his belly as he craves Esmeralda's council.

There are no servants at Francesca's house. The ash from the fire has given way to chunks of sodden wood falling to the earth near the latrines. What a mess, he thinks absently as he makes quick work of returning to the kitchen from the stables after securing a horse outside. Micaela has been left on the pallet near the hearth, in slumber like the old family dog. He bends over her and lifts her head, slowly rubbing her cheeks and calling her name. He needs her awake, so she can move on her own accord. He gently puts her back down and stands to get some water to wet her throat. When he has the water, he tips her head, always listening for footsteps. Micaela's mouth opens and he slips a few cool drops down her throat. A profusion of water and coughing and moaning are the immediate results. He whispers softly in her ear, reassuring her that she will be okay if she follows his every direction. Not trying to scare her as she slowly regains consciousness, Dakarai explains that he has to take her to safety.

"Hush, I think Mama is talking to him now. See how handsome he is, oh, look at those blue eyes. I do hope that he finds me acceptable," Lucia whispers to Ana Catarina and Paloma, as they sit at an empty wedding table. Deciding against dancing with the only available Spanish men in Cartago, most of them widowers or older than Zeus himself, the girls huddle together, taking inventory of the guests. It is unusual for Lucia to spend social time with the girls as they are below her social rank; her mother insists that she keep up her studies in order to eventually make a come out in Spain and not worry about friendships. Yet, today, bolstered by the romance of her brother's wedding and many sips of the wedding wine, Lucia has bridged the divide and joins the girls at their table, instantly launching into giggles and smirks at the dancing, drunken guests. Paloma keeps reproaching the girls as they continue to gauge the size of a man's potential through the front flap of his breeches, screeching behind their elaborate, flashing fans which do little in the late afternoon heat. Paloma, a girl of questionable heritage with her caramel color and curly hair which she spends hours brushing straight into a smooth bun that nary a wisp can escape, is being groomed for the convent and maintains an air of propriety. Closer to the masses, it is her job to remind the girls that they have to maintain their composure in mixed company. Lucia pays her no mind, savoring the day's freedom and the fact that her mother's eye, for once, is not trained on her. Leaning over to whisper in Ana Catarina's ear, she hears Paloma gasp and pull her arm quickly to straighten her back into her seat. Pink from ear to ear, Paloma murmurs something behind her fan to Lucia, but it is difficult to hear with all the guests' laughter and music playing.

"My dear, Señorita Lucia. It seems that your moon cycle has come to visit. There are splotches on the back of your dress which will certainly ruin it if you sit there much longer. You must go change," Paloma strains to maintain a sense of decorum as she makes the grave pronouncement.

"What? Wait. Where is Micaela when I need her? Oh my god, I must go and change. What if Sebastian comes over for a dance? How can I refuse him? Please, let me run home while no one notices and change my dress quickly. If my mother comes, say that I went to the retiring room as I was feeling unwell," Lucia says as she stands up, draping her shawl mid-waist to cover the blood stains, all the while surveying the scene in front of her. Before the girls have a chance to respond, Lucia dashes across the garden once she is certain that her mother is thoroughly engrossed with Padre and the Barrantes family. She can hear her mother's coy laugh as she exits the garden's gate and makes her way quickly across the town, past the church and along the lane that takes her to the back of the house. Before she can open the gate, two things strike her: the entire town is deserted and the lingering smell of burning wood is pungent in the air.

"Micaela, my love, I need you to sit up and drink this water. You have inhaled much smoke and I do not want you to speak, just sip slowly. Please try and stay awake," Dakarai speaks tenderly as he leans the wooden cup along Micaela's full bottom lip. She does not struggle as he raises it again once she has taken the first drink. She refuses to look at him.

Kneeling alongside her, Dakarai keeps a firm arm behind her back, unsure if she will slip back into unconsciousness.

"Here, take another sip. It will be okay," Dakarai places these words into her ear as she resists taking a third drink of water. He can feel her body shudder and within seconds she is coughing and spitting out the water she has just taken in. Trying to calm her as he sees the long, fat tears course down her cheeks, Dakarai lays her back down and is just standing to find a cloth to wipe her face when he comes face-to-face with a gaping Lucia; mouth wide open, hands straight alongside her body.

"What the hell are y-y-you doing here with Micaela? Are you hurting her? Get away from her or I will scream," Lucia says as she gains her breath.

Dakarai takes a deep breath and steps closer to Lucia, with his hands high in front of him to show her that he means to do no harm.

"Señorita Lucia, I was just getting some things that Cook Jenny wants me to bring over to the wedding and I heard Micaela coughing in here, so I stopped to offer her some water. She inhaled too much smoke during the fire," Dakarai says very carefully.

"What fire? What are you talking about? Has she missed the entire wedding?" Lucia asks as she steps around Dakarai to get a better look at Micaela, who remains lying by the hearth on the horse-blanket pallet Dakarai has made for her.

Realizing that Lucia has no knowledge of what has happened to cause the wedding activity to be moved to the new house, Dakarai briefly appraises her, in a soft whisper, that there had been a fire in her mother's bedroom and severe damage had been done to the window and furnishings in the room. Luckily, the remaining slaves and day workers were able to put the fire out before more of the house was destroyed, yet Micaela had been in the upper hallway, trapped by the smoke until they were able to rescue her. He explains that once she awakens, she is to be whipped and sold because the blame of the fire has been placed on her. Dakarai is unsure if Micaela can hear his words. In that moment, he needs to make Lucia an ally; if not, he too will quickly be sold onto the slave markets along with Micaela if she decides to raise an alarm.

Lucia stops in her tracks. A flash of something crosses her face but Dakarai is not able to make it out. She turns and walks over to the center table in the kitchen. Her actions, even as a twenty-two-year-old girl, can decide if he lives or dies. Like a hand washing over his back and his head, memories crash into his mind's eye of a newborn Jendayi, Towela on their wedding day, Esmeralda's head bent in study of her letters as he painstakingly repeats the alphabet, Micaela's oily banana bread, the mother and child icon he has lovingly carved in memory of Towela to be placed on Alvaro's wedding bed and the pain of the moment forces him to close his eyes, calling his ancestors for help to survive. There is too much at stake.

"No, this cannot be right. You must move her to my father's old bedroom down the hall. It has been unused since his death and we will not be disturbed. I will convince my mother not to sell her. I, I . . . it is of no import, move quickly as you carry her," Lucia says to Dakarai as she wraps her shawl more firmly around her waist. Without any more words, Lucia leads Dakarai to a musty, dust-ridden bedroom off the side of the library also used as her father's former office. Though it houses few books in truth, the meager collection is still lovingly referred to whenever her mother tells stories about how Lucia was taught to read by her devoted father. Lucia hates that room, and it is one of the reasons that she insists Micaela read to her from whatever books she selects from the shelves since from her father's death, Lucia has never gone back into the room. The smell of smoke is not as strong on this side of the house and by opening the two large windows once Micaela is deposited gently onto the bed, it is manageable. Lucia exits quickly without an explanation, leaving Dakarai in the full silence of the room.

Micaela's raspy breath becomes a fragrance on the wind that occasionally moves the curtains. The setting sun makes the evening less humid, though the quiet brings the smell of the building rain. Stunned by Lucia's actions, Dakarai stands near the window, unsure of what the next step is going to be. He listens attentively to hear if Lucia is bringing anyone else to the house, but minutes pass without a footstep. Finally, he hears the creak of light steps nearing the door and he is at full alert when Lucia steps back alone through the door. Relieved, he allows his back to release the tension he is feeling. He still has not made a plan but decides that since the ancestors have placed this path in front of him, he will follow it.

"I have never been in a room alone with a man that is not my family, much less a *pardo*," Lucia says, seemingly having regained her haughty composure. If Dakarai is not losing his mind, he could have sworn she has changed her dress into a rich green from the light blue one she has worn to the wedding.

"Señorita Lucia, I beg your pardon. We are in the most extreme circumstances. I am sure that your mother is looking for you at this moment and I think you and I need to decide what the next step will be. I will not hurt you nor Micaela and I am grateful that you are willing to give her a chance. It is surprising that you care so deeply for the fate of a slave." The irony of the moment is not lost on Dakarai as he knows today is to be Micaela's emancipation day as part of his payment for making the Ibarra furniture.

Before Lucia can reply, they both turn sharply as Micaela begins to cry in the bed. It is a strange mewling sound, grasping the hairs on the back of Dakarai's neck.

"Oh my god, look, her dress has blood on it," Lucia stares with horror, backing up to the door.

Dakarai walks over to the bed with firm steps, focused now on Micaela. He knows what the blood means. Dakari speaks to Lucia without taking his eyes off Micaela's form, "It seems as if her time of the month has come. I know someone who can care for her and keep her alive, but you will need to allow me to get Micaela to her. I am still unsure of your desires, Señorita, and time is of the essence."

Lucia raises her voice slightly over Micaela's whimpers in the bed. That is the only sound in the room as Dakarai holds his breath.

"We were raised together, Micaela and I. I knew we were not sisters but we shared everything until my mother explained to me that she was my slave. I owe Micaela this moment. When my father was dying, every day my mother instructed me to go to the library, select a book and read to him in the sickroom for an hour. I have never hated a time more than that in my life. I would take a book off the shelf, caring nothing of the subject, and my father would insist that I sit on the bed next to him and as I read, he would fondle my leg while bringing himself to pleasure, always demanding that I pass him a kerchief in the cupboard to clean himself when done. Then, he would pat my hand and shoo me away until the following day. Never in my life have I wanted the death of another as much as I did my father. My mother never stepped foot into that sickroom that entire year of his slow demise. Then one day, I must have left the door slightly open and Micaela caught the tail end of his moan of completion as I sat reading in a trembling voice, clenched book in hand, legs swinging wildly against the counterpane in terror. Micaela knocked loudly on the door as he struggled to cover his thin, exposed legs and she entered the room, made some excuse and hustled me out. I never laid eyes on my father again until the day of his funeral. Instead, Micaela took up my charge of daily reading and within a month he was dead. And so, here I am at twenty-two beholden to a slave. Micaela is mine and tonight, I will pay my debt. I want you to take her to someone who can help her."

Lucia's speech rocks every nerve in Dakarai's body. To imagine a child having to witness such debauchery at the hands of a relative, but then again, he already knows what the *panas* are capable of; he has seen it too clearly in his seven years enslaved. Shaking his head to get a grip of himself, he states, "Señorita, I will bring Micaela to a trusted friend who can make teas and use herbs to help her injured lungs. However, it is sure death or the auction block if we are found exiting the house."

Lucia peeks out the window and notices the emerging twilight. "When my mother comes home tonight, I will put some laudanum in her tea. She will sleep uninterrupted until tomorrow. Alvaro is not sleeping here tonight, and the slaves are in the attic. I am sure everyone will be exhausted, and no one ever enters this room since my father's death. See the glass door there, I will leave it unlocked so you both can exit once I have gone. When my mother wakes, she and I will have a talk. I will say that I found Micaela dead in the kitchen and forced you to take her body and bury it this evening in *La Gotera's campo santo*. But understand, I will never do this for a slave again. If you betray me in any way, I will sell your precious daughter in Portobello and fetch my family a good price. I must go back to the wedding; it is getting late. Leave quickly," Lucia says as she steps into the hallway and out the front door, quickening her pace as she moves in the direction of the newlywed's house.

Dakarai has no choice but to pick up Micaela's limp body, shuffle out the glass door and pray that Esmeralda will be willing to help.

Micaela is dying. Death is in her skin. The cave of her stomach, holding precious cargo, has settled into a shell; its subsiding heat confirms the life in her has ended. No twitching, no flutter, no faint hiccup reminding her that something else can exist in her dreams beyond the now. Micaela is resolved and does not long for this life. It is a crippled existence, which at one fragile moment pulsed stronger than her child's heartbeat.

There was a time, Micaela remembers, when she and Lucia were younger—Micaela was twelve and Lucia was four—that she always holds in front of her mind's mirror. That day taught Micaela something of the contours of life that gives her the same peace she feels now, as she lies in this bed, fighting for breath. She had been instructed to take Lucia to play away from the house because her father's work was disturbed by their giggles. They held hands and ran to the back of the house that stretched across to a shallow stream. Tentatively, because she knew if her stockings and shoes were lost, she would get a scolding, Micaela allowed Lucia to untie her boots and roll down her silk stockings and dip her pink toes into the crystal cold water. Micaela did not let go of her hand as Lucia dragged her further in, impervious to the fact that Micaela still had her shoes and stockings on. Micaela's comfort was trivial to her pleasure. The hems of their dresses were soaked as they rubbed their feet over the smooth stones in the riverbed, Micaela with her sturdy boots, her mother's hand-me-downs, and Lucia with her toes turned blue with the chill. Lucia looked up at her, face plunged in childhood roundness, as she suddenly bent to scoop up water and splashed its freshness towards Micaela. Her face was in that instant pure joy and for a wicked second, Micaela allowed herself to get swallowed into the moment and she felt free. Splashing in that stream, she felt outside of herself, the possibility of another chance of remembering herself as a child not enslaved, owned and never free. She has only felt that feeling two other times in her life: when they were eating *pan de elote* after stealing it from Cook Jenny's hot pan and when she felt the first butterfly movement of her baby.

Micaela was punished horribly that evening as Lucia caught a cold and had to stay in bed for a week. Micaela went to bed without supper for three nights and only managed to stave her hunger by eating the crusts of Lucia's sickroom fare as she slept on a pallet by her bed. The punishment did not hurt as much as it should have because her secret, that feeling of freedom, rumbled too loudly in her chest. Micaela lies here now, saying goodbye to that life inside of her. It has released her from the obligation to fight to remain.

Micaela can sense the complete darkness and the scent of the air is dry. She cannot place where she is by the sounds around her but there is something insistent in her ear. Her throat gurgles for sound and air and her body wracks with a cough as she tries to open her eyes. The voice comes closer and whispers surround her. Micaela cannot make out the words, but it feels like music. The air changes pressure and her stomach rolls in agony as a firm hand clutches her hips. The urge to pee starts in her jaw which she uses to clamp, and she releases into whoever's hands are caressing her skin. The baby's body travels along the flow as Micaela tries to sit up, grabbing, grabbing to say sorry as she drops into nothingness.

Jendayi

It is impossible to fit any closer into his skin as his heat moves up Jendayi's nose and she inhales fully. Gwelo has better eyesight than she does in the new evening and so he has managed to follow her shadow to the bank of the Reventazon River faster than she anticipated. They are near Dakarai's garden and that is how she is able to navigate this far. It is when she stops that he collapses into her back, winding his arm around her waist to prevent her from falling forward. They stand still then, him breathing into her neck and her shivering for all things to come. He turns her slowly and she stares into his chest, unable to raise her eyes to a face that she has memorized over and over in her head though she has seen it only once in the full sunlight. His kiss is softer than she expected: her first and unannounced. It just covers the corners of her lips and she is greedy for more, yet no skills follow this hunger to determine her next actions, so Jendayi just stands there, licking the corner of her mouth. And with that, he laughs as he covers her mouth fully in a kiss that moves her life into the pit of her belly. They pull back, wishing they had the words to express the thing that now hangs between them. A rustle in the trees and faint barking move them into the present and she holds up her hand against his chest, so he understands that she needs to get her bearings. The barks strangely get louder and a chill moves up Jendayi's spine. Does she dare turn back and take him to her house to ask her father for help? When they left Esmeralda's, there had been no plan except to get him to the river but it is now late and he needs rest and supplies. Only Jendayi knows the way as Esmeralda has never come this far beyond the reaches of her enslavement. But Jendayi's father, he is far too wrapped up in the chaos of the town to even find sympathy towards Gwelo. She knows her father wants to keep her safe at all costs but surely, he will separate them.

Jendayi must have sighed as Gwelo pulled her in for another hug. This man's life was in Jendayi's hands the day she helped him flee the auction yard and she cannot let him down now, even though the chance of failure seems inevitable.

Esmeralda

"What are we going to do?" Dakarai murmurs, hands tugging his short afro.

"What are *you* going to do, that is what we have to figure out, Dakarai," I reply, wanting to remove myself from the entanglements that keep landing at my door. All these years of no notice, only by the gluttonous priest looking to release his loins; the steady rhythm of that peacelessness has defined my life. Now, I am the center in too many life and death stories. It is unfair to feel that I can have value in this community; for once, I am needed rather than the shadow that I have lived as for so long. To pick it up now, that tenuous branch of being necessary, of meaningfulness, makes me feel like a traitor to my own life.

Earlier, when I gave Gwelo a firm hug as soon as the last chain was removed from his ankles and Jendayi was able to help him stand, I said a silent prayer to my mother, a first in all these years since her death, to help these young people see the morning. My life has trained me to live without more expectations than that. The heavy beat of my heart took some time to calm when they left, and I focused on tidying up as the hour was so late.

Suddenly, there was Dakarai's muffled yet distinctive knock on the door. Hair rose on my neck, thinking that he had found Jendayi and Gwelo mid-flight and brought them back to be accounted for. Going to the door, I had tentatively opened it to see Dakarai with a limply hanging Micaela across his arms, the smell of his sweat from carrying such a load filling my nose first. Without a second thought, I stood aside to open the door wider. He moved to put her on the small pallet on the floor, but then thought otherwise and turned with her still in his arms.

Now, Dakarai stands before me. "Mama Esmeralda, she is dying. Her blood runs down my arms and legs and I cannot put her on your bed because it will be ruined. It is too dark to see where I shall rest her otherwise. Forgive me, forgive me…" Dakarai's voice is caught in his throat as he utters these words.

I bend to light my small candle stub and direct him to lay Micaela on the pallet. The smell of blood and smoke fills the small space. Micaela moans softly as she is laid flat. Even in the darkness, I can make out the dark patches of blood on her white apron.

"My son, what has happened? Has she been abused by a *pana*?" I question.

"No, no. She is with child, my child. I did not know until today. There was a fire in the Ibarra house before the wedding lunch and she was caught in the smoke and collapsed. I was able to bring her here because her owner, Lucia, allowed it. But she started to bleed, and I know that she is losing the child. Please, if you can save her, for me," Dakarai groans, tears silently lining the sides of his cheeks.

The next hour is silent work as I make tea and ease it down Micaela's throat. I massage her belly, round and tight, with an aloe-based liniment that cools her skin. After an hour of steady pressure and massage, there is a massive contracting of Micaela's stomach and finally her body releases the life that had lived within her for four months. A girl. A girl child of his making. My heart constricts as I shield its lifeless body from Dakarai and wrap it in my only linen towel.

"I am sorry, my son. This time, the mother is saved but not the child. You will only have to bury one this young morning. I do not envy you the task. Micaela will survive but she must rest for some time without movement because of the blood loss. I can keep her here until tomorrow, then you must move her," I say with barely formed words. I turn into the coming morning light and say, "What you have to do is take your daughter, name her under this moonless sky and then give her to the earth."

Dakarai's crying fills the corners of my skin as I hand the tiny, dead baby into his waiting arms.

Dakarai

Sometimes the most beautiful song comes at the time of death. Accompanying Dakarai's morbid march is the sweet treble of a bay wren, high in the trees, alerting the world of the approaching sunrise. The bundle in his arms is feather-light, so different from the weight of her mother when he brought her to Esmeralda's hours before. How could he have become a father again and then no longer within a single day? All these thoughts swirl in Dakarai's mind as he walks into *La Gotera*, grateful that no one stirs, and along the path to his farm near the river. This is where he will place his daughter, carve her a small headstone with just her name, and place some flowers to remind himself of her beauty.

He has not yet seen her body in the light, only felt the soft contours of arms and legs through the linen. The birdsong is abundant by the time he arrives at his plot. He is glad that his small shed has a spade and other digging tools. He feels that near the big elephant ear tree, famous country-wide, will be the best spot, protected in the shade from the rains and sun that will everlastingly circle the years he will miss watching her grow. He names her *Kweimwe Nguva,* "From Another Time," to show she has been a gift too precious to remain. Already he is growing wistful but as he unwraps the body, no longer as pliant as before, his tears sink into his shirt and bless the earth. So perfect is his daughter, the first of his blood, her tiny fingers and toes all aligned and with a round nose like her mother's. Soft splotches of bruises cover her head and her small chest has caved in slightly, leaving an unnatural dent in her upper body. Clots of blood stick on her skin, tinted a light blue. Stroking her soft cheek before the signs of rigor mortis set in, Dakarai wipes his face and looks down at his bloodied clothes. It is all a mess. Despair fuels his movements as he takes spade to earth, digging a grave that he feels so ready to succumb to alongside his daughter.

Jendayi

Sunday, midmorning after the Ibarra wedding

The morning is full and bright when Jendayi raises her head from the soft mattress in Petronila's house. She hears outside noises, but the curtains have been drawn in the room that she is in, keeping the rainy season's humid scent out. Looking around she can tell that she is in Josefina's room; the lace doilies and dried flowers decorating the small space have all her telltale signs.

"Gwelo," she shouts to herself as she jumps out of the bed and runs into the kitchen of the small two-bedroom house. There, sitting cross legged on the floor near the hearth is Gwelo, smiling with his hands deep in a clay bowl steaming with some delicacy from Petronila.

"Thank you *Negrita*, for guiding me here," Jendayi intones a silent prayer to her missing icon under her breath, as she clears her throat and announces her presence. The previous hours have been a blur once she decided to bring Gwelo here and ask for Petronila's help. It took several hard bangs on the door in the middle of the night to get anyone to let them in but given their state when they arrived, very little was asked of them. Petronila was all business as she hurried them inside, prepared some tea and then arranged sleeping quarters as both nodded off while they sipped the warm tonic. They had missed Josefina, who had been sent out after the wedding with Doña Beatrice's family, who were returning to Matina. Once a year, Josefina delivered her mother's special embroidered tablecloths to the community of Spaniards who lived there. It was such a lucrative venture and Josefina had jumped at the chance for a ride, even after the evening's tiring festivities.

"Come child, sit; you must be starved. Does your father have any idea where you are? I have not seen him since he set out for the wedding yesterday morning," Petronila questions with her back to Jendayi. She bends over a pot at the hearth and carefully spoons out more of the stew that Gwelo is intently focused on. Adding a thick slab of freshly made bread to the top of the bowl and a crude, wooden spoon, Petronila silently places the food in Jendayi's outstretched hands. The smell is so overwhelmingly beautiful that she slides against the wall not far from where Gwelo is crouched and greedily takes a mouthful of bread dipped into the thick broth. The sting of the hot food causes her to grumble but the hunger in her belly overlooks the shot of pain on her tongue as she devours the rest.

"So, our friend Gwelo here has been sharing with me his very interesting journey. Jendayi, you have gone to incredible risks to gain his freedom," Petronila begins as Jendayi covers a burp with her hand.

"You can understand what he is saying?" Jendayi asks incredulously as she moves to wash her empty bowl in a gourd of water.

"He speaks a dialect of my father's language. I have not heard it for many, many years but there is no way to forget the sound of one's father or his people. In this alone, Gwelo is welcome in my home. There are so many dangers, my child," Petronila says quietly, looking directly into Jendayi's exhausted face whose youthful beauty makes her look like her mother's twin. Petronila remembers the first time she met Towela, when she was still a scribe for her father. Both she and Jendayi have the same pleading eyes full of worry, the rounded lips and the firm neck holding a head that was sure to figure matters out in the end. The similarities are startling as their faces, in memory and present, begin to fuse.

"What has he told you? I have no language to communicate with him and know nothing of his story. Mama Esmeralda was able to…" Jendayi replies hastily.

"You should not have involved her in this plan, Jendayi," Petronila stands and hobbles over to look outside her kitchen door, which she then closes firmly. The dog is barking vigorously outside but there is no indication that anyone has come into the yard.

"Gwelo would not be free without her help. But I am sorry," Jendayi admits.

"My child, you put her life at risk. What were you

thinking?" Petronila's tone increases angrily as she returns to her seat by the hearth. Gwelo looks up from the floor, surprised. He shifts and mumbles something quietly which Jendayi cannot understand. However, when Petronila slowly starts to smile, it is clear that she understands what he has said, and it has diffused some of her angst. She murmurs a response and he instantly stands up, hands at his side. His stature and full maleness fill the room and leaves both women gaping as he looks from face to face.

"It is better if we go into Josefina's room to have this conversation. Her window faces the back yard, and no one can pass by and hear our voices without notice," Petronila observes as she painstakingly leads the way back into her daughter's small but tidy room.

Gwelo stands in the doorway until Petronila indicates that he may sit on the bed next to Jendayi. Left alone for a minute as Petronila goes back out to shut the kitchen windows, Jendayi shyly takes in the young man sitting beside her in the full light. He has taken a full bath and is in a proper-fitting shirt and pants, accentuating his handsomeness. His feet are in simple leather sandals that are a bit small as his heels tip over the back edge. Gwelo has soft, soft chocolate skin, even with his charred wrists and ankles, and the deepest brown eyes that smile, as if he has all the time in the world. She remembers their kisses and wants to touch his lips again but knows the inappropriateness of it all. As Petronila shuffles back into the room, Gwelo touches her lips with his index finger while Petronila sits firmly in the rocking chair.

"Come, let us talk now. This boy has asked me to translate his story for you so that he can finally explain who he is. It seems that Esmeralda did not have the time to share his background with you as she is not one for talking. However, he is grateful for her because she saved his life along with your kindness. He has explained to me how you helped him escape the auction, Jendayi," Petronila speaks softly and rubs her hands against her head, trying to soothe its pain.

Gwelo begins speaking in a voice that spreads throughout the room with its musical timbre, yet he is not loud. He and Petronila take turns explaining what he says so that Jendayi can get the full meaning.

"Gwelo is eighteen and the son of a very wealthy Benguela family. They were not involved in the slave trade in their home on the coast of Angola, but his uncle was. Since his parent's family were devoutly Muslim, they thought it would be best to support Gwelo's interests in learning more about the religion. His parents, Lupita and Panzu, also wanted to remove him from the burgeoning slave industry at the coast and his uncle's sudden rise to power and wealth. So, Gwelo's parents agreed for him to go into the interior of Mali and spend several years studying under a cleric who had learned from the famous Ahmad Baba, one of the most revered Islamic scholars in Timbuktu. The journey was to take about two months, moving north and inland, trying their best to avoid the slave traders as they pushed in the opposite direction of the coast with their Black gold cargo. His father sent three loyal servants with him and bags of trinkets and gold to appease those who might threaten Gwelo's chances at success.

Yet, it was in his own house where the deception was laid.

"Unbeknownst to his father, Gwelo's uncle felt insulted that Gwelo was being sent away to study and not profit from the workings of the slave trade, as if the work was not honorable and did not secure their wealth and so he arranged for one of his servants to intercept Gwelo on his way to Timbuktu and hand him over to the *vatengesi vevaranda,* the slave traders. Even with a fight, and the deaths of Gwelo's three companions, he was unable to make his way out from the shackles of the trade. He was sold along with a coffle of others in Angola, on a boat departing for Portobello about seven months previously. He managed to get a message to his father through a market woman on the coast one evening, sharing that he was being taken and it was his uncle who had betrayed them all. Finding his way to the auction in Cartago was easy as he was sold into a group upon his arrival in Portobello and had been forced to walk the *Camino* Royal to the Pacific Coast until they were able to enter the Orosi Valley which opens into Cartago. The thing that saddens him the most is that he was not able to say goodbye to his mother, Lupita."

"I am so sorry, Gwelo. I had no idea," Jendayi states as his story comes to an end. The immense sadness of his uncle's betrayal floods her being. What can she say to this young man? Will he ever be able to return to his home? One can only imagine the horror of his parents, getting the news that their precious son has been captured and sold into the trade by their own blood. Maybe it was best for his dreams to halt in *La Gotera* because really, where can he go from here?

"He wants to repay you for saving his life," Petronila says amid Jendayi's revelry.

"Why? How can he do that? There is nothing to repay. This is who we are in *La Gotera*, people who help each other without asking for anything in return. He should thank Mama Esmeralda, who risked more than I ever could, in helping him," Jendayi states defensively. What was this nonsense about paying her back? She did not help him for gain, rather it was her heart that had acted, and her limbs followed.

Gwelo faces Jendayi as he speaks to Petronila, a pleading look in his hands and expressiveface.

"This is part of his traditional custom, Jendayi. He is indebted to you for his life and will be in your service. He considers it an honor," Petronila explains.

Jendayi laughs crudely in his face, hope crumbling up and down her chest, "Mama Petronila, tell him that the best thing he can do for me is to run far away from this place. That is how he can repay me for saving his life, by saving his own now."

Gwelo makes to speak again but everyone freezes in place as Dakarai's voice is heard calling near the kitchen. Standing abruptly and making a staying sign with her hands, Petronila eases out the door, worry scenting her body as she goes to answer him.

"**L**ucia, *m'ija*, come and sit with me. My head stings so terribly. How long have I been asleep?" Francesca whines from an unfamiliar bed. The smell of smoke wafts in the air, but the curtains' movement allows for it to circulate through the space without any permanence.

Lucia, who has been sitting in a chair near the window, stands and walks close to her mother without touching her. She can see that her mother is still groggy from the dose of laudanum that she had mixed in a glass of wine the previous evening, after the wedding festivities had ended.

She is fortunate that her mother was already deep in her cups and exhausted from the entire event. There was little she had to do to convince her to drink from the wine glass she gave her, as she pulled back the covers on the bed and gently placed her mother into it. Not accustomed to being this close to her mother or doing the job of a slave by undressing her, it took Lucia longer than expected to unbutton her mother's heavily brocaded bodice and corset as well as remove her shoes, stockings, and garters. Her mother's sweaty, suddenly-free body filled the air with woman smells and Lucia had to take a deep breath before shoving the dirty clothes onto a nearby chair. This had been her brother's room. Her mother insists that it still needs to be cleaned regularly, as if she still anticipates his arrival at the door any day, though he is now a married man. Lucia has needed the time to think of what she is going to say to her mother about Micaela and the additional hours of sleep have been helpful for coming up with a plan.

She slept badly, haunted by dreams of burning library books and ships at a distance which she yearns to be on. As soon as the servants begin to move around the house, she gets up to see her mother. After tidying up her clothing and hair, again a task she is unfamiliar with without Micaela's steady hand, she asks for a cup of tea from a passing servant in the hallway. She gingerly steps past the heavy, wet cloth on the floor which had blotted out the fire. It is incredible that the damage was contained to only her mother's room. She sits in a chair most of the early afternoon, at times getting up to pace and sip on the lukewarm tea which has been delivered but almost forgotten. Since her brother's room is on the other side of the stairwell, away from her room and her mother's, it is the farthest from the sounds of the kitchen and stable. Now, the quiet makes her nervous, until her mother eventually rouses from her drug-ladened sleep some sixteen hours since she has been abed.

"Mama, hush now, you need to rest. We are in Alvaro's old room, away from the noise and stench of the fire. Already, the servants are working to clean the space so it can be reconstructed. Come, would you like a sip of water?" Lucia says, as she tries to press a cup of water to her mother's lips.

"Oh, my dear, what a travesty. That Micaela has caused ruin in this house by her carelessness. As soon as I can get out of this bed, I will call Padre to help me get someone to take her to Portobello to market! The journey along the Camino Royal will be swift and they will return with money to fix my house!" Francesca's un-corseted breasts heave as she struggles to sit up amongst the pillows. The effort is too much, and she resettles with a thud. The lethargy of her limbs with the opiate is too drastic to fight and Lucia uses this moment to her advantage.

"Mama, all will be well. I am sure the house will be fixed in no time and it will cost next to nothing. Most of the damage has been contained to a corner of the room and the structure is still strong. You are exhausted after such a lovely wedding and you need your rest. Alvaro and his bride are content in their new home and the festivities will be the talk of the season," Lucia coos, trying to get her mother in a more genteel mood.

"Yes, yes, it was marvelous with all my hard work. Even Isabella thanked me personally, and you know she rarely has two words to put together for me! My goodness, indeed! Moving all the food to the new house, my, it was exhausting. Really, I need a rest after such efforts!" Francesca pronounces, a pink glow coming back to her wan cheeks as her daughter's affirmations perk up her spirits.

Lucia gently re-tucks the blankets under her mother's arm and pats her shoulder gently. She cannot remember the last time she has hugged her mother, and the springy flesh of her skin makes her uncomfortable.

"Mama, there is something I must tell you," says Lucia, as she sits alongside her mother on the bed. Looking down at the lace on the bodice of her cream-colored day dress, Lucia begins to pick at it slowly as she waits for her mother's full attention.

"Lucia, your mama is very tired. Whatever you have to say, can it wait until I am able to…" Francesca waves her bejeweled hands, as her eyes close.

In a sudden outburst, Lucia grabs her mother's hand and says, "Oh Mama, Micaela has died from the fire's fumes. She perished last night as she was left in the kitchen unattended. I was able to get Juan Carlos to remove the body and instructed him to bury her in *La Gotera,* as far away from us as possible. I just cannot bear it!" And with that, she bends her head and weeps deeply. Little does her mother know that she is weeping for the young child who witnessed her father's perversity and the saving hand of Micaela more so than for Micaela herself. She has now paid her dues.

Shocked at her daughter's emotional state and still too confused to take all the information in, Francesca again struggles to sit up on the pillows piled high behind her and attempts to stroke her crying daughter's head. The nostalgia of the moment is not lost on her as she remembers her sweet child, eager to cuddle in her arms after a day of play, during the early days of moving into this newly built house. The possibilities of wealth in Costa Rica and the rise in cacao prices had been a boon for their family and they walked through the door of establishing themselves as the most re-spected colonial family in the country. With a loud sigh, she realizes that those days are long over and the awkwardness of having a fully-grown wailing woman across her lap makes her suddenly disturbed.

"Come, come, Lucia. I know this is all very shock-ing as you were so fond of and incredibly dependent on Micaela. But my dear, she was a slave and can always be replaced. Remember that. It is unbecoming to form attach-ments to those who can be bought and sold. It is not what *we* do. I am very unhappy to hear that she has died and that I will not get my just dues for the damage she caused me. I hope that you did not have to pay Juan Carlos to take the body?"

Lucia sits up, wiping her face with the sleeve of her dress, knowing that her mother will be appalled that she does not use a handkerchief. Her mother's callous response assures her that her lie has worked.

"No, Mama. He was kind to be of service to me. I am sure we will hear nothing more about it. But I have a favor to ask you, now that the wedding is over. I want to leave. I want to go to Spain as you promised so I can have my com-ing out. I need to get out of this country, please, Mama," Lucia pleads, looking directly into her mother's eyes for the first time since she has opened them.

"Leave? Lucia, I, I…must think about it. Our lives are so deeply entrenched here. You must know that Jimenez and I have formed an attachment and I am hoping to one day remarry. Plus, we have so much to do as the leading family in this community," Francesca replies.

"Jimenez? Really, Mama. How can you not see right through him?" Lucia stutters incredulously, shocked that her mother has bought his song and dance. It's all about power and having access to resources for Jimenez, and Lucia has seen his agenda from the start.

"That is neither here nor there, Lucia," Francesca interrupts. "These are my personal affairs and you do not get a say in them. We cannot think of that now when there is this conflict between Spain and France and our families are sending volunteers for the war. We must be a support system for our people. Anyway, it would be unwise to go to Spain now in the midst of a war, my dear. Look, you are just overwrought with the death of your precious Micaela. Why you had so much of an attachment to her, I can never understand. But that is over now. Go, let me rest my eyes and tomorrow I will be better, and we can make more decisions. But mark my words, you must tell Juan Carlos that he has to take Padre and Jimenez to the grave to show where she is in the ground; he must account for her body," Francesca says, then adjusts her head against the pillow and closes her eyes, signaling her need to be alone.

Rather than fight her drowsy mother, Lucia leaves the room without a second glance. She has achieved what she was looking for, though her mother's need for Padre and Jimenez to see the grave is unexpected. This could become a problem if her mother insists. However, she has done the work she set out to do. It is now Juan Carlos's job to deal with the rest.

Esmeralda

In my one working hand, I rub the sharp, curved edge of Dakarai's small saw, which I used to gnaw away at Gwelo's foot irons. I kept this one tool like a thief in the night. Jendayi never remembered any of them on her way out with Gwelo. But I knew. I tucked it under the corner of my mat as they were preparing to leave, plan in mind already. This is how I will say goodbye. This will be my greatest act of redemption, one which will find the justice needed to add salve to the wounds of my people, issued forth so callously by these *panas*. How could it be that Dakarai has to place his daughter, born to death, in the ground without ever hearing her voice call his name? He will never again hear the sounds of his sons' laughter, and it is clear his feet will never touch the soil from the place beyond the sea. Those times are over, and it is this world we must struggle through now. So, I will do my part. Jendayi, in all her youth, taught me that. She gave me the courage unknowingly to dream a plan into action. I will not survive it and for this I am glad. But, to do away with that man who has harmed me so, taken the use of my arm and eye, weakened my spirit so that

I am afraid of the human touch of my brothers and sisters, is my greatest chance at freedom.

With the tenderness of a scribe, I will slit his throat and then cut my wrist. The story of how it came to pass will be my legacy. It may buy time for Gwelo to get away from this hell. In the last year of Padre's coming to me, I have cringed in the corner, fearful of food or water as my body erupts from the violence he lays so carelessly on me, Sunday evenings at his leisure. I have new words now, fancy courage and killing him will be my freedom.

Jendayi

Thursday market, one week later

Jendayi lays the heavy basket down with the vegetables and fruits that she has harvested from their garden. Her father did not have more than a handful of sculptures left haphazardly in his work shed at home in which to sell, but he had tucked them absent-mindedly in the sides of the basket, nestled amongst the papaya and bananas. The last few days have been more difficult than anything she has ever experienced. Struggling to focus on setting up her stall since she is by herself, Jendayi unpacks mechanically, forgetting to smile at her neighbors who are also unpacking for the day's commerce. The census had stopped mid-stream in *La Gotera* as an urgent call for young men to volunteer for the Spanish conflict with France came right after the Ibarra wedding. People were just brushing off the last of the wedding festivities when the alarm was sounded for help to the mother country. Though there were not many eligible Spanish men who could go to war, the ones who could were instantly branded with soldier status and elevated constantly with words of pride for *la patria*. Many just wanted the adventure out of Costa Rica and into the real world, not truly understanding the likelihood of never returning. Yet, their mothers knew. She can hear it at the prayer services that are held daily now that she is given more and more responsibility in the schoolroom. There are rumblings of sending slaves along with their young masters, but these decisions are to be made by the Governor in Guatemala, and not even Jimenez or Padre have any say. So, people are at a standstill. Waiting with bated breath to see their destinies. For Jendayi, it is a good distraction to all the things that are happening in her house.

Sighing deeply, Jendayi goes around to the front of her stall to observe her handiwork. On most days, except during her father's early negotiations about the Ibarra bridal furniture with the *panas*, they have no problems selling their fruit and vegetables, as their produce is fresh and without bruises. They also charge a fair price and have the attraction of her father's craftwork to bring more customers in. Usually, Josefina will stop by at lunch time and they will huddle together, giggling and eating their *tamales,* rice and beans or cassava. Today, Jendayi knows Josefina will not arrive as she is just back from Matina.

The day flies without any respite as it seems that every *pana* household wants to cook elaborate, favorite meals for their sons as if their departures to Spain are imminent. Families stock up on the taut eggplant and tender mushrooms made into their *paella* along with the spicy red onions that cause many an eye to tear. Casually, Jendayi watches Doña

Francesca and Lucia enter the vestry of the church, aware that they are unaccompanied. Used to seeing at least two enslaved workers trailing their owner, Jendayi takes another deep sigh and wishes that her icon was tucked into the pocket of her dress. She has resolved that it has been lost forever and if Don Alvaro and his bride never noticed its absence over their bed, then she is sure her father is not going to be called to explain why it is missing.

As the church bells ring for midafternoon Mass, the steady stream of servants and slaves slow along with the building heat, alerting all about the coming daily rains. Tired, Jendayi turns to sit on the small wooden box that is her make-shift seat and wipes her brow. She can see the legs of people as they approach her stall, but they cannot instantly see her crouched so low.

"And I heard that Alvaro had his way with his sister's slave, Micaela, the night before the wedding. I was told that he was so drunk that he ripped her in half, and she took her life by starting the fire!" comes a voice above Jendayi's head. She keeps hidden so that she can hear more.

Jendayi hears a sharp gasp before the women huddle closer together and begin to whisper incessantly. Holding her breath, she tries not to move in order to hear the conversation of the two *pana* women who have stopped in front of her stall. Hopefully, they will not want to buy anything as she will have to give up her hiding spot and admit to eavesdropping.

"Mercy on that family for their sins. His poor bride, I hear that she is afraid of the marriage bed. Her mother-in-law tells me that she is terrified of all the hummingbirds carved into the headboard, saying they whisper at her throughout the night! It has only been a week! What utter nonsense! I say she is really afraid of the brute who sleeps next to her, not pieces of wood above her head!" comes another voice in reply.

"Well, no matter, hopefully, he is doing his duty by her and will leave her with child, as I am sure he will be called off to war," another firm voice states.

Jendayi does not know whether to stand or sit as she struggles to listen. She knows these women. They are friends of Doña Francesca, wives of slave owners in Cartago and known for their gossip. Grateful when they move on because there is no one to serve them, Jendayi stands slowly, pretending to polish the tomatoes in the pile in front of her. Smiling, she is grateful that this is the story circulating in town among the *panas*. The idea that everyone believes Micaela is dead is a blessing.

"Juana Maria, how is your father? I have heard that he is unwell and has not been seen in town or at his shop since the wedding," Jimenez calls to her while stopping at the corner of her stall.

"*Buenos dias*, Don Jimenez, my father is slowly getting better. He has taken with a very strong *gripe* and the fever has lasted days now. I am out here today by myself so that we can survive as my father is unable to work. I am hopeful that he will be in his shop next week."

"Well, you give him a message for us. Padre and I will be visiting once he is no longer contagious as we need to ascertain the death of the Ibarra slave. He is to take us to the gravesite as Doña Francesca demands. Also, he is needed for the reconstruction of the Ibarra house now that the debris has been taken away. Tell him to mend quickly as much is expected of him," Jimenez stares straight into her eyes, the message clear. With an almost imperceptible nod of his head, he leaves her to enter the church, aware of his lateness.

It is impossible that death has not claimed Micaela, though she so longingly looks for it. They tell her that she had a girl but she was unable to fight against the strain of smoke and fear that hugged her body in the Ibarra house during the fire. They whisper at Micaela how her fingertips were translucent, and her toes evenly curled with the tiniest of nails. Micaela has not opened her eyes to see any of them who come to her ear, pleading for her to wake up and claim the life that remains. Micaela knows there is an urgency that she will not understand, a movement that she must undertake, a hope for something else outside of this exact hollowness of pain. When he explained that he named her *Kweimwe Nguva*, Micaela could not stop the tears from sealing the skin around her head, washing her hair with utter despair. Now, she understands the true burden of slavery. Micaela does not cry because her child is no more, she cries because she understands her death is perhaps a salvation and as a slave mother, after mere months of growing life inside of herself, this should be her moment of celebration. She is being gifted in this death, as she will never know what it is to have her child ripped from her arms and sold at auction in Panama or bred by the Ibarras when she reaches her moon-age and for this Micaela will be told to be grateful. Indeed, she has learned the lessons of her enslavement and now, it is freedom she seeks. Dakarai's arms that cradle her no longer provide solace; the gentle smell of his tenderness is choking as she can feel that he understands that she too has gone away. Luckily, sleep takes her more times than not and so she does not claim her cowardice.

Dakarai

Dakarai cannot wake her, and he understands why. She eats and sips slowly when Petronila and Dakarai alternate with sustenance, yet her eyes remain closed. She even allows Petronila to take her to the bathroom by pulling on her skirt a few times a day, but there are no words. She does not look at any of them. This is grief. He knows it. This all too familiar pit buried so deep inside him, that reminds him that he will never embrace his sons or wives again, he will never sink his toes into the earth of his home—the last fragments of peace he thought this life could offer. Dakarai smiles now, a fool he is. Added to this list, he understands that the only way he can give life to this woman that he deeply loves, lying in wait for a death which will not come, is to release her. It can only be that his ancestors have been wronged that such a price must be placed against his shoulders and he knows he does not get a do-over here, so he waits.

Petronila tells him that every day Micaela grows stronger and that is a good sign as she will be able to leave soon. She must disappear into the hinterlands and hope that she can survive through the rainforests that will take her to the ocean. From there, she can eke something out, maybe a chance at a life, find a helpmate where she can benefit from her own toil if she is careful to avoid the *panas*. The irony in Dakarai loving her is that he is giving her the thing that he has always dreamt of, yet she will not be at his side.

Dakarai has hidden in his house, pretending illness so that he can spend his waking hours crouched alongside Micaela's pallet, wiping her head with lavender water, and pressing a cool drink to her lips. Yet, she refuses to see him. Dakarai tells her the truth, about their daughter who came too early, the perfection of her lips and feet. Micaela hitches her breath and he knows it is pain that covers her heart and she, in some way, blames him for it all. Yes, Dakarai is to blame. He, a free Black man, dared to love an enslaved Black woman, after so many years of being without a woman in his arms, not content to just raise his daughter and mind his business. He did not listen when Esmeralda came with her warning all those months ago. He stepped outside of himself, of his limitations in this skin and for a moment, he remembered himself as the sculptor from across the sea. With her in his arms, he dreamt for the first time in his own language, and it felt right. Dakarai accepts this now. He has caused all of this because he did not know his place in a world that has unfalteringly reminded him of who he is, Black African, former slave and never fully free. There is no greater lesson than humility, he was raised knowing this yet pleasure, even fleeting, made him learn the hard way. And so, he accepts the blame. Their child is dead, and his lover will have to leave him and forge a life into the unknown.

Jendayi

It feels like the day will never end, even as Mass is over and the *panas* and their slaves go home for their four o'clock dinner. Jendayi holds the ripest mango to one side, firm but guaranteed to be succulent as she presses her nail gently into its skin. This Jendayi will give Mama Petronila as she is now beholden to her for the rest of her life. She did not betray Jendayi with Gwelo when her father arrived at her house last week. Sitting next to him in Josefina's room, she almost vomited with fear. She did not know who her father would be most angry with and she wanted to shield Gwelo from a fate he had no making in.

What she had not anticipated was that her father had other things on his mind than looking for his wayward daughter. He begged Petronila to leave her cooking and accompany him back to their house in the most urgent whispers. Jendayi even heard them speaking in Shona, so she knew something must be desperately wrong. Her stomach dropped in thinking that perhaps Nicolaasa Mina had worsened, or even died and she had not done her duty of taking her medicines and the foodstuff her father had prepared. Though the humidity of the day was rising to meet the brewing afternoon storm, Jendayi's entire body was chilled. She placed her hand on her lips indicating to Gwelo not to speak and she tiptoed out of the room. Leaving him in the house, she walked across the dirt yard that divided their houses and gently opened the door to their kitchen. She could hear movement in her father's work shed so she quickly went out to look.

There, on the pallet in the corner was Micaela. She lay without moving and Jendayi noticed faint traces of blood around her ankles and the inner parts of her calves as her dress had not been pulled down properly. Jendayi had cleared her throat and her father looked up, bewilderment in his eyes.

"My daughter, today, you see your father in deep sadness. I have much to explain but for now, I ask that you trust me and keep my confidence about Micaela. No one is to know that she is here, under the risk of death," Dakarai had pleaded.

"Of course, Baba. I will get some clean cloths and lavender oils to ease her." Jendayi exited the room quickly though Mama Petronila followed her slowly, the uneven gait laborious as she tried to reach Jendayi's side.

"There were rumors but nothing to confirm that they had an understanding. Your father has lost so much, and he is a very proud man. He cannot possibly manage one more thing right now. It will kill him to know about Gwelo and your involvement in his escape. Luckily for you, he is focused here and will not enter my house now, unless there is an absolute emergency. And so, I tell you this as you are my daughter. Say your goodbyes to your friend because as the sun sets, he will be on his way along the banks of the Reventazon River. I can see what is between you two and so I will allow you a chance to close, but that is it, Jendayi," Petronila spoke gently, while holding both of her hands.

Without thinking, Jendayi melted into her embrace. It was a first, a rich, deep mother-hug that brought every ache and longing to the surface and with that she cried. Petronila rocked her softly back and forth, rubbing the middle of her back as she leaned further into a tenderness that she had never known until that moment. Her father rarely hugged her, usually just giving a blessing with a kiss on her forehead, and Josefina hugged her only on birthdays, but she now knew the full love embrace of a universe. She sobbed for the missing of her mother, the despair of her father, the never knowing of Gwelo's future, the barely breathing Micaela, the bleakness of Esmeralda's enslaved life. She cried because she wanted her mother and could not picture her face beyond a shadow in her father's description.

When she had emptied it all out, Petronila gave her a small tap on the back and released her. Jendayi wiped her face with the sleeve of her dress, took a deep breath that came out as a hiccup, and whispered, "*Wazviita,* Mama," thanking her for allowing her to fall. She had never spoken Shona to Petronila, but the times called for it. She had quickly gathered the supplies for her father and eased them into Petronila's awaiting arms as she then ran back across the dirt path where Gwelo awaited.

Now, Jendayi packs up her stall and follows the dirt path, the path to Gwelo. It is a goodbye that she cannot imagine. Though she has known him for a matter of days, she already carries him deeply inside of her. He is familiar and it is crushing that she will spend her life wondering what becomes of him. All this she thinks as she enters Josefina's room. She finds him snoring gently across the bed, the house empty except for Picante who has come in and is curled up on the rug in the center of the room. Hushing the dog who sits up eagerly, she slides off her sandals and tucks herself alongside Gwelo's slumbering body. Her movements wake him, but he does not speak, just inches further towards the wall so that their bodies can fit, though the bed is already small, and he is a growing young man. Kissing her fingertips, he intertwines their hands as he puts one arm under her head, so that she can lean onto his chest. Together, they watch their fingers play, as if speaking, chasing, free to be. Jendayi can only bear to look up at him once, when she hears movement outside the house and knows that her time is up. She is surprised to see the pooling of tears in his eyes and when he reaches down with the most tender kiss, everything explodes. She weeps, cradled in his arms, thinking that she had released it all with Petronila.

Hearing someone enter the house, Jendayi sits up awkwardly, disentangling herself from Gwelo, who remains reclining in the bed. He knows he is safe here and this will be his only chance at rest before he flees. Petronila has explained to him that there is a community of free Africans in an area called *Cimarrones,* a small but fertile remote village, high in the mountains towards the coast. If he follows the river and asks those he feels he can trust and barter with, he might be able to get there in twelve days. It is said that many of those maroons who live there still maintain their home language and he might be able to find someone who understands him. Gwelo has been promised some precious silver along with a bag of cacao, some dried fruit and tortilla to carry him along his journey. He also has sandals and a woven poncho covering that will protect him from the mosquitos and rain and can become a blanket at night. He has been made to pledge to Jendayi in front of Petronila that his debt to her would only be repaid if he gains his freedom.

"I must go now. I wish you every safety. I wish I knew words in your language to explain better," as Jendayi says this, Gwelo stands from the bed and steps in front of her. He places his hands alongside her checks, and hoarsely says *gracias,* as he again brushes her lips with the faintest of touches. She greedily hugs him, not wanting the moment to end though already she sees herself outside the door and Gwelo on the way to another life. Jendayi has done her job and that is what he is thanking her for. And maybe he is thanking her for being a small piece of joy in the middle of so much fear.

With the slight knock on the door, Jendayi does not need to be told that it is time to leave. Gwelo squeezes her hand and then releases it, a goodbye they both understood. Petronila stands in the doorframe as Jendayi slips past her and again out the house. This time, no words are uttered between them.

Four Days later

"Jendayi, my mother wants to speak with you. She said that you are to meet her by the path that leads to Nicolaasa Mina's house as she wants you to help her carry some things over there for her care," Josefina smirks, happy not to be selected for that job. She stands just inside the door frame as Jendayi sets a kettle of coffee on the fire.

"Padre needs me to stay after classes today to help make a list of the men who will be volunteering for the war. I am told that a ship will come by October and they need at least forty men prepared for that first journey. Can you ask your mother to delay?" Jendayi replies, annoyed.

"No, she said that you owed some care to Nicolaasa Mina. You will have to make your excuses to Padre. I am sure there are others who can be of service to him. You should not make her wait," with those words, Josefina walks off towards her house, checking the sky for rain clouds.

Unhappy that she has to walk all the way to the church to make her excuses, Jendayi moves quickly along the path outside of *La Gotera*. She meets Padre in the vestibule of the church, and she mutters some words about her father continuing to be ill and that she is unable to help with the soldier list that afternoon but promises to come the next day.

This is outside of the norm for her as Wednesdays are her days off from school, so that she can go with her father to their farm to prepare for Thursday's market. Padre looks up at her strangely, as if not understanding what she has said. He nods and then dismisses her with a flick of his wrist, not even attempting at his normal sign of the cross etched in the air.

As she walks along the path back to *La Gotera,* so many thoughts swirl around her head. She does not have the nerve to give her father the message that Jimenez had shared with her the previous week in the market, but she now knows the *panas* can be tricky. She passes her father occasionally on the way to the kitchen as he continues to brew the tea leaves he has been given for Micaela, but she has not been permitted to enter his work shed. He sleeps there, a constant nurse. Oddly, Petronila has not returned to their home, though each morning Jendayi finds at her door a basket wrapped with warm tortillas and soft bread that comes directly from Petronila's hearth. She knows that she is overdue for a visit to Nicolaasa Mina, and she silently gives thanks that the woman is still alive.

Instead of going to her home, she continues on the path that leads to the farm area of *La Gotera.* The earth is a ruddy brown as the rains over the weekend have been heavy. Every corner of the land is lush; new sprouts emerge on each vine and the color of fuchsia, orange, and pink flowers pop across the horizon. Seeing Petronila lumbering slowly ahead with a fruit-laden basket on her head, Jendayi speeds up to relieve her of her burden.

"Good afternoon, Mama Petronila, allow me to carry that for you please," Jendayi says as she reaches across and moves the basket to her own head.

"Jendayi, I have asked you here for more than a social visit. I have made some arrangements and I need you to convey them to your father. The less people know about this, the better. Come, walk alongside me quickly so I do not have to raise my voice," Petronila commands as she moves her wooden walking stick into her right hand. The stick gives her the extra support she needs for this longer walk, though the pain is evident in her feet as she shuffles forward. As they set pace with one another, Petronila continues, "I have asked Gwelo to wait at two days' walking distance from here at a hunting shed that we used many moons ago so that Micaela can meet with him. I think she is strong enough to make the journey and it will be safer for her to have the company of a young man than to venture into the jungle alone. She has the language of the *panas* and can explain that she is a slave sent to visit a cacao plantation in Nicoya, if they are stopped. Which, I pray to the ancestors, that they are not."

"My father will want to follow her. He loves her," Jendayi answers resolutely.

"My child, he already knows that his love has given her freedom and that he must release her. It will be very hard for him, but I believe this is for the best. She has lost so much with the baby. Luckily, the *panas* believe that she has died from the fire."

"Baby?" Jendayi stops mid-step.

"Yes, you are old enough to know the truth. She was with child, your sister, but the baby was lost when Micaela collapsed in the fire. I am sorry for you all. The risk of being involved with a slave is extraordinary and I hope we all do not bear the punishment for your father's actions," Petronila says gently.

We slow as we near the entrance of Nicolaasa Mina's shack. Weeds and tall grass cover the path near the front door and there are puddles of mud everywhere.

Petronila whispers, "This is her only chance to escape. Nicolaasa Mina's eldest son will be going to Matina the day after tomorrow and he will take Micaela as far as he can until they meet with Gwelo. Gwelo has been told that if after three sunrises they do not appear, then he must continue alone. We cannot risk his freedom for hers. You must tell your father of the plan; prepare her a bundle and he must walk her to the River on the night of the full moon and say his goodbyes. Come, let us now care for our neighbor."

"*Upe,*" Jendayi shouts, using the common Cartago gesture to announce their arrival. There is some scuffling from within and a child peeks its head out the wooden shack door, allowing them to get a glimpse of the despair within.

Jendayi

"**I** just do not understand how he can be so disrespectful as to approach you with such a message for me," Dakarai says, pacing in Jendayi's bedroom. She has begged him for a moment of his time and when he joins her, she is shocked at how he has aged. Gone are the all-black curls in his hair; his face is now framed with gray. His goatee has gray edges as well. It almost feels like she has not lied when she told Don Jimenez that her father was ill. Indeed, his body shows an illness of spirit.

"Baba, too many days have passed now, and your absence is becoming a conversation. You need to resolve with them over your payment for the Ibarra work. But nothing can be done until we follow Mama Petronila's plan, now that Micaela is stronger. She must leave tomorrow night. Mama has arranged for two guides to walk along with her. But the men cannot wait forever. I know they are trustworthy," Jendayi says, almost wanting to spill the secrets of her heart to her father. But Petronila has warned against it; he does not need any extra burdens. The idea that Gwelo is still nearby, within a few days' reach makes her feel like putting on her shoes and running to him.

"If she is to go, then she needs more herbs to take with her to strengthen her blood. I feel that she is still too weak, and she does not speak to me, so I cannot really assess her abilities. I have no more tea and so you must go to Mama Esmeralda this evening and ask for them. I have always told you to leave her alone and not trouble her space because there is much at risk but tonight, daughter, I go against my own words in order to get help," Dakarai says wearily.

"Esmeralda! Baba, that is so far, and the rains are very heavy. I am sure Mama Petronila has some that I can beg a bit from. Should I go there?" Jendayi protests.

"No, Jendayi, only Esmeralda has this special tea that she has made to care for Micaela's childbirth. I know I am asking much from you, but tonight there is no going against my word, if we are to make sure Micaela leaves in safety. I cannot risk being seen since I have told everyone that I am ill and in bed," Dakari says, a strange pleading in his voice.

And so, resentful of having to go into the blinding rain, sharp with rumbling thunder and lightning that makes the night into day, Jendayi wraps her body in her day shawl and covers her head with a farmer's hat, knowing it will only shield her eyes in order to see the few steps in front of her as she makes her way past the Cruz de Caravaca and to the church plaza. The candles on the altar are burning bright. The rain pelts the tile steps. Jendayi notes that, oddly, the church doors are ajar, though there is no special Mass that evening. Assuming that Esmeralda is cleaning, instead of going directly to her shed, Jendayi dashes up the slippery steps into the vestibule, not bothering to touch her head with Holy Water at the font. She calls out but does not hear or see anyone. The whirling storm makes music around her and it feels strangely safe standing inside, though she is dripping wet.

A sudden bolt of thunder and a flash of lightning illuminates the room, slamming one of the front doors closed and outing several candles on the altar. Jumping with fright, Jendayi remembers Josefina's story of the dead brothers; one who remains pleading for forgiveness night after night. Overcome with an ominous feeling, she shakes herself, remembering her errand and makes her way through the nave, genuflecting hesitantly, as if Padre will show up at any second to scold her for not showing the required respect.

Crossing the altar and walking out the side door towards the schoolroom and Esmeralda's dilapidated shack, Jendayi struggles as the rain slashes across her face once she is back outside. The brief respite inside the church has been a foolish choice on her part because now the chill wracks her spine as her wet clothes cling to her skin. Knocking lightly at first on the tin door, Jendayi hears some movement inside though with the storm around her, it is hard to discern. Sure that Esmeralda is inside, Jendayi pushes the door open, calling out softly that it is her. Another muffling sound reaches her as she eases herself in from the rain and pulls the door shut behind her. When she turns to focus her eyes in the dark, lightning illuminates the small room and the acrid smell of blood overwhelms her.

"Oh, no, no, no, Mama Esmeralda," Jendayi screams into the storm and the room and the blood and the pain that she sees in front of her.

Esmeralda

I never expected you to come and stand witness to my life. It is done and let me look at you quickly before I too say goodbye. That heavy body heaved its final time across my back. I did not anticipate that he would struggle so much against the razor edge at his throat as he was in the ecstasy of climax. I chose the exact moment, letting him release his seed in me one more time, the rancid smell of his sweat, semen, after-dinner drinks and wet clothing fought with the shiny tinge of blood as it spurted everywhere. I slit him carefully, as he threw his head back in pleasure, across the jugular and the corresponding arteries, digging deep with all my one-arm strength, to make sure he would never survive. I know I took him unawares, yet he pushed against me. It was too dark to see his face, which I will never have to do again. I disengaged myself as his blood pooled against my pallet and I slit my wrists. Now, the pain is beyond words yet the storm outside focuses me, and I feel something like power for the first time in my life. You have come to trust me, and you now see that I have killed a man, a holy man of the panas who has enslaved my body in ways that are so destructive. He is the reason why I only have one good working arm and eye. I cannot hide from you in the way that your father wants you to be protected. I say these things because I have seen your strength. I am not asking you to be here and stand witness. Turn around slowly and go back to the life that you know. In the end, it will bring you comfort to pretend this was all a dream during a bad storm. But know my child, as I say these final words to you in my head and heart, the life of a slave is a place of silence. You are never allowed to use the voice inside your head to create visions of anything except dread because you do not belong to yourself.

And now you come. I can sense your mother bent over you, wiping the tears from your eyes as you hold my head. Your hands are so gentle but I feel your pain fresh on my skin. It is done, my child.

Jendayi

The strobing lightning flashes illuminate a ghostly murder scene, a replica of the curse between brothers which already define the church. Padre is lying face-down in a seeping pool of blood as Esmeralda lies inches away from him, still conscious though struggling with breath as the blood drains out of her wrists.

Jendayi tries to gather her wits. She rushes to the clay pots near the wall, looking for something to tie Esmeralda's wrists long enough to get help. Her foot kicks something across the floor as she bends to find the candlestick. The lightning is occasional as the storm begins to move away from town. Scrambling to light the small candle stub, Jendayi is overwhelmed by Esmeralda's rasping breath. As the candle comes to life, Jendayi realizes that she has kicked her missing icon of *La Negrita*. Grabbing hold of it with relief, the tears form deep in her chest and spill without thought down her face as Esmeralda's breath begins to lessen.

Crawling over to cradle Esmeralda's head in her lap, Jendayi calls her name softly and whispers, "Mama Esmeralda, it's me, Jendayi. I am here now and will take care of you. Look, the icon is here too. This is a message from my mother. I know she is saying that you are safe and she will cross you over. She thanks you for protecting me."

Esmeralda tries to speak though only a gurgle emerges. Jendayi bends closer to her head to hear her words, as her tears mingle with Esmeralda's.

"Letter…Goo-oo-ing home, sweet Jendayi," Esmeralda says with her dying breath.

"Oh no, Mama…oh please," Jendayi weeps with Esmeralda's dead body in her lap.

The thunderclap revives her from the death scene and slowly, Jendayi eases Esmeralda's body onto the floor. The dirt is sticky with blood which has pooled between both bodies. Jendayi sees that Padre is without pants and it is only then that she understands what has transpired. Choked with agony and rage, Jendayi impulsively places the icon in Esmeralda's right hand as a parting gift. Wiping her streaming eyes and nose, Jendayi sees her father's tools that she had forgotten in her rush to get Gwelo to the River for his escape. Wavering back and forth as to whether she should cover Esmeralda's body, she decides against it so that it is clear no one is witness to this betrayal. She uses the water in a small clay pot to wash the blood off her hands as she gathers the tools and wraps them in her soaking cloak. The bile in her stomach threatens to come up as she turns to blow out the candle and make her final farewell to Esmeralda, who has been a true friend.

Before she blows out the flame, her eye catches a piece of paper near where the tools were placed. She bends to pick it up and notices, as she looks closer, that her name is meticulously written across the top. Tempted to read it in the staggering light, the hair suddenly rises on the back of her neck, telling her that she must leave the dead in peace.

Jendayi climbs into her bed, every inch of her skin chilled from what she has seen. She had returned with speed in the rain, bursting into the house and crying for her father, who came running from the work shed. Trembling and with little breath, she explained what had happened at Esmeralda's, collapsing in his arms with body-moving sobs. Together, they sat on the floor of her room, weeping in shock at the news. He had no words of comfort for Jendayi, only his arms and his tears kept her together. It was only when he was conscious of her teeth chattering does he help remove her sodden cloak and hat. He went to the kitchen and busied himself with heating water for a hip bath. He left the steaming water in the tub in her room, lit a few candles, then excused himself so she had the privacy to bathe. However, he paced outside her door until he heard the sloshing of the water as she stepped out of the tub. He called through the door to ask if he could come in and retrieve the tub but she had already donned her nightdress and climbed into bed, weeping quietly. He now clears the tub, moving mechanically. He whispers a good night to her, unsure if she hears his words as he returns to Micaela in his work shed.

Jendayi waits for her father to leave, her face dry and tight from all the tears she has shed.

The pain in her chest is dense as her body continues to shake from the grief she has witnessed. Going over to remove the letter Esmeralda has left for her, which she tucked under some clothing on her chair before she stepped into her bath, she brings the sheet to the candle now. Leaning in, she reads,

Jendayi,

If you are reading this, then you know that my story is an old story, one that has been timelessly written on bodies like ours by men like him. I am sorry.

But I have other words to say, which is my gift to you, daughter of my heart. Beg your father my forgiveness as I have stepped ahead of him in this tale but there can be no one who stands in the way of you knowing your full truth. As I was cutting through Gwelo's chains, he told me a little bit about his family. He missed his mother, so terribly and in trying to remember her voice, he shared with me a story that she told him over and over when he was a child to protect him from the Portuguese. His mother, Lupita, had a best friend who was a master sculptor. She was married to a man who also carved. They lived near the Zambezi, a six-day journey from the Benguela coast. Only once a year would Lupita get to see her friend, when she came with her husband to sell their Shona sculptures. On an unexpected visit from her friend, Lupita introduced her to the poet, Agostinho, a young man famed for his political verse throughout the country. Their connection was instant and when Lupita saw her friend five months later, it is evident that Agostinho was the father of her friend's budding child. It is during that time when her friend tries to find Agostinho to tell him the truth about their child, that she is captured by the Portuguese, along with her husband. Gwelo learned to be wary of the Portuguese because he understood that they can come upon you unawares. And the name of Lupita's dearest friend was Towela and her husband was Dakarai. This is your mother's story, Jendayi, and your own. Take your truth now, knowing I share it in love.

Jendayi, cherish the precious freedom you have. Understand that you have taught me a bit of laughter and the possibility to have power within myself. I never saw that with my mother. She was bent in the fields, yet today, I straighten the backs of my people. The knife that will slice Padre's neck provides the music for the lesson these panas need to learn. They can no longer dictate my life as I too have heard the song, and it is the one I have always known how to sing. If I can beg you as a bit of vanity, hold the memory of me a bit tenderly; an old lady who has gone to rest.

Always,
Esmeralda

The scandal that follows the discovery of the two dead bodies, betrayed by the eventual stench of their rotting corpses a day and a half after it was noticed that Padre had gone missing from the schoolroom and confession, rocks the entire town for weeks on end. There are rumors that Esmeralda had bewitched him as it was clear from his naked loins what they had been engaged in. The church in Guatemala sends a delegation to try to tamp down some of the talk, hoping to divert the attention away from Padre's indiscretion to the conflict in Spain and the urgent need for soldiers. Blaming Padre's death on Esmeralda, the church buries him quietly in the *campo santo* and it is never revealed what happened to Esmeralda's body. A new Padre is requested to come on the ship in October which will return the first round of army volunteers to Spain.

And so, several months pass and the talk about a slave killing the man who owned her slowly eases out of the mouths, but not the minds, of the people who live and work in Cartago. The Africans in *La Gotera* hold an all-night vigil for Esmeralda, praising her strength in hushed tones, though most had never met her personally. Her shack is razed to the ground, though the leaves surrounding it seem to be forever tinted in shades of blood.

Dakarai weeps inconsolably, his tears a mixture of saying too many goodbyes. Micaela had left with Nicolaasa Mina's son towards the riverbank as planned and their goodbye was bittersweet. To then find out that Esmeralda was also gone made his gut constrict and he remained in bed for several days, deep in a fever of grief. Jendayi had come and gone with soup and tea; even Petronila had stopped in to wipe his weary forehead with a lemongrass infused cloth, but for the most part he was left to his own demons. And for this he was grateful. Jendayi would sit alongside his bed, humming softly. One day, when he turned in the bed to adjust his pillow, he saw her whittling away on a tiny piece of wood, tender long fingers holding the carver's knife with expertise. She smiled at him, bashfully, as if asking for his approval. But there she was, a daughter, the image of her mother in all ways and he felt such relief that he had not lost her as well. The perfect little bird in her hand took his breath away and for the first time in weeks, he slept without screams in his head.

Finally, he resolves to get up, bathe and venture into Cartago, weeks after he had last left the Ibarra house on that fateful wedding day. He promises Jendayi that he will not stay long at his shop, but he has to begin work again; if not how will they eat? He also needs a long-overdue conversation with Don Jimenez.

Surprisingly, Jimenez is too distracted by the church scandal and the newly arriving priest to place much stock in Dakarai's presence in town. Jimenez passes by his shop one morning, assuring Dakarai that the two other Ibarra house slaves had been manumitted and moved to Alvaro's as paid servants. Dakarai does not have to make much pretense when he arranges with Jimenez to visit Micaela's burial site as he took him to the newly dug grave of Nicolaasa Mina, who never overcame her childbed fever and perished quietly three nights before. Her children were taken in by the community as they could not survive alone. Petronila decided to take in the twin girls, who were barely four. Only Jendayi and Josefina understood her mother's gesture and it humbled them.

Now, Jimenez stands over the fresh grave as Dakarai remains somber at his side. The space between them is fraught with all that has transpired over the last year and words do not seem adequate. The show suffices for Jimenez and he quickly walks to his horse and leaves *La Gotera* to take the news back to Francesca, already the thought of Micaela a remote one in his head.

October comes and with it the ship from Spain. Many *panas* and their slaves go to the Pacific coast to bear witness to its arrival. Jendayi spends three days a week keeping up the school room as the children come back to continue their basic education. She adds some games and songs, which had been prohibited during Padre's strict lessons. She also tells stories about her people from across the sea to the children, rather than just use the ones from the Bible as Padre had insisted.

One day, as she clears the slate boards, she hears her name called from inside the vestry. She dusts her hands and bends to fasten her sandals carefully. Hearing her name called for a second time, she replies loudly that she is on her way and rushes out the door. However, she is met at the altar in the church by Jimenez and a man unknown to her.

"Juana Maria, you have been called three times. Have you not heard our summons? Padre Victor has just arrived from Spain. I want you to give him a tour of the grounds and then help him get settled into the Parish House. The cook and serving maid are already preparing lunch. Make sure to take him to the library and share information about how the schoolroom works and what current lessons you are undertaking with the children," Jimenez says pointedly. Jendayi curtsies and does not look directly into the face of the new Padre. From a quick side glance, she can see he is a much older, corpulent fellow, vastly different from the previous vicar. The church has done its homework this time around.

"Blessings, Juana Maria," Padre Victor says, approaching her. Jendayi takes a step back, saying, "Padre Victor, I will be happy to show you the grounds and then the library in the Parish House. I believe the previous Padre left many of the schoolbooks and our learning instructions at his desk." Padre Victor nods and turns to thank Jimenez, who obviously wants to return to his duties in town. After Jimenez leaves, Jendayi waits for Padre Victor to exist the church through the Sacristy, leading to the schoolroom and the burnt-out area where she had once whispered secrets with Esmeralda and Gwelo.

Padre Victor pokes his head into the schoolroom, his disinterest evident on his face as he glances around but does not cross the threshold. Jendayi tries to peek past his round body to make sure she has left everything tidy. He turns abruptly and says, "Juana Maria, show me where it happened." Jendayi does not need to ask him what he means, she simply nods, a dull ache springing inside her stomach. She has been loath to walk past Esmeralda's death place since she has returned to the schoolroom. The dead brothers come to mind whenever she walks through the center of the church, past the altar and around to the back kitchen next to the schoolroom, avoiding at all costs the residue of pain still lingering there. She is willing to take a mournful ghost, forever seeking the forgiveness of a brother he has killed in cold blood, rather than face the emptiness of Esmeralda's space, knowing she will never return.

As they walk silently past the open kitchen where empty clay gourds lay awaiting to be filled with water, the air warns them in advance of smoke. Though there is nothing left of Esmeralda's shack, the charred limbs of trees and fragments of what must have been Esmeralda's possessions intertwine with the destroyed walls and roof of the shack. The ash lays thickly against the earth. Death and despair fill the space, and Jendayi wants to rush away. "We must say a prayer over this space as it is one that contains deep sin. Bow your head, Juana Maria, and let us recite the Hail Mary together," Padre Victor says as he clears his throat and raises his right hand to make the sign of the cross in the air.

"Hail Mary, full of Grace, the Lord is with thee. Blessed are thou amongst women and blessed is the fruit of thy womb,

Jesus. Holy Mary, mother of God, pray for us sinners, now and at the hour of our death. Amen," intones Jendayi and Padre Victor in unison. Just as Padre Victor clears his throat to utter a final benediction, Jendayi gasps suddenly, cursing herself for alerting Padre Victor to what she has seen at the center of the burnt rubbish. There, laying on top of a broken branch is her icon *La Negrita*, which she had placed so lovingly in Esmeralda's hand as she lay dying. Instinctually curious, Padre Victor shrewdly follows Jendayi's gaze to the icon.

"What is it? Get it and bring it here," Padre Victor commands with his hand outstretched.

Jendayi carefully tiptoes across the ash, soot, and dust to retrieve the icon. The stone is now black from the fire but remains intact just as her father carved it. She is probably the only one who would recognize it now. Closing her eyes quickly, she rubs it in joy. Turning around once again to face Padre Victor, she walks over to him.

"I am sure it is nothing, just a piece of rock," Jendayi states, reluctantly handing over *La Negrita*.

Padre Victor examines it quickly and then, sucking in his breath, he proclaims, "Do you see what this is? Out of death and sin has emerged our Holy Mother, answering our prayerful petition. This is a divine sign that She has found favor with my arrival, and it is up to me to change the tides of this country. You are a very special girl. I am sure that our Sacred Mother will anoint your path, even as a *parda*. It will be remembered in our history that Juana Maria was the one who discovered the icon of our Blessed *Negrita*. I must write immediately to Spain to announce the miraculous appearance of Our Virgin. And look at her, so lovingly carved, black as the deep sea. We will build a church in her honor. You may leave and come back tomorrow to show me the library, Juana Maria, as I must share the news of our *Negrita*."

Jendayi's legs tremble as she listens to Padre Victor's words about her icon. He leaves her frozen in the same spot as he hastily walks towards the Parish House with the icon in his hand. No longer afraid to stand witness to the plot of land that once housed Esmeralda, she turns back and walks so that her toes in her sandals touch the edges of the ash that have piled and formed layers against the brown earth. Bowing her head, she whispers, "Thank you Mama Towela and Mama Esmeralda, I will take care of our *Negrita* and always call your names."

As the weeks pass, Padre Victor has several *pardo* men build a small, thatched hut over the land which housed Esmeralda's former shack, clearing it, and planting new trees. In this space the icon is placed and venerated until a church can be built in Her honor. Every day on her way to the schoolroom with the water needed to clean the church for yet another enslaved woman that was quietly purchased with Don Jimenez's help, Jendayi stops and greets her *Negrita*, sharing the news of how her father finally had been teaching her to sculpt. And so, at this sacred site, Jendayi whispers and laughs and at times cries, sharing her life with her mother and Esmeralda. Those who see Jendayi believe she indeed is the most pious *parda* of the time.

Acknowledgments

What a journey! This book's idea started from a chance visit to the Basilica to see the icon of *La Negrita* in Costa Rica to a family decision to leave New York and relocate fully to Costa Rica so I could answer the clarion call to tell this story. There are so many spirit-warriors who rode this wave with me and there is not enough paper in the world to thank them properly. I am them and they are me. I thank my ancestral team of my grandmother, Leonora Robotham, my grand-aunt Beatrice, my Tia Marjorie, my godmother Maisie and my great-grandmother, Ruth Gourzong as they started me on this journey and cleared every path with the most graceful winds.

There were so many people who disregarded my work; agents, editors, presses—people who said they would read my work but never did more than skim and then come back with a form letter no. I want to thank them first as they were my motivation to keep moving and insisting that this story come to life.

I want to thank Dr. Elizabeth Nunez for being the first person to read the first 50-pages of this novel and provide me with vital notes for revision.

I am so grateful to have been led (via a Facebook private group of writers seeking literary agents) to the incredible Lisa Pegram, my editor at Jaded Ibis Press. You were the first person in the publishing world who dealt with my novel gracefully because you read it and truly got it. I thank you for having faith in my writing and for supporting my dreams! Here is to a writer's life! I also need to thank the amazing team of folks at Levee Break Lit for my spectacular publicity! I must also shout out the AfroLatin@ Forum for supporting my work unconditionally from day one.

The first time I workshopped this story, just a short ten-page excerpt that perhaps is now part of Chapter 2, was at my first Tengo Sed Writing Retreat in Costa Rica, January 2015. I had just moved to Costa Rica and wanted to be amongst my writing people, so I created a retreat which has now turned into an exclusively curated spiritual gathering of BIPOC every January. This was my first time writing fiction after a life of academic publications and sharing my work in community finally felt safe. This book could not exist without my Tengo Sed family: Anton, Katarina, Racquel, Tonya, Delida, Alicia, Tawana, Yndia, Kathryn, Kinitra, Janell, Michele, Vilna, Tiffani, Todne, Cazzie, N'deye, Courtney, Maria, Rosie, and Gabrielle. I love you all so much.

I want to thank Kathryn Sophia Belle for envisioning and manifesting La Belle Vie writing group which allowed me the structure and community support to re-draft and finalize the novel over two years (and was a life-line during COVID).

I do need to take a moment to especially hold up Yndia Lorick-Wilmot, Tonya Cherie Hegamin and Sindi Gordon who were my absolute spirit-sisters through this entire journey; celebrating me through the milestones of manifesting this work. THANK YOU for being superb examples of Black womanhood. I am humbled to have you in my life.

I would also be remiss if I did not mention all my family and friends who supported me through this process: Ki-sha Clarke, Bongi Bangeni, Ron Cummings, Eddie Paulino, Caylie Hoffmans, Karol Perez, Jamie Philbert, Erica James and Arlene Hendricks, my sisters-in-law Selina, Nyangu and Shila and my incredible mother-in-law, Catharine Ajizinga Chipembere and the Chipembere/Okeyo/Hamilton families. To my AfroCentral American@ posse: Javier Wallace, Pamela Cunningham, Laura Hall, Margaret Simpson, Marva Spence, Carmen Hutchinson-Miller, Maria Fernanda Batista, and Kendall Cayasso. To my yoga teacher and mentor, Carmen Valverde and the sanctuary of Yoga Batsu. It was through your example that I became a yoga teacher. Thank you! You are so loved.

In loving memory for those who I lost through COVID times: Miriam Jimenez Romain and Dr. Bheki Peterson; both who were integral to my growth as a writer and thinker.

Since this is my book, I need to acknowledge that Kes the Band (from Trinidad and Tobago) was the ENTIRE soundtrack to my work, giving me the perseverance to keep dreaming and just finding joy in the midst of this eight-year grind.

I celebrate being part of a massive AfroCosta Rican family—the Gourzongs. I give thanks for my *Tias* (Sylvia, Jean and my late Tia Maj), my cousins (multi-generations) but especially Carolyn Gourzong, as she took me to the beach when I needed the expanse of the sea to dip my prayers in and she celebrated, loved me up and encouraged my work on our family history.

I thank my parents, Vicente and Norma for letting me fly, even when it was scary. To my sister, Xanthe and brother, Stephen—thank you for putting up with me, my long-distance requests, my shopping lists, and for always catching me in a pinch—every single time. I am so grateful.

To my gorgeously amazing children, Jabulani Neo Masauko and Aminata Baila Bahati. I want you to be proud of me. Both of you are parts of my heart walking outside my body and what joy you bring me. Thank you for choosing me to be your mother. It is the biggest honor of my life.

I could never end without thanking my husband, Masauko, my-ride-or-die. He is the first person I gave the manuscript to read in its entirety when I was done with it. I was shaking in my *chanclas* as he stayed up late into the night reading. To be honest, his opinion is the only one that really matters. Masauko's feedback was invaluable but it was when he started quoting lines from the book randomly that I knew why I fell in love with him over 25 years ago and continue to fall in love every day. Thank you, my darling, what a beautiful life!

Works Cited

Hartman, S. (2007). *Lose Your Mother: A Journey Along the Atlantic Slave Route*. New York: *Farrar, Straus and Giroux*.

Lohse, R. (2014). *Africans into Creoles: Slavery, Ethnicity, and Identity in Colonial Costa Rica*. Albuquerque: *University of New Mexico Press*.

Meléndez, C. and Ducan, Q. (2012). *El Negro in Costa Rica*. San Jose: *Editorial Costa Rica*.